PRESIDENTIAL TRAIL

John Lock

Whiteley Publishing

Published by Whiteley Publishing Ltd
First soft cover edition 2013

ISBN 978-1-908586-29-2

1

A bead of sweat formed in the middle of his furrowed brow before slowly trickling down the side of his nose onto a glistening, sun tanned cheek to drip silently onto the collar of his light grey, Blue Harbour shirt. The damp material clung to his taut, muscular frame as he viewed the surrounding roof tops and old, dust ravaged windows through the standard, telescopic sites of the Accuracy International AS50.

Kane squinted through the narrow, fixed scope as he slowly, very slowly panned from right to left, noting every detail and comparing them to the previous scan. In the distance, an open top cavalcade wound its' way down traffic free streets, now filled with supporters and onlookers alike as the Presidential candidate, ignoring his security staff's pleas, stood proudly in the open top Jaguar XF, lapping up the supporters adoration and presenting himself as a perfect target.

Security was tight, very tight. SWAT, FBI and local security forces peered down from every rooftop and vantage point. The intelligence information was sparse and vague, stating only that the popular candidate and probable new President of the United States would be assassinated during the run up to the election.

Dale Edwards was a fit, energetic forty four year old Managing Partner of a very successful law firm. The past few months had been spent on the campaign trail and had seen his popularity go from oblivion to front runner for the Presidency. In the late 1960s Dale's father, Peter, had moved from the UK to concentrate on developing the New York arm of his expanding Chemical business. Within a few months of opening his New York office he had started dating his Personal Assistant Catherine and after a whirlwind romance took her back to his home town of Cardiff where on a cold but sunny June morning they were married in the pomp and ceremony that surrounded Llandaff Cathedral. After three weeks honeymooning in the sun kissed Caribbean they finally returned to New York to continue their empire building. A year later Dale was born and as soon as he was old enough, he was bundled off to the best boarding schools.

Catherine fought hard to keep Dale at home, stating that there were plenty of excellent schools in their neighbourhood which would give Dale a good standard of education but Peter would have none of it. It made Peter into a man, as it had his father before him and now it would do the same for Dale.

During those often boring boarding school years Dale would look forward to the secret weekend visits his mother Catherine would make while his father was away on his many overseas visits. At the end of term, he was usually whisked back to the UK to keep in touch with his British relatives whilst his father spent most of the so called vacation evaluating the progress of the UK side of his business. Peter had two sites in Wales, one just outside of Cardiff and the other in Barry and both were overseen by his very capable brother Kevin. There was also a site in Chessington, Surrey which was mainly R & D and was Peter's personal 'baby'. Kevin had stopped asking questions about the site years ago and was now only interested in the 'Welsh Empire' as Peter had often referred to it.

After a somewhat stormy education Dale joined Johnson & Harbuckle, a respected New York law firm and specialised in Company law. Dale built up an impressive company portfolio and within seven years had set up his own law firm Edwards International. Calling the firm just Edwards seemed to lack something and maybe it was his father's influence but the 'International' addition appeared to give the name worldwide acceptance.

Dale frequently visited the UK and on a recent trip to London was so impressed with his test drive of the Jaguar XF 5 litre V8 that, much to the amazement of the showroom manager, he not only ordered and paid out the $125,000 for it, there and then, but also ordered another $60,000 worth of enhancements, including the open top convertible conversion.

When it eventually arrived, Dale used it on all his canvassing trips and the gleaming Jaguar with it's Italian Racing Red metallic finish, soon became his trade mark, being noticed wherever he went on his desired Presidential trail to the Whitehouse.

After addressing a packed assembly of ardent supporters, he now began the slow drive through the streets of Dallas, standing proudly in his trademarked pride and joy basking in the adulation of the many supporters and well-wishers, ignoring the suggestions of his personal advisor David Butane, ignoring the frantic pleas of his security staff, ignoring history.

Using the back of his forearm, Kane wiped the sweat from his forehead, clenched and unclenched his left fist several times and lifting up the barrel of the AS50, he squinted through the sites and began to slowly traverse from left to right. As he focussed, his target slowly came into view. It took just three seconds for him to confirm the target which was less than 500 metres away but he had to be right.

"Zach, end block, second window from the left, two floors down. You got him?"

"Yeah, it's him alright and he's setting himself up for the shot." Kane's partner was sat by the window at the far end of the dusty, deserted room, steadying his grip on the black, Canon 18 x 50 Binoculars to re-confirm his identification. "You gotta take him… NOW."

Kane's finger slowly pressed against the curved, steel trigger, allowing himself one more brief, confirmatory second before releasing the .50 BMG cartridge with deadly accuracy. He could scarcely believe Leidmeister had presented him with such an easy target.

To Dale Edwards the distant crack of the AS50 was nothing more than a car back firing. To some of the local security forces, the relief that the Presidential candidate was still standing, waving to the crowds around him, was more than evident. The SWAT teams and FBI increased the speed of their sweeps before settling back into their routine surveillance.

Kane continued to peer through the telescopic sights. The lifeless body, hung motionless in the open window. A Russian VSSK Vykhlop sniper rifle, specially adapted for long range usage, pointed aimlessly to the sky.

"Target eliminated, sixth floor, west side tenement building." Zach's voice was calm and collected as he spoke into the hand held radio. The sound of car doors slamming echoed up the old, weathered, stone walls as three FBI agents burst into the tired, paint flaked entrance of the tenement building, two taking the stairs whilst the third took the lift. After six flights of stairs the two agents paused to get their breath and check their bearings before running down the corridor to the last door on the left. They again paused for a couple of seconds, but hearing no signs of movement, stood back and began to kick open the faded, brown painted, door which gave way on the second attempt. Moving quickly and methodically, they swept through the small, dingy hallway into the sparsely furnished room where the prone, blood soaked body lay draped on the open window sill.

Kane Rhodes quickly removed the telescopic sights before sheathing the AS50 back into the soft, brown leather case. The dull ache in his neck and back were the result of six hours surveillance, the last sixty minutes of which were spent scanning through the sights of the scope. He paused briefly to reflect on how relatively easy the mission had been and not what he would have expected from someone with Leidmeister's background.

"You wanna go take a look while I keep up the surveillance," Zach drawled. "Give me a call on the radio when it's a done deal."

"Okay, then next stop a coffee shop."

"And I thought you Brits only drank tea?"

Kane gave Zach a brief, sarcastic smile as he opened the door and made his way to the staircase but he could not shake off this feeling of doubt, something was missing, but what?

He jogged down the remaining two flights of time worn, wooden stairs and out into the brilliant, warm June sunshine. As he walked towards the car, the covered AS50 butt tucked under his shoulder and the barrel cradled in the nook of his right arm, he scanned the old, paint flaked windows of the tenement building and pondered over the events of the last few days. There was something wrong, considering what he had learned about Leidmeister over this short period, he could not help feeling that this was too easy and he was soon to be proved right.

A young girl peered through the grime at three kids playing in the park then glanced at the man walking towards the car with a long, thin, brown bag under his arm before retracing her stare back to the park. An old man on the second floor looked left and right down the street but quickly disappeared from view when he caught Kane's inquisitive stare.

Kane looked across to the distant buildings, too far for the human eye to identify the corpse he had just created. It seemed ages ago since Kane had received his final briefing on the scant information received at MI6 Headquarters in London. The only real lead they had was when they arrived in Dallas and were informed that Henryk Leidmeister, a known assassin with links to Al Qaeda had been positively identified landing at Dallas airport. The rest 'a suspected assassination attempt on a Presidential candidate' was pretty vague.

Kane was sent out with two other British operatives, each were eventually tasked with identifying and helping to remove Henryk Leidmeister, who although of German descent, was born and grew up in Reading, England. At eighteen years of age, he joined the 8th Paras and excelled at virtually everything, quickly attaining the rank of sergeant. Shortly after his last promotion he was drafted to Hereford but after failing an SAS selection at the final hurdle, mysteriously left the army with a conditional discharge. His journeys took him to Libya, with intermittent trips to Ireland, presumably to support the IRA splinter groups though nothing could be proved and then onto Afghanistan and Syria where he had been linked to several international 'events'.

Kane had previous experience of Herr Leidmeister in Pakistan, which was why he was hastily picked for this mission. A Taliban informant, who was to be escorted to Paris and then onto London, was taken out minutes before Kane had arrived to collect him.

It had been a very warm June morning and the battered white taxi, bearing several scratches from not so near misses, wound its' way down from Islamabad International airport into the heavy traffic of the capital. The traffic ground to a standstill a few blocks away from Kane's destination. Kane decided it would be quicker to walk the remainder of the journey, so having paid the driver; he exited the car onto the bustling sidewalk. Placing his blue, Travel hold-all bag at his feet, Kane breathed in the heavy, spicy mixture of aromas emanating from a nearby delicatessen before straightening up, his alert blue eyes scanning the surroundings to get his bearings while the relentless waves of bodies jostled him back and fore. Eventually, his eyes focussed on the familiar outline of the Sargreb office block, diminished in the distant skyline. Noticing the sidewalk was less congested near the shop fronts, he picked up his bag and carefully weaving in and out of the oncoming flow of pedestrians, made his way across the width of the pavement to a large, empty shop front. Here the heaving crowds were mostly going in the same direction as him and he let himself be taken up by the flow.

A sharp, echoing bang pierced the warm mid-day, air and cut through the endless chatter of people dashing about their business. No one took much notice but Kane's ears had already identified the rifle shot. He peered down the busy street and allowed his gaze to search out the quieter Blue Area district on the horizon, its tall colourful, advertisement banners reaching to the sky. He hastened his pace, sometimes having to turn sideways to squeeze through the busy sidewalk. The people congestion began to ease slightly and Kane's strides broke into a crisp, determined rhythm until the edge of a large travel bag, protruding from an open doorway, caught his left leg just below the knee, forcing him to an abrupt stop. The flow of pedestrian traffic carried on behind him and as his left leg had nowhere to go, he found himself being turned towards the doorway which framed the statue like figure of the travel bag's owner. For a split second Kane stared into the cold, grey, blue eyes which appeared more bulbous due to the hollow, pale skinned, western cheeks and the short, cropped blonde hair that barely covered the flat crown. The head dipped immediately and without a word pushed past Kane out onto the busy street. Kane watched as the man darted in and out of the almost stationary traffic to be swallowed up in the crowds on the opposite sidewalk. It was then that Kane finally recognised the distinct smell of cordite, which had already started to drift away.

Ten minutes later, Kane emerged from the spacious, Sargreb building lift to walk down the thick, red carpeted corridor to the offices of Continental Holdings Inc. One of several cover bases used throughout Pakistan and one of the few known to the host nation. Outside the main office door, two men were deep in conversation and did not notice Kane until he was almost upon them.

"Excuse me, Sir, can I help you?" Enquired the taller of the two as Kane reached out to open the door.

Kane surveyed the pensive face that now stood in front of him, the dark, pock marked skin punctuated by two bushy black eyebrows and a thick jet black moustache.

"Yes, I've come to collect something, my name's Rhodes, Kane Rhodes."

"Can I see some identification please, Mr Rhodes?"

Kane pulled out his passport which the moustached man scrutinised somewhat apprehensively, scanning the photograph and comparing it to the lean, tanned figure in front of him.

"Wait here a minute please Mr Rhodes." He stated as he opened the door just enough to pop his head through and have a brief but inaudible conversation with whoever was inside.

After a few more seconds, the door was fully opened and Kane was ushered into a large, well-furnished, reception area. A dark skinned lady with long, jet black hair and large, brown eyes briefly looked up from her telephone conversation before resuming her call. Although Kane did not know the Urdu language well enough to decipher what she was saying, there was an obvious trace of panic in her deliberation.

Kane's eyes scanned the surrounding rooms which adjoined the large reception area. Two of the doors were open and the sound of heated male voices echoed from the large office at the front of the building.

"This way please, Mr Rhodes." The moustached man led him toward the sound of the animated voices. On entering the room, Kane did a quick recce of his surroundings, starting with the two Pakistani interrogators who were still stood arguing in the centre of the room, then onto the window, with it's neat little hole in the centre and the tell-tale surrounding spider's web where the bullet had pierced it on route to the intended target. On the floor to the right of the now silent men, was an upturned chair and the crumpled, blood stained body of the informant Kane had come to collect.

"How long ago did this happen?" Kane asked, bending down to examine the body.

"About ten minutes ago, maybe twelve," The taller of the two men replied. "We had just started the interview."

"Did you get much out of him before he was shot?" Kane continued, rising to walk over to the window and gauging the trajectory of the bullet in relation to where the chair would have been.

"No… we had only just started…"

Kane looked briefly at the two men before returning his attention to the window. Having roughly determined the angle inside the room, Kane continued to follow the probable trajectory route, through the window, to the sun lit buildings in the distance. A quick visual trace along the road he had walked down, back towards the identified buildings, confirmed it as the area where he had heard the shot and came face to face with the close cropped, fair haired westerner with the cold, grey eyes. A picture that had already been stored in his memory banks.

"What do you want us to do now?" The second interrogator asked timidly.

"What would you normally do in a situation like this? Have you called it in?"

"Yes."

"Then that's all you have to do for the moment, they'll take care of everything else. Who knew the informant was going to be here at this time?"

The two interrogators looked at each other before the taller, slightly overweight one responded. "Well, there were the men, who delivered him this morning, us obviously and Major Henry Morgan and his staff."

"Where was he kept before?"

"I don't know, we were only told about it yesterday. You need to speak to the Major."

After several lengthy telephone conversations with his superiors, Kane was eventually recalled to London and on the flight home he pondered over the events of the last twenty four hours. This had been a routine trip and the Taliban informant, on the surface, had been categorized as one of the many who try to secure monetary rewards for sparse and often manufactured information. MI6 however, had discovered that he was the brother of Abdul Hussein, a British citizen who had been reported missing by his wife a few weeks ago. His frequent visits to Pakistan had been flagged up to MI6 and added to their surveillance list and it had been further compounded when he had booked his luggage onto a flight from Heathrow to Islamabad on the 20th May but failed to board. This resulted in a two hour delay whilst all the luggage was removed from the plane and his single brown Pierre Cardin suitcase, once quarantined, had been examined by the bomb squad. The search proved fruitless as the case contained all the basics for a scheduled two day trip abroad, but it still did not explain his disappearance.

Back in London, Kane stood in the small office in the MI6 headquarters and looked down at the cold, murky waters of the river Thames. Pleasure cruisers filled with sightseers chugged back and fore and a lone canoeist rose and dipped his way across the white tipped crests in the wake of the tourist traffic. The view from the tinted, toughened window was a welcome break from the intense scrutiny of the IBM Monitor. For the last hour and a quarter Kane had been searching through hundreds of computerised files and photographs in an effort to identify the cold grey eyes of the cordite smelling stranger from just twenty four hours earlier. It was a slim, very slim lead, but Kane's instincts and extensive field experience heightened his belief that the stranger was connected to the assassination. Seven minutes later Kane enlarged the computer image of the cold grey eyes of Henryk

Leidmeister.

The hair was longer and darker, the skin smoother and younger but there was no mistaking the cold grey blue eyes and the hollow pale skinned features that had been the stranger in the doorway. Henryk Leidmeister's file gave full details of his army training and proficiency at sniping but the rest of it appeared to be supposition, vaguely linking him to several high impact assassinations, all with the same long distance method of operation. Several calls to Interpol in Paris and the CIA in Langley produced more sparse information, but enough circumstantial evidence to identify Leidmeister as a prime suspect in at least three highly reported assassinations.

The information obtained from the Taliban informant, prior to his demise, was also sparse. He was unwilling to divulge any more information until he had been paid to secure a new, safe future away from potential Taliban reprisals. Kane sifted through the transcripts of the last interview Ahmed Hussein would ever give.

Apart from confirming his name, the only tangible bits of conversation was his initial 'taster' that a prominent American would be assassinated. The only other times Ahmed spoke was to state that he would not divulge any more information until his future had been secured and he wanted to be paid by June 27th.

Kane read through the transcripts again and again. There was no mention of a specific amount of money, just that he wanted to have a safe, secure future. Why did it have to be paid by 27th June, was there anything significant about the date? Who was the prominent American allegedly earmarked for assassination? Was this a genuine informant or just someone cashing in on the ever growing information market?

Kane inserted the memory stick into the front of the console and loaded up the recorded interview. The session was brief, coming to an untimely end just after the bullet tore through the glass window entering the top of Ahmed's head just above his left temple and exiting through his lower right jaw. The tape confirmed the written transcripts and did not add to the verbal information obtained. Kane replayed the interview several times, each time concentrating more and more on Ahmed's body language and tone of voice. Ahmed spoke perfect English but there was a hint of anxiety in the brief dialogue which did not match the calm, deliberate statement about a prominent American or the request for a safe, secure future. If he had been trying to sell useless information he would have demanded payment there and then and the body language would have shown his eagerness to get paid and get out of there. Ahmed, however, seemed totally relaxed, safe and the only hint of anxiety was when he mentioned that he needed to be paid by the 27th and his voice rose slightly with an underlying sense of urgency.

It was on the seventh replay of the tape that Kane noticed one of the interrogators, furthest away from the window, was sat back in his chair and further away from the table than seemed necessary. On all the interviews he had sat on, it was natural for interrogators to sit close to and even lean on the table, to get into direct eye contact with the interviewee and to identify any tell-tale signs of someone who was a bit lenient with the truth, but this guy seemed uninvolved. Kane magnified the image and re-running the tape, concentrated on the first interrogator. Throughout the brief interview he appeared to be glancing furtively at the window and he had thrown himself backwards immediately the bullet had entered the room. His fellow interrogator had taken a full two seconds to duck his head, look at the window and then back to the falling body before following suit.

Repeated viewings of the interview further strengthened his belief and he carefully closed down the file and selected the safely remove option to extract the memory stick and head off to the Section Leader's office.

Bill Johnson had been a section leader for six years and had risen up from the ranks of field operative to his current position. His receding hairline and wrinkled, well-tanned skin, advanced by his passion for sun bathing during a five year posting to the Middle East, made him look older than his forty nine years. Bill specialised in anti-terrorist activities and as such, sat on many an interview which had often resulted in obtaining crucial information that had played a big part in thwarting potential terrorist threats.

Kane quickly briefed Bill on the outline of the case and having explained about the informant and his subsequent assassination, loaded the memory stick and asked Bill to concentrate on the interrogators. Bill watched the brief interview through slightly squinted eyes, focusing his attention on the two Pakistani interrogators. When it had finished, Bill asked Kane to play it again and this time he lent forward to concentrate on a specific part of the screen. As the bullet crashed through the window for the second time Bill uttered "The bastard, he knew it was coming!"

"This would explain how the assassin knew where and when to get at his mark." Kane responded, before explaining about his brief encounter with Henryk Leidmeister in the shop doorway.

"What else have you got?" Bill enquired as he rose from the black leather, high back chair and strode purposely towards a large, brown, filing cabinet.

"Not much really, just what you heard on the tape and the fact that a person that looks like Leidmeister was in the vicinity when it happened. But the fact that this guy was taken out so quickly means that there has to be a leak somewhere and my initial investigations would make me believe that not only was the informant genuine but what he had to offer was obviously well worth the risk. I just wish I had a bit more to go on than a prominent American and 27th June."

"I might be able to give you a bit more in that case," Bill smiled as he retrieved a file from the top drawer of the cabinet. "A friend of mine, Chas Wiltson, my counterpart with the CIA in Texas, was coming over at the end of June for a visit but had to put it off for a week because…" Bill's voice trailed off as he placed the open folder in front of Kane. The opened page showed a picture of Dale Edwards, the current forerunner in the presidential election race together with a list of dates. "He had his leave stopped because this guy is scheduled to attend a canvassing rally in Dallas on June 28th… the day after your informant's deadline."

"It's pretty weak Bill, are we clutching at straws here?"

"Well, we've got to start somewhere, trust your gut instincts. If we're wrong, we're wrong, but if we're right and didn't do anything about it…! You contact our office in Islamabad, tell them what you've found out and get them to investigate our friend on the tape. On second thoughts, time's running out and if we are right about this guy, he might be able to fill in some of the gaps. Get them to pull him and find out what he knows. While you're at it, send me the file on Leidmeister. I'll send it to Dallas together with the information we have to hand and put the ball in their park."

Kane strode back along the corridor with renewed vigour, leaving Bill to pick up the phone and give Chas Wiltson the story so far… 'What time is it in Dallas?' he thought to himself as the line connected.

Time moved quickly, It was now three days since Kane had informed

Bill Johnson of his intuitive beliefs and within an hour and a half of that meeting finishing, he had been finalising travel arrangements for himself and two other agents, Brian Jones and Neil Bishop, for their trip to Dallas the following day.

After consulting with his superiors Chas Wiltson had specifically asked for Kane and anybody else who might be able to identify Leidmeister to visit Dallas in a non-operational role. The intention being, to brief their teams with as much information on Leidmeister as they could get their hands on. The CIA had apparently uncovered two separate pieces of information relating to a terrorist activity that would receive substantial press coverage and Bill's assumption of the main presidential candidate being assassinated fitted the bill. MI6's feed, together with Dale Edward's stubborn refusal to change any part of his canvassing tour, including his open top cavalcade, sent alarm bells running throughout the FBI and CIA.

Once he had fed in the relevant details, it had taken Bill Johnson just five minutes to come up with four names of serving officers who had either been in the Paras at the same time as Leidmeister or anywhere else on his brief dossier. Two of the names were discounted after brief telephone conversations with the individuals concerned, but both the remaining two, when asked to describe Leidmeister, matched the army photograph now on file but more than that, matched Kane's description of the blue grey bulbous eyes. Brian Jones had been with MI6 for just over two years and was on the same SAS selection course as Leidmeister, except he was more successful. Neil Bishop was currently serving with MI5 and had joined the 8th Paras after Leidmeister's return from Hereford and in response to Bill's questions added that Leidmeister always appeared to be a sinister loner who kept himself to himself before being booted out, or at least he assumed he'd been booted out. MI5, who are responsible for anti-terrorism and espionage in the UK and Ireland, often work closely with MI6 who are responsible for anti-terrorism and espionage on an International level. However, it still took longer to get Neil Bishop temporally seconded to MI6 than it did to make the travel arrangements to Dallas.

2

Asif Khan sat by the small, wooden framed window, swathed in the dim evening light that seeped, eerily into the cold, dark apartment. The well-furnished room now felt more like a jail cell as opposed to the party atmosphere of two short days ago when he celebrated his thirtieth birthday.

'Where are you?' he muttered to himself as he glanced up and down the dimly lit street looking for his unusually late wife. The events of the day had made him realize it would not take them long to discover that it was he who had betrayed the firm, he who had been able to pass on information that had suddenly drawn much attention from his benefactors.

A chance meeting with an old school friend, Rashid Gazar, in the Monal Restaurant, Islamabad, nearly five years ago, would change Asif's life forever. The meeting was brief and the customary business cards exchanged with the expected promise of getting in touch soon. Asif had been somewhat surprised when two days later he received a phone call from Rashid asking him to meet for lunch the following day, again in the Monal restaurant, his treat. Asif was never one to pass up a free meal and readily accepted, it was only after the call had finished that he began to wonder why Rashid had wanted to meet him, after all, they were not that friendly in school and never seemed to have much in common. Asif sat back in his chair staring through the open slats of the cream coloured, vertical blinds, his thoughts slowly drifting back to his wife of three weeks and the previous night's romantic evening spent in their new apartment.

Asif turned up early for his mid-day appointment and was surprised to see Rashid already there, sat at a table waiting for him. As he made his way towards where Rashid was sitting, one of the waiters walked up to him and asked if he had booked a table.

"I'm meeting a colleague." Asif responded, smiling to himself at the confident, authoritative tone in his voice. He brushed past the waiter and extended his hand to the now standing Rashid who grasped it warmly with his right hand whilst his left hand reached up and cupped the back of Asif's neck, pulling his head down to rest against Rashid's bearded cheek, more like brothers than old acquaintances.

Once Rashid's grip had been released, Asif stepped backwards and sitting down in the chair opposite, immediately unfolded the burgundy, monogrammed napkin to place on his lap and give him time to compose himself after the unexpected warm welcome.

"Thank you for coming my friend, it is good to rekindle old friendships, can I get you a drink?"

"Just water please." Asif responded, mainly because he was unsure what else to order as the novelty of eating in high class restaurants was still fairly new to him and decided he would take his lead from Rashid when it came to ordering the food.

"How are you settling down to married life in your new apartment?"

Asif looked up from the tablecloth into Rashid's dark brown, hooded eyes. "I don't remember telling you I was married or that I had an apartment."

"You didn't, I made it my business to find out. Two months ago I was travelling back from Nurpur Shahan and just as I was entering the Diplomatic Enclave you walked past in deep conversation with Yousef Ahbrim, one of my many Jewish friends. With my contacts it did not take too long to confirm your identity and here we are today."

"So why am I here today?" Asif asked cautiously, feeling a little uneasy that his personal life had been peered into.

"Simple," Continued Rashid, "I'm more of, what you might call an entrepreneur, with many different business interests. My success has been down to my networking contacts with business colleagues or friends. They give me information which could help my businesses and in return I give them information which might help them. You work with the British Embassy so information on forthcoming Business delegations and the right contact names would be very helpful to my import and export businesses. I also have a small, but well accepted Media Company which would benefit from being on your list for Press releases. In return, I will endeavour to supply answers to whatever information you may require."

"Well, I am afraid I will not be that much use to you Rashid. I get most of my information from the papers."

"Okay, who compiles your press releases?"

"Peter Harrington-Smythe, but you could get that information from any of the freely distributed contact lists."

"Could I get straight through to him or do I have to go through one of his subordinates?"

"You've got to get past his secretary first and she's a real Rottweiler. Yasmin will not put you through unless the call is expected. She will take your name, number and reason for your call and pass the details to Harry who will decide whether or not it is worth a return call."

"Harry, who is that?"

"Peter Harrington-Smythe is a bit of a mouthful and as we have several Peters, he became known as Harry."

"See, you learn something every day. Right, where's the menu? I'm starving."

The meal passed by with polite conversation, mainly Rashid asking what Asif had been up to since he left school, what his hobbies were, what his plans were for the future. An hour later Asif was back in his chair staring out of the cream coloured blinds, reflecting on his re-kindled friendship.

A week later Rashid called and asked to meet for a cup of coffee. Asif had a morning meeting and could not make the suggested 11.00am time but agreed to meet at 2.00pm.

Throughout the morning Asif kept drifting back to Rashid's telephone call. He had sounded excited and as if he genuinely wanted to see him again, so it was a very curious Asif who sauntered into the Polo Lounge at five past two.

"Asif my friend, take a seat." This time Rashid did not get up from his chair or offer a handshake, simply extending his open hand to the chair opposite. Asif barely had time to sit down before Rashid pulled out a narrow white envelope from inside the left pocket of his black, soft leather jacket and grabbing Asif's right hand with his left, deposited the package into his palm.

"What's this?" Asif blurted, a startled look spread across his face.

"The information you gave me about Yasmin and Harry enabled me to get straight through and I am now not only on his preferred Press release list, but also on the invitation list for future dignitary functions."

"But I can't…"

"I insist," Rashid interrupted, rising from his chair, "now I must go, consider it a belated wedding present in exchange for your help. Speak to you soon."

Asif's mouth was still open as he watched Rashid disappearing through the door. He glanced down at the white, woven envelope and then back to the door before carefully opening the edge of the packet. His eyes widened as he flicked through the bundles of bills inside. 'There must be 50,000 Rupees here', he thought to himself, suddenly feeling vulnerable at handing this amount of money in such clandestine circumstances. The brief feeling of guilt was soon forgotten as he thought of how the money could be used to impress his new bride. After all, the information he had passed over was already in the public domain as such, so it was not like he was selling trade secrets and 50,000 Rupees was not that much really.

Over the next few years, they would meet up every two to three months, whenever Rashid called. After each meeting Asif was given a package and each time it was more than the amount before. The extra income eventually enabled him to move to a bigger, more modern apartment and furnish it with some of the finer things in life. Asif's wife, Zelda, had assumed the extra income had come from the several job changes within the British Embassy or promotions as Asif had preferred to call them. Over the last year things had changed and Asif had started to feel uneasy with his business partner. Rashid had started to demand information on various events or individuals relating to the Middle East, in particular some sensitive details to do with the British and American involvement in Afghanistan.

Shortly after Osama Bin Laden's demise, Rashid contacted Asif and demanded information relating to how the Americans had uncovered Bin Laden's stronghold in Pakistan. When he could not offer any tangible information Rashid became very angry and sinister, referring to the 'help' he and his family, stressing the word family, had received in the past and what would happen if all that stopped, or worse, if his employers had got to find out. Asif had been very careful with his spending so as not to draw attention to himself and as such had a considerable amount of money stashed away for a rainy day, but if the Embassy did find out he was getting paid for passing information, then he would end up losing everything, including his beloved Zelda.

"I am not involved in that side of things, I just gather initial information from people before they are passed on to the senior staff."

"Then who does?" Rashid snarled through gritted teeth.

"It would be one of the Area controllers."

"Who?" Rashid snapped, the patience now gone from his voice.

"Mohammed Azir." Asif blurted out the name of the first Area controller he could think of, sensing that a negative response could escalate the tension into something more sinister.

A faint click indicated the call was ended and Rashid had gone. Two days later the mutilated bodies of Mohammed Azir and his family were found in their burnt out car.

On hearing the news, Asif became overcome with fear and phoned in sick with a stomach bug. The taught, nauseating feeling in his stomach was down to him struggling with his conscience and concerns for his and Zelda's safety. Should he come clean to his bosses and lose everything and if he did, would they be safe? Every time the phone rang his heart skipped a beat and beads of sweat would immediately form on his forehead to trickle down the side of his nose onto his thick, black moustache. Zelda often commented on how long it took him to answer the phone and on a couple of occasions he had literally grabbed the phone from her hand causing her to enquire, rather forcibly, if he was having an affair. He quickly dismissed her accusation, stating that he did not feel well enough to go back to work and did not want to be persuaded back if he felt he was not ready. After a full week off, he was eventually forced to go back to work or be marched off, by Zelda, to the family doctor.

It was at the end of his first week back that Rashid finally made contact. Asif, lulled into a sense of false security, stuttered his response to Rashid's "Good morning Asif, are you feeling better?"

"F… f… fine, I've been ill, I…"

"I know Asif, but I trust your stomach bug has gone now. How's your wife Zelda, has she been looking after you? She must have because you are back in work and carrying on your normal duties. By the way, is there anything you think I should be aware of?"

"N… no, just catching up on paperwork."

"Well, be sure to let me know if there is anything and I mean anything, you think I might be interested in."

"Yes, I will, I er…"

“We’ll speak soon then, bye.” The line went dead and Asif was left mouthing words that would not come out. Was he responsible for the death of Mohammed and his family? Were he and Zelda safe?

He lent forward onto his elbows and placing his head in his hands, racked his brains for any information he could supply that would put him in good stead, but news about the installation of a new telephone system or the redecorating of the entrance hall would not earn him any favours.

A few days later Asif was called into conference room 2 at the end of his corridor. Zelda had laid on a surprise birthday party the night before which, considering the circumstances, he had thoroughly enjoyed, but was now feeling rather the worse for wear. Having knocked on the solid oak door, he opened it just enough to see into the room and squinted through the gap. The dark oak panelled walls, with crystal semi chandelier wall lights, made the room appear smaller than it actually was. A dark mahogany, oval shaped table held pride of place in the centre of the room. At the far end of the table, three taut, pale faces looked up briefly as he entered, before dropping their gaze back to the open files that lay disarranged on the table in front of them.

“Ah, Asif, come in man, don’t dawdle about in the doorway.” The Major boomed without looking up from the file in front of him. Major Henry Morgan was head of Embassy security and was famed for his blunt, no nonsense attitude.

“Spot of babysitting for you my lad, one of these rag heads wants a new car by the look of it, but London seem interested enough to send someone to pick him up. Fellah by the name of Ahmed Hussein, I want you to meet him in the Sargreb office, he’ll be delivered to you at 9.00am sharp. Before you hand him over to the London chappie, see if you can get any more out of him, he has been a bit tight lipped up to now and I still think this is a fool’s errand, personally I’d kick his arse back over the border where he came from. Come on man, hurry up, haven’t got all day.” He growled, waving a well-thumbed green pocket file at the now rapidly advancing Asif.

Returning to his office, Asif spent the next forty five minutes ploughing through the transcripts of the initial interviews, all of which produced very little information apart from an intended assassination and his insistence that he would not divulge any details until he had secured the safety of his future.

Could he make this sound interesting to Rashid? Would it put him back in the good books? Will it buy him enough time to disappear? He quickly dismissed the last thought, he had nowhere to go and would have to explain to Zelda why they were going to start a new life elsewhere. He lent forward to pick up the handset of the gleaming, black phone that now adorned his aged, light oak veneered desk, then stopped, suddenly remembering the brief operating instructions the engineer had given him when the system was installed earlier in the day. "… and if you want to play back a telephone conversation just press #690…" He could not risk his call to Rashid being recorded and taking out his cell phone, keyed in the telephone number on his Nokia 3200.

Three rings later and Rashid answered with an abrupt "Hello?"

"Rashid, its Asif. I have something for you." He paused, trying to think of how he could make the information sound more important. Rashid did not speak.

"I have to pass on an informant to our London office. He has some information which... "

"Hussein?" Rashid interrupted, an air of excitement in his voice, "Asif, is it Hussein, Ahmed Hussein?"

"Yes… how did you…" Before Asif could continue Rashid again interrupted.

"We need to meet… NOW!" It was a demand rather than a request. "Meet me at your place in an hour, don't be late."

"But…" Rashid had already hung up, leaving Asif trying to find a logical excuse to leave the building and at the same time wishing he had suggested somewhere else to meet. What if Zelda came home early?

Fifty minutes later Asif was pacing up and down the floor of his banner covered living room. Balloons and 'Happy 30th Birthdays' covered the main wall. Two loud thuds on the door stopped him in his tracks. He turned and cautiously started to make his way towards the door when another two louder, impatient thuds echoed around the apartment. As he opened the door, Rashid, quickly followed by another tall, fair haired man, brushed past him into the room.

"Where are you meeting with him?"

"The Sargreb Building, it's on…"

"I know where it is, what floor and specifically, what room? Speak up Asif, you know what happens to people who do not cooperate."

A cold, sharp pang of guilt shuddered through Asif's body as he realized Rashid had been responsible for Mohammed's death and that he was now probably condemning Ahmed Hussein to a similar fate.

"I would like to see for myself." Henryk Leidmeister interrupted, his cold, grey blue eyes piercing into Asif's very soul.

"I can't... you need passes."

"Tonight, I'll meet you outside, 8.00pm." Leidmeister turned to Rashid and nodded.

"Well done, Asif, I won't forget this." Rashid stared deep into the frightened, dark rimmed eyes for several seconds before turning and sweeping out through the door which Leidmeister had already opened, a thin, menacing smile spread across his face as he nodded to Asif, closing the door behind him.

It was a long time to 8 o'clock. Asif's sub conscious went into overload, all sorts of frantic thoughts raced through his mind. 'Wait a minute,' he thought, 'when he said outside, did he mean outside the Sargreb Building or outside here? What if I go to the Sargreb and he's waiting here, will he come up and tell Zelda?'

The hours dragged by, increasing his built up anxiety.

"You ill again?" Zelda asked in a pointed but concerned manner.

"No, I just need to sort some things out for tomorrow, I'll go down to the office and finish off, it will be done then." Asif involuntary scratched his head. Did any of what he just said make sense?

Zelda stared at him with a puzzled look and then shrugged her shoulders. "Well, don't be long, you still have a birthday present to unwrap." She pouted, tilting her head slightly to one side, a broad, warm smile lighting up her face.

There was still an hour to go, but after forty five minutes of shuffling papers back and fore, he put on his coat, kissed Zelda several times and left for his appointment, electing to take the stairs rather than the lift, that would kill a few more minutes. Exiting the building he paused and took long lingering looks in both directions before starting the five minute walk to the Sargreb Buildings. Asif slowed as the main entrance came into in view.

"Which floor, front or back?"

Asif jumped noticeably as he turned to see Leidmeister's cold, grey blue eyes, staring, uncaring, waiting for an answer.

"Front, sixth floor." He mumbled.

"Good, let's take a closer look, come on." Leidmeister strode off and one backward glance was enough to get Asif following in line. They skirted around the building, stopping every now and then whilst Leidmeister checked the front of the building and scanned the horizons in all three visible directions.

"Which office will he be in?" Leidmeister asked, as he quietly took in his surroundings.

"That one." Asif responded, nodding towards the sixth floor.

"Which window?" Leidmeister snapped, annoyed at the lack of preciseness in the response. Henryk Leidmeister was a master of fine detail and perfection and did not suffer fools gladly.

"Er, fifth… no sixth from the left."

"Are you sure?"

"Yes… sixth." Asif responded having re-checked the window three times.

"What time are you meeting with Hussein?"

"9am. He's being delivered at 9am."

"Delivered? How?"

"I don't know, other Embassy staff I assume, but I wasn't told."

Leidmeister sighed aloud. It would have probably been easier to take out Hussein on route but he now had to make do with what he had.

"Asif listen carefully, you must do this right, there must be no room for errors. I want you to make sure Hussein is in plain view of the window at all times. There must be no obstructions and when the time comes, I must be able to see him clearly."

"What are you going to do?" Asif blurted, knowing full well what Leidmeister had in mind.

"Should this not work, then we will have to meet again tomorrow, but Asif. In war, everything must work."

'War, what war, what does he mean by must work?' The thoughts raced through Asif's tired, confused mind. Before he could summon up the courage to ask he realized that Leidmeister was fast disappearing out of sight, starting his search for a good vantage point, a search that would take him most of the night.

The following morning after a sleepless night, Asif arrived early at the Sargreb Building and studied the contents of the room which would be used to talk to Ahmed Hussein. Four wooden framed, blue padded chairs were place around the plain oak veneered table in the centre of the room. Asif removed one of the chairs and placed it against the wall next to the door. He glanced up at the Hitachi flat screen above him and the high quality web cam secured on top. This was used for conference calls and 'fact finding' meetings such as the one he was about to have. His tired, defeatist mind kept going back to Leidmeister's comments from the night before, when he suddenly realized that he was pulling the table closer to the window.

'What am I doing?' he thought to himself, 'I am setting someone up to be killed.'

Asif slumped into the chair, put his elbows on the table and holding his head in his hands, began shaking his head back and fore but he had no choice.

The day had gone exactly as he had dreaded and his fear and anxiety quickly turned to anger when he stared down at lifeless, blood soaked body sprawled on the blue carpeted floor. A dark, crimson outline began to spread around Hussein's shattered head and slowly seep across the thick, blue pile of the carpet. The rest of the day was a blur. Asif had given his statement as to the day's events and his growing anger at allowing himself to be manipulated by Rashid and Leidmeister had been assumed by Major Henry Morgan, as frustration, that there was nothing he could have done to prevent it – an assumption that could not have been further from the truth.

The early evening haze found Asif sat by the small, wooden framed window, waiting impatiently for his wife Zelda, to return home. When she did, he would whisk her out of the apartment and drive to his cousin's on the border with Afghanistan. Then all he had to do was work out how they could both disappear, from Rashid, Leidmeister and the long arms of the Pakistani and British Governments.

A creak from somewhere behind jerked him out of his semi trance and as he turned he saw the cold, calculating face of Henryk Leidmeister.

"How did you get in?" He shouted, now standing, his face just inches away from Leidmeister's.

"You seem a bit flustered Asif, what happened today?" Totally ignoring Asif's question.

"You know what happened today, you killed him."

"No, what happened after he was executed."

"Executed…?" Asif turned back to the window. "Well, I cannot go back there now, they are already investigating how you found out he was there and you need to be careful too, someone saw you." Asif suddenly realized he was no longer afraid and began to feel quite proud of his direct, almost confident manner.

Leidmeister lowered his right hand back to his side, the six inch stiletto blade still visible.

"What do you mean, someone saw me. Who?"

"The agent, the man from London, he described you in detail, you bumped into him in the street after you killed Hussein."

Leidmeister flashed back to the doorway and instantly remembered the tanned rugged face of the stranger who had blocked him in the doorway. It was a face he knew he would see again.

"Where is this agent now?"

"He's on his way back to London; you did not leave him with anything to collect."

"What information did you collect from Hussein?"

"The same as he told everybody else, that someone prominent in America would be killed and that he wanted a lot of money."

"Did he give any date when this would take place?"

"No, the only date he said was when he wanted his money by and that was the 27th June."

"Does this agent from London know about this?"

"Of course, he has all the transcripts of the previous interview and the one this morning before it was… terminated."

"Anything else?"

"No and as soon as Zelda gets back we are gone."

"That is what I am here for, so that you may join her."

"What do you mean join her." Asif asked as he turned to face Leidmeister. He did not notice the thin, shiny blade, nor did he immediately feel it slide between the third and fourth ribs to puncture his now fast beating heart. Asif's hands slid slowly down Leidmeister's chest, following his body as it collapsed effortlessly to the floor. His eyes slowly closed, darkness began to set in as Asif left to join his beloved Zelda.

3

The flight from Gatwick to Fort Worth International was spent swotting up on the brief bits of information from MI6, Interpol, CIA and some very basic army data which portrayed Henryk Leidmeister as a brilliant tactician and potential leader except for one major flaw. He was not a team player and had been described by the assessment board at Hereford as a psychotic individual.

Having collected their luggage from the baggage area, they were met at customs by two CIA operatives who, after a very brief introduction, quickly whisked them through security and out into a waiting black Cadillac. The flight had been long and tiring and Kane, having given up on trying to make polite conversation with his hosts and only getting one word responses, allowed his eyelids to flutter gently to a close before being roughly wakened what seemed like seconds later, by someone kicking the outside of his shoe.

"We're here," This grunt came from the taller of the Americans.

Kane's eyes opened and then squinted momentarily to take in his immediate surroundings. A large, sandstone building loomed in front of him with six wide, spotlessly clean, concrete steps leading up to a large revolving glass door, the bare aluminium frames reflecting the late afternoon sunlight. Two larger glass doors stood on either side, apparently locked as the constant flow of human traffic rotated in and out of the middle entrance.

"Leave the bags; you can pick them up later." Kane ignored his host and reached down to pick up the dark blue travel hold all before alighting from the car and overtaking Neil Bishop as he strode up the steps two at a time.

Once inside they were ushered straight into a large ornamental lift whose shining brass, gleaming mirrors and red thick piled carpet seemed totally out of place to the cold, sandstone building exterior. The lift raced silently to the tenth floor where a gentle ping opened the two sliding doors onto a well-lit, red carpeted hallway. On the far wall, two brass mounted wall lights shone down on a glass coffee table flanked by two high backed, red leather chairs, outlined by shiny brass studs. Kane exited first and glanced left and right. A large, tinted, glass door stood on either side of the hallway and identical, wide passageways could be seen trailing off into the distance. The tall American brushed past Kane and opened the door to his right, his entourage in hot pursuit.

"Where are we now?" Neil bishop enquired of Kane as he marvelled at the length of the never ending corridor.

"Your guess is as good as mine, but it looks as if we're about to find out." Kane responded, as the tall American opened the third door on the right and waved them through.

Chas Wiltson rose from his chair and slowly circled the large, dark green leather topped, desk to greet them. His huge six foot eight frame and broad shoulders gave the impression of someone who had been used to keeping himself in shape, but a couple of years behind a desk had developed a round pot belly which he did his best to hold in.

"Hi, Chas Wiltson, welcome to Dallas." He boomed, holding out a large, friendly right hand.

Kane introduced himself, quickly followed by Brian and Neil whose right hand had just been swallowed by Chas' vigorous handshake.

Chas nodded at the soft, padded chairs that lined the walls, "Please, take a seat. Our boy looks like he flew in to Dallas airport, from Islamabad, the day before yesterday, just under twelve hours before we put surveillance in place. We've had two positive IDs from customs, based on the computer enhanced photograph you sent over and the airport's CCTV footage more or less confirms it, even though he did a good job of keeping his head down. We traced the taxi driver who remembers dropping him off at the junction of Main Street and Lamar but that's where it ends. We've checked all the hotels in the area but got diddly squat."

"So where do we fit in?" Kane asked, trying to find justification for their visit. "You already have all the data and the photographs with the updated computer enhancements. There doesn't seem to be much more we can offer you in a non-operational role."

Chas let out a long deliberate sigh and moving slowly back behind the desk, lowered his heavy frame into the plush, brown executive chair which gently creaked as it absorbed his full weight.

"Okay, I'll level with you. The information we have is not conclusive but it's probable. That dick head Dale Edwards has refused to alter his itinerary in any way shape or form, making him even more of an open target. Take a look outside, our guy could set himself up in any of the hundreds of buildings that look down on Main Street or any of the other streets that form part of his God dam glory hunting cavalcade. I haven't the man power to cover all the angles and if this shooter is as good as we've made him out to be, then he'll find himself a loophole somewhere to take his shot. Edwards might not be the President yet, but for my money, he's as good as and I can't afford another JFK. So gentlemen, we need to find Leidmeister before the 28th. He doesn't seem bothered about changing his appearance, but even with some sort of disguise, you three should be able to recognize him on contact. So, in answer to your question, for the next couple of days, you guys are going to pair up with some of my people on a site seeing tour and turn Dallas inside out. Zach will take you to your Hotel to freshen up and three of my men will meet with you about eight o'clock to sort out tomorrow's search areas. Enjoy your stay gentlemen and find our man."

Three brief handshakes later and the trio were dismissed to the corridor where Zach the tall American, was waiting to take them to the hotel.

After a long, leisurely shower, Kane towelled himself dry and put on a fresh change of clothes. A brief, but enjoyable meal later in the Hotel's restaurant, was brought to an abrupt end when they were joined by Zach and two other agents. They went through the usual courteous introductions and then made their way up to Kane's room to start dividing up the blocks from Main Street, Lamar Street and Elm Street to the outskirts of the City.

Kane had been paired with Zach who was surprisingly different to his stoic, daytime behaviour and proved to be a wealth of knowledge when it came to the more seedier areas of downtown Dallas. As they shared out the following day's territory, Kane stared at the street map in front of him and tried to work out locations where he would set himself up if he were to take the shot. The main route of the cavalcade would be well covered and the height of the surrounding buildings would limit any longer range opportunities to specific junctions.

"Zach, can you get hold of a chopper?"

"I can try, if you give me a good enough reason to risk fronting up to Wiltson."

"I think our guy may already be holed up in, or at least very near to, his proposed vantage point. He's had forty eight hours to identify several possible shoots and even the most amateur would-be assassin would have zoned in on one by now. Add to that the fact that he may know we are onto him, he is unlikely to be venturing out very far."

"So why do you need the Chopper?"

"Security on and around the main route is going to restrict his movements and the repeated sweeps would mean he could not stay in any one place for long. The further away from Main Street, the fewer the sweeps and the less chance of being stumbled upon, but it also cut down on shooting opportunities. We could identify these vulnerable areas far quicker and easier from the air and concentrate our searches in areas along any potential lines of fire."

"Don't want to take the wind out of your sail my friend, but we have already set up a door to door sweep up to two blocks from every junction." Zach replied with a smug look of satisfaction.

"Two blocks, Leidmeister was four blocks away when he took out my informant in Islamabad. Now do you see why I want a helicopter?"

"Hey," Brian interrupted. "How come you get to fly and we get the foot pounding?"

"Pecking order Brian," Kane smiled, "Pecking order."

4

An hour and several phone calls later, Zach had managed to track down Chas Wiltson and having listened to his ranting about Limeys on a pleasure jaunt finally agreed to getting a Helicopter and Pilot arranged for 9am the following morning, but he would be expecting substantial progress or Zach may find himself looking for alternative employment.

"I've put my neck in the noose for you Kane, so we better come up with something tomorrow." Zach was used to Chas' rants and although he was in full agreement with him that foot pounding and door knocking would have a better chance of uncovering Leidmeister than flying around Dallas, there was also something about Kane, his quiet, confident manner, his ability to make the unthinkable, probable, which he had to admit, he found inspirational, to the point that he was now carrying out mundane, routine tasks with a renewed vigour.

At precisely 8am the following morning, Zach pulled up outside the hotel to find Kane sat on the step waiting for him.

Opening the passenger door Kane climbed in, "Good morning Zack, how are you this fine, sunny morning?" He greeted in an over exaggerated English accent.

"I'm fine your Lordship, are we ready to go?"

"Sure thing pardner, where we all going?" Kane smiled in his best Southern drawl.

"Kane, you can't even speak English properly, let alone American," A broad grin spreading across Zach's face as he accelerated out into the flow of traffic. "Fort Worth," He continued, "we got a two hour slot from 9.15am."

The traffic was unusually heavy, the centre of Dallas would be a traffic free Zone as from tomorrow so everybody was trying to get their business done today.

Just over an hour later they were both buckling up and watching the pilot go through his pre-flight routine. The blue and white, Bell 429 was bigger than he expected and Kane, having elected for the seat next to the pilot, peered through the cockpit window to make sure he could get a good view. Zach meanwhile, was sat in the seats behind, he was not that keen on flying 'but it had to be done' he thought to himself.

"Okay guys, where do you want to go?" The pilot asked, glancing at the open street map lay out on Kane's lap. The snaking route of Dale Edwards' canvassing cavalcade was highlighted in orange, right through the middle of Dallas. Kane had identified the main junctions on the proposed route the previous night and drawn several, thin, black triangles, the tip of these were at the selected junctions and the remainder of the triangle fanned out to show an area where it might be possible to line up a shot.

"I'd like to check out these areas," Kane replied, pointing to the black triangles, "How low can you go?"

"Well, we can pick up a Starbucks if you want, is that low enough for you?"

"Good, I might keep you to that." Kane smiled as he turned around to see Zach staring at the pilot and slowly shaking his head.

The pilot finally got clearance for take-off and headed for the first triangle on the map. He hovered back and fore, slowly descending at Kane's request, before tilting the nose and ascending in a forward line to another part of the triangle. Kane scanned the buildings below and followed the view to the centre of Dallas in the distance. Every now and then he would ask the pilot to drop lower and he would take several photographs on his TZ30 Super Zoom Travel Camera before asking the pilot to move on to another part of the triangle. They had already used a half hour of their time allocation and were only just starting on their second of the eight triangles highlighted on the now well-worn street map.

"What are you like at flying backwards?" Kane asked rather nonchalantly.

"Buddy, I could fly this thing upside down, on its tail or inside out if you want me to."

A faint groan was heard from behind as Zack turned to look out of the large, side window; he had only just got used to the tilting but did not fancy any more acrobatics.

"If we can start here," Kane pointed to an area near the proposed route just below the tip of the triangle, "and then hover back for about 1500 metres." Kane continued.

"You got it." The pilot replied, tilting the nose of the Bell 429 and accelerating to the point indicated on the map.

They repeated the manoeuvre over and over, on all the remaining seven triangles and each time, Kane would take a video clip as well as several snapshots, before eventually setting down at Fort Worth, still with ten minutes left on their flight time allowance.

"Now what?" A relieved Zach enquired.

"Now we find a computer and narrow down our search." Kane, having unbuckled his seat belt and said his thanks to the pilot, alighted from the helicopter onto the warm, oil stained tarmac to stride back to the office with Zach in tow.

It took another hour to get back into Dallas and set Kane up with access to a PC. Once logged in, Kane quickly uploaded the stills and video clips while Zach searched out two cups of coffee. Together they trawled through the pictures and clips, narrowing down the options and circling areas from where a hit could be made. Two hours later, six circles had been drawn on the map.

"Right, we had better make a start." Kane stated, tapping the first circle with his pen, before stretching his arms high above his head to relieve the tension. Rising from his seat, Kane collected the map and travel camera and headed for the door.

"Jeez, when are we going to eat?" Zach complained, "my stomach thinks my throat has been cut."

"We'll grab something on the way, there's a hot dog stand on the corner."

"Oh yeah, great." The sarcastic reply.

They soon arrived at the first circle, or rather egg shaped area, on the map and having got out of the car and took to opposite sides of the street. Zach had one last look at the computer enhanced image of Henryk Leidmeister before folding it away into his jacket pocket. The first building was a delicatessen with two floors above. Zach flashed his badge and showed the computer enhanced image to everyone he encountered. Kane was doing something similar on the opposite side of the street, but flashed his British driving licence, it worked every time.

By 9am they had decided to call it a day and Kane walked back to where they had parked the car to wait for Zach who was trying to extract himself from an 'overly helpful' old lady. As he approached the car, three Hispanic youths were busy removing the rear alloy to match the one they had just taken off the front.

"Oh great, just what I needed." Kane uttered out aloud as he headed for the nearest target. His policy had always been attack is the best form of defence and tonight was no different.

Hearing the approaching footsteps, the tall, skinny youth spun around, tapping the end of a crowbar menacingly into his left palm. "What you want man?" He sneered.

Kane took two steps forward and grabbed the bar with both hands pushing it forward and upward into the bridge of the startled youth's nose. Blood immediately poured from his broken nose as the crowbar fell to the floor, clanged a couple of times before rolling under Zach's jacked up red, Chevrolet Cruze. Instinct made him lean back as a bony, tattooed fist flew in front of his face. Kane grabbed the outstretched arm and turning his body completely around, brought the arm and the following body with him. Leaving go at the last possible moment, the second target smashed into the side of the car before collapsing in a heap on the damp, dark street. As he released his grip, Kane allowed his body to dip forward as his right leg spun around to catch the third and final statue like target square in the chest. The round kick was intended for the head but it was enough to send the recipient sprawling onto his backside. The frightened youth scrambled to his feet and ran off clutching his chest, quickly followed by the other two.

Kane turned around to see Zach stood in the middle of the street staring at his beloved car.

"Thanks for your help." Kane shouted sarcastically but with the hint of a smile in his voice.

"I was going to join in," Zach replied, "just couldn't make my mind up on what side. Hey, you dent my car?" Zach blurted out as he strode over to the buckled, body shaped, dent in the driver's door.

"Never mind the dent; it will match the ones on the other side. Can you get these back on or shall I call our friends back to help out?" Kane asked pointing to the front wheel lying flat on the floor and enjoying the banter after the monotony of the day's door to door trudging.

Zach tightened up the rear wheel and put the lock nut back in place.

"Jeez, they even used my own tools."

Kane helped him to locate the front wheel onto the four protruding bolts and Zach set about locating and tightening the nuts. The clatter of the brace hitting the floor, followed by some choice swear words, made Kane turn around just in time to see Zach jumping to his feet and holding his right hand.

"Jeez, I've broken my goddam finger."

Kane walked over and smiled as he gently lifted Zach's hand up into the light from the distant street lamp.

"You big baby, it's not even scratched," Kane mimicked, noticing the index finger was already starting to swell. "You get in the car and I'll finish off here. Are you alright to drive or do you want me to do that as well?"

"Fun-eeee. Just make sure you put that on tight." Zach replied, climbing behind the wheel.

Kane put the tools back into the trunk and an hour and a half later they both emerged from A & E with Zach's index and middle finger strapped firmly together.

"Well, at least it's not broken." Kane stated.

"It might just as well be," Zack retorted, "it hurts like hell."

By the end of the following day they still had one area to search, but now it was too late. Tomorrow was the 28th.

Kane, Brian and Neil had been called to an 8 pm meeting in the CIA offices in Main Street which started with a ten minute catch up briefing with Chas, before being led away to the main meeting room to join what Kane guessed to be between fifty and sixty people crammed into the small but brightly lit office. The bodies parted silently to let Chas' large, sturdy frame glide to the far end of the room, closing ranks behind him and leaving the six men jockeying for position in the doorway. An enlarged, aerial view map of Dallas spread across the far wall, beneath which Chas Wiltson and Dan Reagan, his FBI counterpart, were already deep in conversation.

Five minutes later Chas' voice boomed out for quiet as he prepared to address the assembled audience. He spoke directly to each group in turn, indicating an area on the map behind him with a long, tapered pointer. As he finished with each group they left to collect the equipment needed for the task in hand until eventually only Kane and his five colleagues were left, still huddled in the corner of the room.

"Right guys, come a bit closer," Chas called with a short wave of his hand. "I think if there were to be an assassination attempt on Dale Edwards tomorrow, it would more than likely come from somewhere along the route. Dan, however, thinks your view…" Chas was staring directly at Kane, "… on a possible long range shot, is worth investing in, so over to you Dan."

Dan Reagan at five foot nine was nearly a foot shorter than Chas and about a hundred pounds lighter. Taking the pointer from Chas, he started to trace a circular area on the map. "These are the areas you have covered and we have mobile units following up in each of the locations. The remaining area is too large to get a proper sweep done in time so we intend setting you guys up in vantage points to link up with my guys on the ground. If you see him, holler, we'll do the rest."

"So are we to be just look outs?" Zach asked, pointing his question at Chas.

"No, you guys will remain in your pairs and will be issued with a rifle and scope, one for each pair." Chas turned his head to look at Kane and continued, "Our British friends will be issued with Binos and a radio to keep in contact with our FBI colleagues on the ground, but I don't need to tell you guys the seriousness of this job."

"Er, Sir…" Zach interrupted, holding up his strapped fingers.

Chas looked at Dan and then back to Zach, "Okay, you two can swap over, but Kane, no shooting unless it is absolutely necessary and for God sakes, if any of you have to take aim, don't pull that trigger unless you are absolutely positive he's our man. I have enough paperwork on my desk as it is and I certainly don't want anymore; and Kane, remember, your role is supposed to be non-operational."

The meeting finished and having been issued with their equipment, Zach and his three British friends set off back to the Hotel.

"Pick you up about 6am, okay?" Zach suggested on the way back to the hotel.

"Yeah, that's fine. I'm going to spend some time with Brian and Neil trying to identify some good vantage points which we can investigate first thing tomorrow but your guys don't have to stay."

"Fine by me, tomorrow's going to be long enough as it is," Zack replied, pulling into the kerb outside the hotel. "See you bright and early."

Shortly after 6am the following morning, the three pairs set off to their designated areas. Kane and Zach found a suitable vantage point on their second attempt, whilst the other two pairs took a little longer.

Even with both windows open, the empty room had a heavy, musty smell. Recent visits by local kids and passing vagrants had left an array of litter strewn across the bare, grimy, wooden floorboards. The stench of stale urine emulated from the corner of the room, but Zach, who was nearest, did not seem to notice. Kane was resting on the open window sill, scanning the far off buildings with his telescopic sites, thinking if he could see Leidmeister, then surely he could see them, but if he was in the vicinity, it should be enough to deter his actions and maybe even force him out into the open. A bead of sweat trickled down his cheek onto the collar of his Blue Harbour shirt.

Using the back of his forearm, Kane wiped the sweat from his forehead, clenched and unclenched his left fist several times and lifting up the barrel of the AS50, he squinted through the sites and began to slowly traverse from left to right. As he focussed, his target slowly came into view. It took just three seconds for him to confirm the target which was less than 500 metres away, but he had to be right.

"Zach, end block, second window from the left, two floors down, you got him?"

"Yeah, it's him alright and he's setting himself up for the shot." Kane's partner was sat by the window at the far end of the dusty, deserted room, steadying his grip on the Canon 18 x 50 Binoculars to re-confirm his identification. "You gotta take him… NOW."

Kane's finger slowly pressed against the trigger, releasing the .50 BMG cartridge with deadly accuracy. The target collapsed, slumping half out of the open window.

Leaving Zach to continue his surveillance, Kane had packed up the AS50 and having secured it in the trunk of Zach's car, placed the keys in his pocket and walked briskly towards the old tenement building, checking the cold, murky windows of the buildings that surrounded him. Kane raced up the six flights of stairs to the corridor. The exercise felt good after hours being cramped in the same position.

As Kane approached the final door he shouted ahead "Guys, it's Kane, I'm coming in."

“In here…” The instant response came from somewhere deep within the room.

Kane walked carefully through the small hallway and into the sparsely furnished room. One of the FBI agents was standing over the body, which was still half hanging out of the window, whilst another continued his painstaking search of the apartment. The third was going through the purse of the old lady slumped in a floral covered, high winged armchair, her head tilted to the side and a large, dark red patch clearly visible through the strands of her thin, grey hair.

“You do this?” The agent stood by the window asked, staring down at the motionless form. “That was some shot man, straight in the head.”

Kane looked back at the young excited face in front of him and guessed this was his first real assignment, after all, nobody really expected Leidmeister to be here. Kane glanced at the body hanging out of the window. Then down at the small crowd of people forming below.

“We'd better get him in.” Kane said forcibly.

“No,” The sharp retort came from the agent by the armchair. “The lab boys are on their way, they'll take care of it.”

“Well, if he slips down any further he'll be joining those looking up at us.” Kane snapped back.

The Agent walked across the threadbare brown carpet and stared down at the body. The waist and top torso were over the edge of the windowsill and only the legs remained inside.

“Get me something to secure him.” He barked to the young face by his side. As if on cue, the body started to slip further out of the window and Kane rushed to help the Agent pull the lifeless form out of the window and prop it, sitting upright, against the wall. Kane noticed where the .50 BMG cartridge had entered the left side of the corpse's head, taking half his ear with it and leaving a large hole in the back of his skull, pieces of brain tissue clearly visible. The closely cut blonde hair was now matted with blood which had also trickled down over the cheeks in three separate lines. Kane was about to turn away when he retraced his thoughts. Cheeks? he thought to himself as he bent down to take a closer look.

Leidmeister's cheeks were hollow, these though thin, were not as prominent. The matted hair and blood stained face masked the features, but there was something wrong with the cold, grey blue eyes, this was not the face of the man in the doorway. Kane stared for several seconds at the corpse's lifeless left eye. Sirens wailed in the background and numerous tires screeched to a halt on the weathered tarmac below. Kane reached over to the small, mug stained, coffee table and picking up a discarded envelope, tore off a strip and began folding it into a firm, slender stick.

"Hey, what you doing?" The FBI agent demanded, as Kane ignoring his question, began to scrape away the thick grey blue contact lens to reveal the natural brown iris.

"Don't know who this guy is," Kane stated as he rose from the floor, "but it's not Leidmeister." Then he turned, walked out of the apartment, down the stairs and out onto the traffic filled street below.

5

Several hours, two written reports, two lengthy interviews and numerous cups of coffee later, Kane sat at the corner of Zach's desk, reading through his discharging a firearm report. The two officers conducting the last interview had been very thorough, leaving him in no doubt that the shot was not necessary and there were other things he could have done – yeah, right!

"Don't worry too much about the paperwork, Chas will get that report closed off for you after what you have done." Zach stated, replacing the telephone handset. "That was him on the phone, wants you guys in his office now. Probably wants to personally thank you." A hint of sarcasm in Zach's voice as he rose from his chair. "We'll pick up Brian and Neil on the way."

Kane, Brian and Neil sat impatiently in Chas Wiltson's office waiting for him to finish his telephone call with Dan Reagan. It had been over ten minutes since they had been ushered into the office and beckoned over to the three padded seats carefully lined up in front of the large mahogany desk. Kane stared at the scuffed leather top on Chas' desk as he strained to pick up the conversation on the telephone but all he could hear was Chas' somewhat sympathetic voice.

"Thank God it wasn't our watch. The killing of a presidential candidate will certainly cause heads to roll and some big ones at that." Chas briefly looked up at the three Brits before continuing his conversation. "What time was he shot?"

"Shot." All three of them picked up on the question and gave one another puzzled looks. Kane waited for Chas to end his call and before the handset had been placed back in the cradle, bluntly asked, “Dale Edwards? Shot?”

“No, not Edwards, Bob Jollinger. He was shot and killed an hour ago in Memphis on his way out to a promotional dinner.”

“Did you get the perpetrator?” Brian interjected, with a renewed interest after the foot slogging and stake outs of the last few days.

“No it was a rifle shot, came from an office block over 900 metres away. Found the cleaner, dead under a desk, but so far, nothing else.”

“Leidmeister?” Kane posed the question, trying to find something that would tie everything together.

“Who knows.” Chas replied, “At the moment your guess is as good as mine. None of this makes sense at the moment, but anyway, you guys don’t have to worry about it anymore. You have been booked on the 8.30pm flight back to England tomorrow evening, so thanks for your help and enjoy the rest of your stay. Oh and Kane, I spoke to Bill Johnson, he has been trying to get hold of you all day.”

“Yeah, battery died, haven’t been able to charge it yet.”

“Well, use this one and give him a call.” Chas replied, holding out the handset from the desk phone.

Kane dialled the number and a few moments later he was put through to his section leader.

“Kane, the very man.” Bill seemed genuinely pleased to hear Kane’s voice and taking a deep breath, continued. “Chas has filled me in on what’s been going on over there but I have something which should be of interest to you. The man on the tape, the interrogator, it looks as if he was on the take. They found a considerable amount of money stashed in his apartment and two suitcases packed and ready to go.”

“Has he admitted to it?” Kane asked hopefully. If he had started to give information then they would soon have some of the answers they were searching for.

“Nope, he can’t admit to anything. They found his body on the floor of his apartment, been dead a while.”

“How did he die?”

“Stabbed through the heart. No sign of a struggle, so he obviously knew his assailant.”

“Didn’t they bring him in for questioning as we asked?”

“No, some Major Morgan, security chief, said he’d already interviewed him and didn't think he was involved. Even gave him a couple of days off as he had only recently returned to work after an illness. They only went to his apartment after they found his wife stuffed into a skip not far from where she worked. She'd been stabbed through the heart too. Anyway, the Yanks are taking it from here so I'll see you in a couple of days when you get back."

Kane said his farewells and replaced the handset. Chas looked up at him, "Problem?" He enquired, like Kane, he was searching for answers that would wrap this whole thing up into one tidy ball.

"The cleaner in Memphis, how did he die?" Kane realised he was assuming the cleaner to be male, but Chas did not correct him.

"Stab wound, through the heart I think, why?"

"Sir, do you mind if I dig around for a bit."

"Officially, you are off the case, but if you want to spend your last day here digging around then fine, just don't shoot anybody and I want to be the first to know if you do find anything."

"Yeah you got it, could we borrow Zach for the day?"

"Well, I was going to get him to show around Dallas before you went but if that's how you want to spend your day then fine."

"Whoa, don't forget me." Brian interrupted.

"Nor me," Neil added. "I want in too."

"Okay," Chas conceded, "but stay out of trouble."

Three handshakes and three goodbyes later the trio left Chas' office and headed down the corridor, picking up a bewildered Zach on the way.

"Hey guys, wait up, where we going?" Zach asked as they squeezed themselves into the lift.

"Can you take us back to the area we were in today?" Kane asked Zach, trying to get himself more room but only succeeding in getting a scornful look from a middle aged lady having stepped on her ankle.

"What, now?"

"No, in the morning when we can see the area in the daylight. It's okay; we got your boss' permission, provided I don't shoot anybody." This got another scornful look from the now concerned lady who quickly exited the lift as soon as the doors opened. "In the meantime, you can buy us dinner."

The following morning Zach pulled up outside the Hotel in his red Chevrolet Cruze. Neil and Brian jumped in the back and Kane sat in the front passenger seat. During the twenty five minute journey, Kane relayed his conversation with Bill Johnson, adding a few more details to fill in some of the gaps for Zach.

"So what are we going to do here?" Zach asked as they pulled up at their destination.

"Well, we'll just knock a few doors and flash Leidmeister's picture; it's enough of a resemblance to yesterday's shooter and should jog somebody's memory."

"Aww great, just what I wanted, another day of bloody door knocking." Neil moaned, climbing out of the car and selecting a likely place to start.

"I haven't got a copy." Brian added.

"That's okay," Kane answered, opening the glove box. "There are a few here."

"Zach, can you get me back into the apartment?" Kane asked, nodding to the old tenement block with the Black and white outside. A young woman in a low cut, red top and tight white hot pants was taking her pet dog, which looked like a cross between a poodle and a Rottweiler, for a leisurely walk. Both Kane and Zach allowed themselves an extra second to take in the view before Zach responded.

"Yeah, sure, but don't expect to find anything left in there. Forensic would have removed anything and everything. Are you looking for something in particular?"

"Don't know yet, just like to get a few more pieces of the jigsaw."

"Huh?" Zach was none the wiser, so pulling out his ID, he got out of the Cruze and walked over to introduce himself to the two young officers, currently admiring the way the woman bent over to caress and ruffle the scruffy white, lucky dog. Zach approached the car just as the woman was lifting the dog and turning it around to face the direction they had just come from. Her ample breasts threatening to bounce out of her tight fitting top as she continued her teasing.

"Guys," Zach interrupted the startled pair, shoving his ID through the open window. "Just going to have a look around again. Don't bother getting out, we won't be long. Carry on with what you were doing." Zach continued, glancing at the woman and then back at the two officers with the schoolboy blushes. The woman, considering her playtime over, dragged the dog back down the street while Zach and Kane entered the building and climbed the stairs to the sealed off apartment.

"What are we looking for?" Zach asked, ducking under the tape which is magically supposed to keep everyone out.

"I really don't know, Zach. There are more holes in this case than a sieve, nothing seems to fit together." Kane answered as he glanced around the room and the blood stained wall and floor.

Zach went to the window where the shooter's body had been dangling out before being unceremoniously pulled in to rest against the wall. He gazed down at the road, the woman had gone and the two young officers were peering through the windscreen to the apartment above. Zach let his gaze move down the street to the building where they had been staked out, then traversed across towards the Main Street area. He squinted slightly as he tried to make out recognisable buildings or street junctions, then moved his view left and then right again, this time slower. Crouching down, he repeated the process, before standing back and walking back over the threadbare carpet, looked out of the window at the other end of the musty room.

Kane smiled as he noticed him crouching to look through the window before walking to the other one.

"Lost something?" He asked jokingly.

"Yes." Zach replied, a perplexed look on his face, "Main Street."

"What…?"

"Take a look for yourself, there is no way you could see onto Main Street from here. You would have to go probably to the next block to see the junction clearly.

Kane stared through the window, skimming the distant roof tops and allowing his focus to rest on the roof of a light coloured concrete building which was the only part of Main Street visible.

"But he was taking aim, you saw him," Kane stuttered, now more confused than ever. "The rifle, it was a VSSK Vykhlop, used for long range work, what else could he have been aiming at?"

"Birds, tin cans, who knows." Zach turned back to look out of the grimy window, still patterned with blotches of powder where forensic had painstakingly lifted every fresh fingerprint. "I saw him taking aim and yes it was towards the Main Street area, but he could only have been aiming at someone on the same level as the roof. The only people allowed on the roof tops yesterday were the security personnel and it wouldn't make sense to shoot one of them but then nothing makes sense at the moment."

"What do we know about this guy anyway, apart from the fact he's not

Leidmeister, or is he and we're going off on the wrong track?" Kane blurted out, looking for inspiration.

"Well, he had a French passport saying his name was Henri Devaux, it seems to check out so far and Interpol don't have anything on him."

"Okay," Kane sighed as he headed for the door. "Let's join Brian and Neil on the streets and see if we can dig anything else up. There's not much time left and I'd like to get some sense out of this before we catch our plane back to Gatwick. All the neighbours have been interviewed so let's concentrate on the streets, parents taking kids to and from school, the mailman, anybody that would have noticed something out of the normal daily routine."

Just over an hour later, Kane crossed the street to where Zach was trying to politely end the conversation with yet another clingy old lady and seized his opportunity when he saw Kane.

"Ah, there's my lift. Sorry Mam, I have to go, nice talking to you." Then Zach spun around and headed off to meet Kane, not waiting for a response.

"What is it with you and old ladies?" Kane joked. "Did you find out anything?"

"No, she was just taken with my boyish charm."

"Then try your boyish charm on that one over there." Kane nodded to the woman walking her poodleweiller.

They both walked over to the woman in the red top and very short white shorts. She smiled as they approached.

Zach tried to maintain eye contact as he produced his badge. "Excuse me Mam; we'd like to know if you've seen this gentleman before?" Zach unfolded the computer enhanced photo and held it in front of her face.

"No, sorry, I've already told your friends I don't know him."

"Could you take another look please, madam," Kane interrupted. "You may have seen him going in or coming out of one of the buildings at the end of the street."

The woman looked Kane up and down. "Are you English? I love the English accent."

"Er, Mam, could we get back to the picture." Zach moved the well-used photo between her and Kane, feeling a bit narked that Kane was receiving the glad eye and not him.

The woman glanced down again at the picture. "No I told you, I ain't seen him coming out of anywhere…" Her voice trailed off, then staring at the picture again, continued. "Wait a minute; he could have been the other guy."

"Other guy?" Kane asked, moving around to look down at the picture.

"Yeah, about three maybe four days ago, there were two guys coming outta the building on the end, one I didn't see very well."

"What about the one you did see, did he look anything like this?"

"Well, he had a hat on and his collar pulled up, kind of mysterious looking, nearly tripped over my dog. Had eyes like yours, blue… only… colder."

Zach looked over at Kane and nodded. "Thank you Mam, you've been a great help."

"Always willing to assist gentlemen." She responded, giving Kane another once over.

Kane smiled and turned to face Zach. "Let's grab Brian and Neil and get back to the office."

"Thank you madam." Kane finished as he turned to join Zach for the walk back to the car, leaving the woman with a very disappointed look on her face.

Ten minutes later, having picked up a very grateful Brian and Neil, they were working their way through the traffic when Kane turned around in his seat to speak to Brian and Neil. "You guys knew Leidmeister, what would you say was his single, most memorable feature?"

"His eyes." Came Neil's immediate response.

"Yeah, I'd go along with that." Brian joined in. "They were kind of weird… lifeless."

"Cold…" Kane thought out aloud.

"Yeah, that's right; cold." Neil confirmed

Getting back to the office, Kane sat himself at the corner of Zach's desk and started scribbling some notes.

Zach sat down in his chair and turned to speak to Kane. "I was in the office with Chas yesterday evening, being told to take you guys on a tour of Dallas and keep you out of trouble until your plane left. It was Chas who phoned your guy in London. Our shooter Henri, or whatever his name is, had a return flight to Islamabad booked for last night and a healthy wad of hundred dollar bills in his inside pocket. Now I couldn't hear both sides of the conversation, but Wiltson was obviously concerned about something."

A frown etched into Kane's face as he leaned back in th
the only one. If we look at what we have so far, we have
of an informant plus two other killings in Islamabad, v
money found in Islamabad and another stash here on ou
a presidential candidate assassinated and another one that could
not have been a target. We also have a dead cleaner that may have been killed in a similar way to the other two killings in Islamabad. It's a safe bet that Leidmeister took out the informant, but did he commit the other two killings? If he did and the Memphis cleaner went the same way, then Leidmeister assassinated the other presidential candidate, Bob Jollinger."

Zach thought pensively for a moment before adding to the confusion. "Forensic said the old lady had been dead for at least forty eight hours. That meant the shooter would probably have been in the apartment all that time. Definitely enough time to realise he did not have a clear shot at Edwards, so why didn't he move on and if Edwards wasn't his target, what was he aiming at? He was definitely going to shoot at something, no doubt about it. But at what?"

"Unless this was a red herring!"

"Red herring?" Zach asked perplexed.

"If Leidmeister did kill the Pakistani interrogator, maybe he got something out of him first. Perhaps he thought we were onto him and changed targets, but then why would he go to such lengths to make out that Edwards was the target? Or was the target Jollinger all along and this was just to throw us off the scent?"

"I could understand it if it were the other way around," Zach replied, his brain kicking into gear as small pieces of a jigsaw started to fit into place. "Edwards is the running favourite, so if he had been the target then Leidmeister would have been here and this other shooter in Memphis. But, having gone to all this trouble, if this is a terrorist set up, why didn't they make sure of killing both candidates? That would have doubled the media impact."

"Perhaps Edwards was never the intended target after all," Kane replied, his brow creased with concentration. "It could have been that Jollinger was the hit all along. If Leidmeister thought we knew anything then what better way to throw us off course. All this shooter had to do was drop one of our security guys to cause panic and heighten our belief that Edwards was the target. It may even have relaxed the security around Jollinger."

"You taking the shooter out would have had the same effect." Brian commented.

Neil looked down at the creased photographic print out. "Leidmeister is obviously the hitman," Emphasizing the word the. "So Jollinger must have been the target all along. I'm willing to bet that this guy Henri Devaux is a novice, they weren't bothered about him being discovered, just as long as it drew attention away from Jollinger. That's why they went to all the trouble of making us think he was Leidmeister. So yes, I reckon your guy in Islamabad did tell Leidmeister we were onto him, but whoever put this all together at such short notice, must have some powerful and influential backers and why would Jollinger be a more important target to them than Edwards?"

"Well, perhaps Edwards was the target but as Kane suggested, they changed to Jollinger when they thought they had been found out." Brian responded.

"But then they could have done this in reverse and had our guy Henri go to Memphis, drop a couple of pointers to alert us to his presence and we would have been concentrating there instead of here," Zach contributed. "Christ, this is getting confusing. It still doesn't explain why, having staked out the area, got the gear and the man in place, they did not go after Edwards as well. The risks would have been the same and it looks as if Leidmeister helped him set this up, so they would definitely have worked out that if they had gone four windows down they would have had a clear view, albeit a very distant view, of Main Street junction?"

"Or, perhaps they want to keep Edwards alive." Kane commented. Like Zach and the others, pieces of the puzzle were starting to fit into place, but not the way Kane expected them to.

Kane's close down meeting with Chas was very brief. The fallout from Jollinger's political assassination was already having far reaching effects. Having been summoned to Langley for a briefing, Chas had first appeared disinterested in Kane's report, that is, until he had mentioned that the shooter had no clear view of Main Street junction and would not have been able to have taken Edwards out.

"So why was he there?" Chas had stopped packing his briefcase and sat back down in the large, brown executive chair, a puzzled frown etched on his face.

"We're still trying to work that one out." Kane replied. "It looks like either he knew we were onto him and changed targets, or Jollinger could have been the target all along."

"All this written down somewhere?" Chas asked as he stood and collected up some red pocket files and his brief case.

"It will be, I'll finish off my report before I leave."

"Ah yes, you're back to England today, is Zach up to date on all this?"

"Yes Sir." Kane sensed he was about to be dismissed and felt uneasy at not being able to finish the job.

"Well, have a good trip back and thanks for your help." Chas responded holding out his overly large right hand.

Kane shook the hand and turned to walk out of the open door.

"Kane," Chas called out. "I mean it, thanks for all your help. I may be speaking to you again when you get back to England. There are too many loose ends to tie up and what is it you English say, many hands make light work? I'll be in touch."

They both nodded and Kane made his way back along the corridor to Zach's desk to complete his report.

6

The flight back was long and tiring. Kane had been on several long haul flights in the past few weeks and was still trying to find a mental framework to conclusively tie the events of the past few days together. Unfortunately, Neil was wide awake and in between playing computer games on the seat console in front, kept coming up with his own theories on the assassination attempt that never was.

Kane suggested that due to the time delay they should try and get some sleep and seeing that it would be the very early hours of the morning when they arrived back in England they should meet at MI6 headquarters at about 12 noon.

"How do I get in?" Neil asked, "Do I need a special pass?"

"Hark at him!" Brian laughed, "He thinks we're all like James Bond, expensive cars, complicated gadgets and a special card to allow us access to all areas. Just go to reception like everybody else and we'll come and get you."

Kane smiled and settled back in his extended seat, Neil was a fresh faced ex-para, who had somehow managed to get transferred into the Military police before ending up in MI5. He was ambitious, a thinker not a fighter, though he wasn't afraid to mix it as he had proved on two tours of Afghanistan and numerous 'friendly' encounters extracting brawling squaddies from local pubs and he had two scars to prove it! But Kane had warmed to him over the last few days. He liked the way he thought outside of the box and was not afraid to suggest things no matter how farfetched they may sound.

Brian was quieter, more reserved. He had the ability to size people up very quickly and was seldom wrong. Kane had worked with Brian twice before, once in Libya and the other time in Somalia where a hostage investigation had gone wrong and they had walked, somewhat knowingly, into an ambush. If the rebels had opened up instead of taking them prisoner they would not have been here today.

The rebel leader at the time, Raoul, enjoyed inflicting pain. The local villages were full of one armed men and women whom Raoul had delighted in chopping off a hand or arm if he suspected they favoured the government regime. He also got bored with the many hostages he had taken over the last eight months and amused himself by sending some of them back piece by piece until the demands had been met. Some he decided were not worth keeping alive and delighted in coming up with new sadistic methods of giving them a slow, agonising death, to entertain his drug crazed 'soldiers'.

A British couple had been seized a week earlier whilst trying to pay for the release of their kidnapped daughter. They had hastily cashed in all their savings and frantically borrowed from friends to try and meet the ransom demand for their daughter, whose right ear had been sent to the British High Commissioner in Nairobi six days previously. They flew to Somalia with promises to pay the remainder as soon as their house had been sold but as they had only come up with half the amount, the rebels took them captive in Hargeisa and sent a further ransom demand together with two right ears.

Kane and Brian were working in Uganda and Kenya on different assignments and had been quickly diverted to Somalia to try and locate the whereabouts of the hostages and then feedback enough confirmed information for an extraction. Two SAS pods were already on standby in Nairobi waiting for the details so they could develop and implement a plan of action. The British Government wanted a quick response and the terrorists had already been identified as a splinter group of Somalia's Islamist al-Shabaab militants, who were so high on drugs and adrenalin that they made little effort to cover their tracks and moved on to new locations every few days.

Kane posed as a journalist with Brian as his cameraman and made it known they would pay for useful information that they could use in their news reports. Journalists were often prime targets for kidnappers but it was also a quick way of asking questions without raising too much interest –

apart from their worth as a ransom prize.

By the end of the first full day of 'news hunting', they had paid for eight newsworthy items of information, all small amounts paid in dollars, but eagerly accepted by the starving locals willing to chance the wrath of the rebels for helping the Westerners in exchange for food. Three of the snippets related to the two British tourists and all three suggested they were being held nearby, but nobody knew or was brave enough to say where. They had opted to share a room and Kane and Brian took it in turn to sleep while the other kept a watchful eye out for any unwelcome visitors.

They had just left the hotel and were walking down the dry, dusty road towards the outskirts of Hargeisa when an ageing, green Freelander pulled up alongside.

"You want see British people, you pay much money, yes?" A voice called out from inside the battered, green chassis.

Kane lowered his head and peered in. "What British people?"

"They have lovely daughter, very good," The man smiled, his white teeth framed by the blackness of his skin. "I take you, you pay, yes?"

"No, you tell us where and we will decide if it's worth paying for." Kane replied, staring into the driver's bloodshot eyes, the large pupils now squinting as he sized up the westerner who dared to correct him.

"No, no my friend, you pay me and I take you to someone who tell you about them." A big grin spread across his face as he lent across the ripped and scuffed passenger seat to open the creaking door.

Kane looked up at Brian and saw the concern in his face. "Okay. Ops on."

They had already discussed the risks they were taking in their efforts to try and get information quickly, but if a situation arose, which meant they could be getting close to determining the hostages whereabouts, but also putting themselves in danger, then 'ops on' would be their code to alert one another to be ready for anything.

"Just one thing," Kane continued, looking back to the driver. "We do not have any more cash with us and will need to go to the bank, but I am not drawing any out until I know what I'm paying for."

The bloodshot eyes narrowed, the smile disappeared for a few seconds then slowly spread back across the sunken cheeks.

"Get in, I take you." The smile was there, but the eyes portrayed something different.

Brian got in the back and sat behind the driver, while Kane eased into the front passenger seat and slammed the creaking door behind him. He could not help noticing the door and dashboard were covered in dark red splashes, some of which had dried and were starting to flake. Judging from the way the driver was struggling with the manual gear box, it was easy to assume that the streaks were from the previous owner, but there were other things to concentrate on now.

"So how much further?" Kane asked as the last remnants of the town faded behind them. "I thought you said it was just on the outskirts."

"Yeah man, don't you worry now, soon be there."

"And where exactly is there?"

"We here now, you see, up there." The grinning driver smiled even wider as he pointed to a ramshackle farmhouse about four hundred metres off the road.

"That's far enough." Kane ordered, snatching up the hand brake.

"Hey man, what you doing?" The driver remonstrated as the Freelander skidded to a halt.

"Now whose up there and how many?" Kane was about to ask again when four heavily armed rebels eased out of the bushes about 500 metres in front and walked slowly towards the car.

"Your call, Kane." Brian whispered, sliding up the right leg of his blue Levi jeans and feeling for the handle of the hunting knife strapped to his calf. Both he and Kane had opted for the knives strapped to their legs as opposed to carrying hand guns which, if searched, may be more difficult to explain, seeing as they were supposed to be neutral reporters, than a knife, even a concealed one.

"No, chill. See what happens." Kane had already noticed a fifth Kalashnikov carrying youth in the mirror who was slowly approaching the car from about one hundred metres to the rear, index finger testing the tension of the well-used trigger, eager to pull it again.

"This what happens, you get out." The driver snarled in response, whilst removing his hand from under his sweat stained, blue cotton shirt to reveal an old Makarov semi-automatic pistol.

The gun was inches from Kane's face and he could easily have disarmed him but one pistol against five or more Kalashnikovs was not the odds he favoured.

"Okay, it's cool, I want my story, you want the money, we're getting out." Kane replied opening the creaking door and nodding to Brian to do the same.

The youth approaching the car from the rear stopped as first the front passenger door and then the rear door opened and the two westerners got out. He levelled his gun towards them and continued his approach.

"I thought we weren't going to let ourselves be taken." Brian remarked sarcastically as Kane walked around the back of the car to join him.

"When the odds are better, or you have no choice, then go for it," Kane whispered, "In the meantime, it looks as if we may get the information we came for, now all we have to do is get out."

"No talk." The driver shouted as he got out of the car, motioning with his pistol for them to walk towards the four fast approaching youths, their ageing Kalashnikovs slung low in front of them. The youth that had appeared from the bushes to the rear of the Freelander was now using the length of his weapon, sideways on, to push both Kane and Brian towards the oncoming quartet, his smile broadening each time they stumbled forward at the force of his shove. Meanwhile, the driver leaned into the cab and retrieved a menacing looking, rope handled machete from its' hiding place underneath the driver's seat. Kicking the door shut, he turned and jogged towards the two westerners who had now stopped to be surrounded by their captors.

Kane could not understand the Somali language, but now and then he picked up on an Arabic word but still not enough to determine what they were joking about. He glanced around at the sniggering rebels. Their guns were all strapped over their shoulders and around their backs so there would be no easy way to disarm one of them, let alone have enough free movement to use the gun with any effect.

"Any ideas?" Kane murmured quietly to Brian, but not quietly enough.

The flat blade of the machete slammed down onto Kane's left shoulder causing him to dip slightly.

"I said no talking," Shouted the driver, walking around to face Kane and placing the edge of the machete against the tip of his nose. "Maybe I send your nose to your wife, eh, you want that?" He continued slowly sliding the blade down the bridge of Kane's nose causing a small line of blood to trickle effortlessly down the side of his nose and on to his chin.

"No Abu, enough." A voice boomed out from somewhere on Kane's right. Kane glanced to his side as a large, muscular form emerged from the sparse undergrowth. A red, sweat soaked bandana was roughly tied around his head and he was flanked by two equally large figures, Kalashnikovs at the ready.

"Raoul…" The driver started before carrying on in his native Somalian tongue, occasionally waving the machete in Kane's direction.

"My friend not like you, but if you buy my guests then maybe I not give you to him," Raoul sneered at Kane before continuing. "You have money?"

"I can get it," Kane replied, sensing that how and what he said next could be the difference between life and death. "We just need to agree on how much its worth. I'll phone my boss with the details and the money should be transferred across the same day, then it just needs both our signatures," Kane paused to look at Brian just long enough for Raoul to know that Brian would be needed too, "and we can draw the money out."

Abu started gesticulating again in his native tongue, although Kane could not understand the language, the gestures were enough to show that Abu did not trust him.

"You make phone call." Raoul ordered as his large pupils pierced directly into Kane's unflinching stare.

"Sure, but I need to go back to the hotel first and get the details." Kane replied.

"One million dollars." Raoul sneered, his wide grin highlighting the sparkling white teeth in a now fixed smile.

"No chance," Kane immediately responded, his mind racing to find a response that would sound genuine. "Our banker's draft limit is only $50,000."

"Well, that will buy you one ear, which one will we send back?" Raoul stepped towards Kane unsheathing his machete, no longer smiling.

"Wait," Brian shouted, picking up on Kane's comment and trying to make it sound more feasible. "We could probably get that raised to $50,000 each so you would get $100,000, but we still need two signatures and it won't look very good in the Bank if he has parts missing."

Raoul stared into Kane's alert, china blue eyes for a few more seconds before shifting his attention to Brian. "You stay here." Then turning back to face Kane continued. "Make the call, Abu, you and Massa go with him and bring him back in one piece." Another big grin formed across Raoul's face which Abu returned. It didn't matter whether they got the money or not, the westerner's fate would still be the same.

Abu, pushed Kane all the way back to the Freelander, revelling in his power over his submissive captive. When they reached the battered green car, Abu made Kane get into the back seat and climbed in next to him, the old Makarov semi-automatic pistol pointing into Kane's midriff. Massa climbed behind the wheel and stalled the engine on the first attempt, before jerkily starting off to turn the car around back towards Hargeisa.

After five stuttering attempts of driving forward and four in reverse, Massa, eventually managed to turn the car around until it faced in the right direction. Kane knew he had to act quickly and concentrated on how he was going to grab the Makarov, shoot Massa and then deal with Abu. He would have to wait until they were out of earshot or the sound of gunfire might panic the rebels into doing something drastic, though they all looked so stoned they probably would not even hear the shot, but he couldn't take that chance. He was also aware that he had to get back and pick up Brian's trail while it was fresh. The ramshackle farmhouse could have been a ruse and if they had another vehicle nearby, then they could already be loading Brian onto it.

Massa's driving confidence grew and a half mile down the road he went to change into third gear but as his left foot went down onto the clutch it also came into contact with the foot brake causing the car to dramatically reduce speed and both Kane and Abu lurched forward.

"Fool." Abu snapped, before uttering a tirade of abuse in his native tongue. Kane seized his chance and as he slowly straightened up, his right hand slid the leg of his loose Khaki trousers over the handle of the hunting knife. His grip tightened on the bone handle and in one movement he lifted the knife and flicking his wrist to the right, lunged upwards, driving the blade through the underside of Abu's chin and into his pickled brain. His left hand simultaneously reached out for the pistol from an already limp hand. Abu had been in mid-sentence when his end had come, but Massa had not even noticed, he was too busy trying to start the stalled engine which had now suddenly sprung into life. Kane gently dropped the pistol to the floor and reaching over with both hands cupped Massa's chin with his right and a greasy clump of matted hair with his left. One quick twist and tell-tale crack later, Massa slumped onto the steering wheel and the car stuttered forward to stall once more.

Kane picked up the pistol and having climbed out of the rear seat, ran around to the driver's side to retrieve the keys from the ignition. He was too close to drive the Freelander, they would hear the engine and be alerted, but if Brian's captors had a vehicle, he would need to have some means of following them. Pushing Massa's lifeless body to lie across the passenger seat, Kane put the car in neutral and turning the wheel strained to push the Freelander into the side of the road. Abu sat upright in the back seat his eyes wide open, the handle of the hunting knife clearly visible beneath his now motionless chin. Kane reached back and grabbing the handle pulled sharply downwards. The blade extracted with a long slurp and Abu fell slowly sideways to rest peacefully along the blood soaked rear seat. Wiping the bloodied blade against the worn rim of the driver's seat, Kane stepped back and closed the door. After making a quick check to ensure the bodies were not visible to any passing vehicle, he set off along the dusty road, jogging back towards the ramshackle farmhouse at a fast but comfortable pace, keeping close to the bushes that lined both sides of the road.

After a couple of minutes, Kane began to focus on the outline of the farmhouse which was starting to emerge in the distance. Slowing his pace to a walk, he moved into the bushes and began picking his way through the edge of the brush as quickly and quietly as he could. Muted voices could be heard in the distance and peering through the edge of the brush, he squinted in the direction of the farmhouse on the other side of the road. Several figures could be seen trudging towards the dilapidated building, but he was too far away to identify if Brian was among them. Withdrawing back into the brush, Kane continued, quietly picking his way along the many animal trails that criss crossed throughout the undergrowth, towards the spot where the Freelander had stopped previously.

"Yaz..." A voice shouted out six or seven metres in front of him. The call was answered from the far side of the road and Kane carefully inched slowly to the edge of the brush to peer down the road to where the response had come from. He did not understand the Somalian conversation that ensued but it was enough to identify that there were only two of them talking. He squinted his eyes and slowly scanned the opposite brush until, at about eight metres down, he could make out slight gesticulating movements each time the other person responded.

The conversation appeared to stop and Brian waited a further two minutes before continuing to move stealthily forward. The dark, crouched form of one of the sentries, left to guard the approach, could just be seen through the undergrowth barely two metres in front. Kane weighed the gun up and down in his right hand, it would be heavy enough for what he had in mind. He continued to inch his way over the warm, sandy soil before finally lunging forward through the brush and cupping his left hand over the guard's mouth, brought the butt of the Markov crashing down onto the top of the red and white spotted headscarf tied loosely around the now bloodied head. A further blow to the temple followed as Kane eased the lifeless body to the sandy floor. Tucking the pistol into the waist band of his light Khaki trousers, Kane relieved the hapless guard of his Kalashnikov and crouching back down, slowly carried on, picking his way silently through the brush.

An inquisitive voice mumbled incoherently on the other side of the road. Kane carried on inching forward, being careful not to move any of the tall foliage around him. The voice mumbled again and a tall, skinny youth emerged from the bushes looking up and down the dusty highway before sauntering across the road, his weapon swinging nonchalantly by his side, held midway in his right hand. Kane turned slowly on his haunches to face the oncoming youth, gently bouncing up and down, preparing his calf muscles for the surge that was about to come. Placing the weapon on the dry, sandy floor, Kane laced his fingers around the bone handled knife and poised ready to spring.

He put the boy's age at about seventeen, maybe sixteen but age did not matter, he was yet another hurdle to be overcome. The boy passed by, within one metre of Kane's lair, a mischievous smile spread across his face as if he had been playing hide and seek and had just found the hider. He stopped and peered through the brush at the motionless form of his comrade in arms. Kane charged out of the bush, the boy turned, dropped the gun and catching a glimpse of the stained steel blade began to form the word 'no' or the Somalia equivalent but it was too late. Kane's left hand was already awkwardly clamping the surprised youth's mouth whilst the right was pushing the blade further into the frightened boy's chest. The force of the charge brought them both crashing to the floor. Kane withdrew the knife and still clamping the boy's mouth, changed the grip he had on the handle and raising the knife above his head, sent the blade crashing down into the blood soaked chest and all became silent.

Kane glanced up and down the road. The tall foliage obscured them from the farmhouse. Jumping to his feet he grabbed the boy's legs and dragged him into the nearby brush, then, dusting himself off, Kane retrieved the first Kalashnikov before returning to the road to collect the one left by the boy. Carrying one in each hand he began to jog down to the start of the winding, track worn road that led to the farmhouse and hopefully Brian.

Turning onto the dirt track road, Kane jogged from bush to bush, about five metres at a time, only pausing to listen for tell-tale voices and hoping no more guards had been posted in the ever thinning brush. The farmhouse was now in clear view, a solitary figure sat on the top of three, rickety steps that lead up to a large open door. At the side of the house an old red Dodge van was having its' rear wheel washed by the second guard relieving himself over the dust covered tyre, the continuous splashing barely audible. Then a new noise caught Kane's attention, as the sound of sobbing from within the semi derelict house could be distinctly heard in the mid-morning silence.

There was very little cover left and there was no possibility of approaching the farmhouse from the front without being seen. He would have to go back down the dirt track a bit and work his way through the brush around to the rear of the house, but that would take time. Having finished his ablutions the second guard zipped himself up and walked around the front of the house, passed the guard on the steps to peer into the open doorway. After a few moments he called to the guard on the steps who stood up and joined him in the entrance. They stood laughing for a few moments before entering further into the room.

Kane seized his chance and sprinted towards the red van. It took just ten seconds to cover the distance but it was uphill and carrying two weapons drained all the strength out of him. If he was seen now he doubted that he would have enough energy to defend himself. Standing with his back flat against the side wall of the house, he gulped down mouthfuls of warm, dry air and tried to regulate his erratic breathing. A piercing scream from inside the house tensed every muscle in his body and he slid sideways along the cracked and flaking rendering to the edge of an old sash window. Peering through the corner of the dust covered pane, Kane could make out two figures on the floor. One was Raoul, obviously pleasuring himself with the sobbing girl and two more leering figures were stood just inside the doorway. Scanning around the room Kane noticed a fourth sat in a chair, cradling a weapon and barely inches away from his viewing point. Ducking down under the window Kane shuffled to the other corner and slowly leant forward to look at the far end of the room.

Brian was clearly visible, his arms stretched up and his wrists tied to a wooden beam. Two other figures were similarly tied next to him but their bodies appeared limp and their heads were resting motionlessly on their chests. Kane checked the Kalashnikov and leaving the other weapon on the urine streaked floor, began to make his way around the front of the farmhouse. Moving quickly up to the open doorway, a creaking floor board spurred him forward into the opening. Firing two short bursts into the backs of the startled onlookers he turned and squeezed off a burst into the seated guard in the corner whose weapon flash had already sent a stream of bullets to pepper the door frame just above his head. Kane sent another two second burst into the now silent guard before turning his attention to Raoul who was fast disappearing through the open back door soon to be out of sight. The Kalashnikov clicked empty and Raoul disappeared.

Kane stepped over the sobbing girl who was trying to cover her naked body with the tattered remnants of a light blue dress. Pulling out the knife Kane quickly cut both of the bonds that held Brian captive. Rubbing both aching wrists Brian scrambled over to retrieve the weapon from the seated, silent sentry, his head rolled back, his wide bloodshot eyes staring up but seeing nothing.

"Where did he go?" Brian shouted, flattening himself against the wall.

"Out back," Kane replied, "What about these two?" He continued, glancing at the motionless, blood speckled figures of the two dangling, older captives, both missing an ear.

"I think they're dead, I have…" Brian did not get to finish as a hail of bullets ran along the edge of the ceiling and down the far wall.

Kane crouched down instinctively and turned to face the back door just as Raoul, flanked by two henchmen, charged into the room. The guards traversed their well-used weapons, spitting bullets in all directions, but Raoul was only focussed on Kane and lunged forward, machete raised ready to strike. Kane lifted the empty gun in an effort to defend himself but Raoul's flying leap had already brought his heavy, bulky frame crashing down onto Kane's twisted torso, pinning him to the ground. The glinting machete blade rose high in the air as Kane helplessly struggled to free his trapped arms. Raoul shuddered as a burst of gunfire riddled his back and shoulder, the force sending him tipping forward to crash on the floor. Brian turned his attention from Raoul to the two henchmen who were now aiming their bursts in his direction. Two bullets drilled through the top of Brian's right thigh forcing him to collapse onto the shell covered floor, but still managing to empty the remainder of his magazine into the first of his assailants.

Kane meanwhile had wriggled himself free and drawing the Makrov from his waistband and using Raoul's torso as a shield, began to pump single bullets into the last remaining guard. The guard faltered, stumbled, sank to his knees and finally keeled over as the fifth bullet drilled through the centre of his forehead.

Silence reigned. Kane stretched his neck to look through the open back door into the yard beyond then turned around to look out through the empty front doorway before turning his attention to Brian. "You okay?"

"Yeah, I will be," He replied, blood seeping between his fingers as he pressed his hand over the two neat holes in his thigh. "Is that all of them?"

"I hope so," Kane grunted, pushing Raoul's lower body off his right foot and raising himself to stand upright. "How are you for ammo?"

"Empty." Brian grimaced as the adrenalin slowly subsided and the pain of his wounds took over.

"Here, take this." Kane offered, passing one of the henchmen's weapons to Brian and collecting up the other. "I'm going to have a quick look outside. I'll be coming in the front way so make sure it's not me before you get trigger happy."

Kane slid out the back door and glanced right and left before crouching down low and quickly making his way to the far right rear corner of the building. Pausing briefly to listen for any other movement, Kane spun around the rough rendered, edge to stare down the empty, open side of the farmhouse, weapon at the ready. Satisfied that there was no obvious threat, he made his way back to the other corner of the farmhouse and repeated the process with the same result. Kane walked slowly down past the red Dodge and stopped briefly to pick up the Kalashnikov he had left earlier.

Moving around the front of the building Kane shouted, "It's me so don't shoot."

"Come on in; better see to the girl, I think she's hurt."

Kane walked into the room, furtively scanning the fallen bodies for any sign of movement before walking over to where the scantily clad girl lay. Part of the left side of her head was missing and a short trail of bullet holes peppered her left shoulder and chest. "I'm afraid she's had it." He almost whispered as he looked down on the abused, scratched, bruised body trying not to imagine the fear and humiliation she must have gone through.

"I thought I heard her crying." Brian added sadly as he struggled to his feet.

Kane turned his head to look at the other body lying a few feet away. Raoul's cold, brown eyes were wide open, frozen in death. Kane wished he hadn't died so quickly. A soft whimper from behind him made Kane spin around, "She's alive!" He shouted, dropping his weapon and wrapping his arm around the dangling captive's slender waste to take her weight while the other hand reached for the bone handled knife to cut her free of the bonds that held her.

Placing her gently on the ground she began to sob in soft rhythmical bursts.

"Better find her some water." Brian suggested.

Kane rose and started to look around for any bottles of water the rebels may have brought with them. He doubted if there was any water in the system, let alone if it was safe to drink. He paused in front of the remaining hostage. His lips were blue, but apart from a missing ear and a six inch superficial cut on his chest, there was no visible signs of any other injury, neither was there a pulse when Kane carefully checked his wrist and neck. Kane quickly cut the ropes that supported him and lowered him gently to lay peacefully on the floor, then rising to step over the two prone henchmen walked into the kitchen area where three, large bottles of Evian stood upright on the worktop. Two had already been opened but the third was untouched. He selected the latter and strode back into the room. Undoing the top he bent down next to the woman and gently lifted her head to rest the top of the bottle against her mouth and allow the water to trickle over her lips which remained closed and the rhythmical sobbing began again.

Kane lowered the head gently back to the floor and placed the top back on the blue plastic bottle. "Right, we'd better get you two off to hospital. Are you okay to walk?"

"Yeah," Brian replied, as he wrapped and tied his shirt around his blood soaked thigh. “Then we’ve got to explain what happened here.” He continued shuffling towards the front door.

Kane bent down and placing one arm around her back and the other under her legs, gently lifted the frail, still sobbing lady off the floor. She allowed her head to nestle into Kane’s chest and seep in the sense of warmth and security, trying unsuccessfully to block out the horrors of the last few days.

Kane looked down at the tear stained face and gently whispered, “You’re safe now.”

He turned carefully sideways through the doorway, hoping that they had left the keys in the Dodge. Not that it mattered if they hadn’t, he would carry her back to the Freelander, in fact he would carry her all the way back to Hargeisa if he had to.

7

The Boeing 747 slowly descended out of the black, English sky to land at Gatwick Airport in the early hours of June 30th. Having collected their baggage, the three of them agreed to meet at 4pm in the MI6 Headquarters at Vauxhall Cross. It was a bit later than originally planned because Neil had to report into the MI5 Headquarters across the river in Thames House. MI5 is responsible for combating Terrorism and espionage in the UK and Ireland and as such, Neil's superiors were interested in finding out if there were any links between the operations in the States and Abdul Hussein, the British citizen who went missing several weeks ago.

Kane looked down at his watch, 3.35am. The taxi taking him to his Kingston-upon-Thames apartment was weaving its' way in and out of the M25 traffic, still busy even at this time of the morning, though nothing like the car park it often turns into during the rush hour. Just over half an hour later, Kane turned the key in the front door lock, de-activated the alarm and walking into the bedroom, dumped his blue hold-all on the floor, removed his coat and collapsed onto the bed, where he remained for the next six hours, drifting in and out of welcoming, intermittent sleep.

Despite the pillow that Kane had placed over his head some two hours earlier, the warm, end of June sun continued to light up the room and stir him from his fitful slumber. He moved his legs over the edge of the bed and sat there for a few seconds, yawning and rubbing his face before standing and stretching his arms high above his head, accompanied by yet another long yawn, then headed off into the bathroom.

Having decided that a jog was probably the best way to wake up, Kane donned a pair of dark blue shorts and a white Nike vest. Tying up the laces on his white and blue Adidas trainers, he started to plan the route of his run in his head, but then accepted that he would probably follow his normal routine anyway.

Kingston-upon-Thames was busier at this time of the day than on his normal early morning jogs and as he glided in and out of the pedestrian traffic, past the car park and the Irish Pub, he focussed his attention on the river in the distance. Easing his pace to a gentle rhythm, Kane jogged past the Albany Canoe and Rowing Club and down onto the well-trodden footpath by the side of the river. Having decided he would jog his normal route, he carried on for two miles before turning around and increasing his pace, headed back to his apartment, thinking about what he could have for breakfast, or was it lunch?

At 3.35pm, Brian got the phone call to collect Neil from reception and brought him up to the first floor meeting room B where Kane, Bill Johnson and two other people sat around a long rectangular table, deep in conversation.

"This is Neil Bishop, our MI5 colleague," Brian introduced, as he ushered Neil into the now silent room. "Kane you already know," Brian continued, "and this is Bill Johnson, our section leader, Tom Flannery, our head of department and agent Alison Jenkins."

Neil nodded his acknowledgement and sat down next to Brian.

"Right, Neil," Tom Flannery started, "Just to bring you up to date, nobody has claimed responsibility for Jollinger's assassination as yet and our friends in the States are anxious to find out if Edwards was a target or not. They are following up on Henri Devaux, the would-be assassin in Dallas and also on how Henryk Leidmeister got into the country, that is, if it was him in Memphis. They have asked us to re-check everything that happened in Islamabad right back to our missing guy at the airport."

"Excuse me, Sir," Neil interrupted, "Abdul Hussein is no longer missing, he was brought into Thames House this morning after contacting Scotland Yard earlier in the day."

"Why wasn't I informed? I thought we were supposed to be working together on this." The department head's cheeks started to glow red. There was always a bit of rivalry between MI5 and MI6 and he did not like the idea of them getting to the suspect first.

"If I may, Sir," Neil continued, "knowing that I was coming here for a de-brief, my superiors thought that I could update you on the information they had already obtained."

"Well, come on man, get on with it." Tom was quietly seething but also curious as to what information Abdul Hussein, whom he had expected to be dead, had to offer that might shed some light on the subject.

"Abdul Hussein works as a research lab technician for a chemical company based in Chessington and makes frequent business trips to Pakistan on behalf of the company."

"Yes, yes, we know that man, what else have you got?" Tom Flannery was not a patient man at the best of times.

"His brother phoned him just after he had checked in his luggage and told him that both their lives could be in danger. Apparently, Ahmed Hussein had been lured into working for some kind of drugs lord with links to the Taliban. Three days before Abdul was due to fly to Islamabad, Ahmed was sat in a warehouse office with three other drivers and their boss, a guy named Rashid. They were told to leave when a tall, fair haired stranger arrived carrying a small, black leather briefcase. The rest of the information is pretty vague but Ahmed had gone back to the office and stopped outside the door when he heard them talking about killing a presidential candidate on June 28th. Somehow or other they found out he had been listening and went after him. He hid under a lorry and heard them talking about where he lived and that he had a brother in England who was due to visit again. We assume that if they had not found Ahmed, they would have used Abdul to get to him. From Ahmed's description, Abdul thought he had seen someone similar in the airport coffee shop and on the way back from check-in he literally bumped into the same guy, his cold grey blue eyes seemed to be eerily confirming his innermost thoughts. Abdul panicked and left the airport and went into hiding. But just before I left he identified the stranger as Henryk Leidmeister."

"How did he get out of the airport without being seen?" Kane asked

"I don't know, but before I left we had confirmation that Leidmeister was on the plane to Islamabad, under the name of John Chantler.

"Have we got an address for this warehouse?" Bill Johnson enquired.

"Sorry, that's all I've been told, but George Daniels said that if I saw you to tell you he would be couriering the interview transcripts over to you and that you owe him a couple of pints."

Tom Flannery cleared his throat, "Thank you er..."

"Neil, Sir." He responded with his name.

"I don't think we need to detain Neil any longer, unless you have any more questions Bill?" The department head continued.

"No, I'll go through the transcripts when they get here and ring George Daniels if I have any queries."

"Right, thank you for the update, you can return to Thames House now."

Neil stood up. 'That's it,' he thought to himself, 'dismissed, my brief career with MI6 over.'

Kane gave him a friendly wink as Neil turned in the open doorway to say goodbye and head off down the corridor with Brian in tow.

"Right, gentlemen… and lady." Tom added as an afterthought, "I'll leave you to sort out what happens next but I want us to take the lead from here. See what you can dig up in Islamabad, find this Leidmeister fellow and get to the bottom of all this. It's all yours now Kane, get me some results."

Collecting his files together, Tom pushed back his chair, rose to his feet and strode purposely across the floor. Opening the large, wood panelled door he turned and addressing the group as a whole offered, "Good luck gentlemen," This time not adding the word lady, "I'm counting on you." Then exited the room, leaving the door to close effortlessly behind him.

"Well, that seems simple enough," Alison broke the silence. "All we have to do is find Leidmeister, get him to tell us what it's all about and that's it, job done."

"We?" Kane responded staring straight at Alison. They had worked together before but that had been purely information retrieval. This was something different and Kane sensed this could get ugly.

"Yes Kane, Alison speaks the lingo and we need some answers while the trail is still hot, well warm at least." Bill intervened, pausing to give both of them a concerned look.

"You sending her to Pakistan?" Kane asked.

"Who's her?" Alison asked pointedly.

"Okay you two, you're both going to Islamabad," Bill interjected before passions got heated, "just need to sort out some cover stories, in fact, seeing as you act like it, it might be worthwhile sending you out as man and wife."

"Well, there could be some perks to it." Kane mused.

"In your dreams." Alison's quick retort.

"But just to make sure." Bill grinned, "I'm sending Brian out there with you. Right, let's get down to business, work out what we need to get, where from and more importantly, how you are going to do it."

"What did I miss?" Brian asked as he re-entered the room.

"Nothing yet," Bill retorted, "you're going to Islamabad with these two, now pull up a chair and let's get to work."

For the next three hours they sifted through the various bits of information and numerous files trying to establish a pattern or possible source that would aid their enquiries, pausing now and then to add key points to the rapidly filling whiteboard. The transcripts of the interview with Abdul Hussein had been delivered and read through several times but apart from what they had already been told, no fresh information was apparent. Bill had phoned George Daniels over a couple of points and also asked if Abdul Hussein had an address for the warehouse but all Abdul could offer was that it was somewhere near the centre of Islamabad and the lorry his brother drove had some sort of Palm tree logo on the door. Bill finally stood up, stretched his arms high into the air, yawned and surveyed the tired faces sat around the desk.

"Okay guys, let's call it a day. The only real lead we have is this warehouse, so I'll get our number crunchers to try and get you an address while you three sort out your passports and travel arrangements."

"Just one thing, Bill," Kane interrupted as he rose from his chair. "How much can we rely on our office over there? If there was one leak, there could be more?"

"That investigation is still going on so in the meantime, carry on using your cellular phones channelled through the secure line on the central desk. I'll prime them that they will be your main contact and to respond to whatever information requests you may have. Apart from local knowledge, it may even be quicker."

Kane turned to join Brian and Alison as they made their way down the corridor to the Data Compliance office where forty five minutes later they were presented with their new identities and passports.

"Richmond?" Alison questioned reading the surname on her passport.

"Well, at least you get to keep Alison as your Christian name." Kane retorted, seeing as he had personally selected the surname. It was common practice to retain the Christian names in case there was a slip of the tongue in potentially awkward situations.

"The name would be alright if you didn't have to share it." Alison replied, trying to restrain a slow, secret smile that had had started to form at the corner of her mouth.

She had always admired Kane for his directness and for a few seconds the thought of being 'married' to him began to form vivid pictures in her mind.

"Now, children," Brian broke in, "you two sound just like my mum and dad."

"Charming!" Kane added, "Better get familiarised with these new identities and decide what we are going to do first. There's a flight out tomorrow night, do you want to sort out the travel and hotel arrangements?" Kane continued as he stared into Alison's green blue eyes, a broad smile spreading across his face."

"You bet I do, I'm not sharing a double bed with you." There was a hint of laughter in her voice and a smile on her lips but it was the twinkle in her eye that Kane noticed the most.

Alison was a very attractive lady. Kane could not work out whether her eyes were green or blue, they appeared to change every time he looked at them. Her long flowing hair accentuated the outline of her figure hugging dress and Kane suddenly realised he was staring straight at her and she was doing exactly the same to him.

"Right," Kane broke off trying to regain his air of authority and turning his attention to Brian. "While Alison sorts that lot out, you and I can work out where we are going to start."

Alison dutifully left them to it, but still felt miffed at having to do the mundane secretarial duties whilst they discussed the forthcoming operation. 'Really is a man's world…' she thought to herself. She was never one for being 'backward at coming forward' and suddenly found herself questioning why she had let Kane 'dismiss' her from the discussions, but then his directness and take control attitude had always appealed to her.

"What are you grinning at?" Kane snapped at Brian, who just stood there with a broad smile and knowing look.

"Body language," He replied, "and you two have got plenty of it."

"Piss off, you moron. We go back a long way and like the banter, but that's all there is to it, so let's get on with the job in hand."

"Anything you say mate, you're the boss." Brian responded with an even bigger smile.

The following afternoon the Qatar Airlines flight took off from a rain soaked Heathrow Airport, rising through the thick, dark clouds to eventually break through into dazzling sunshine. Kane settled down to another long flight, it seemed that most of his time lately was spent on long haul flights. Alison had retrieved her Kindle from her hand luggage and shifted around to get a more comfortable seating position before engrossing herself in the latest Danielle Steele novel. Kane reclined his seat and closed his eyes, allowing his thoughts to drift to the last visit he made to Pakistan and the events that had followed. Eight hours later they were landing at Islamabad International airport and Kane was surprised that, much to the annoyance of his 'wife', he had spent most of the travelling time fast asleep.

"Oh, you are still with us?" Alison sarcastically remarked.

Kane looked at his watch and mentally added on the four hours difference.

"Well, it is 6.30am here, time to get up," He replied, just as sarcastically, before stretching his cramped body as much as the confines of the seats would allow. "Did I miss breakfast?" He continued, but his question fell on deaf ears.

A short while later they had cleared the customs area and were on their way to the Islamabad Marriott Hotel, stopping briefly at a well-stocked sports shop for Kane to pick up a hunting knife and leg holster. Brian had been sat towards the back of the plane and was now following behind in another taxi. Seeing Kane stopping to visit the sports shop, he told the driver to stop and asked him to wait whilst he also went into the shop. They had already decided, from an information gathering point of view, that they would be better off if they appeared not to know one another, so this was an opportunity to briefly catch up. Kane had already made his purchase and was walking out the door as Brian approached. There was no opportunity to talk so Kane grabbed the handle of the knife through the blue plastic bag and waved it a couple of times, long enough for Brian to determine what he had bought and to get one for himself. Kane climbed back into the cab and barely had he closed the door before the driver shot out into the early morning traffic. Ten minutes later the taxi driver pulled up sharply outside the Marriott Hotel and Kane opened the rear door and stepped out onto the freshly cleaned sidewalk. The smell of heated rubber from the taxi's tires filled his nostrils as Kane wondered if they had any tread left. Having emptied the bags out of the boot onto the sidewalk the driver snatched the generous fare Kane offered and climbing back into the cab, once again accelerated out into the traffic.

"Remember that guy at the customs desk?" Kane asked as they both squeezed through the front doors into the hotel foyer.

"Not really, why?" Alison replied, her face screwed up in concentration trying to recall his features.

"He looked at my passport the other week when I was here, under my real name. Surprised he didn't recognise me."

"Sorry babes, your face isn't that memorable." Alison laughed as they made their way to the large square reception desk in the middle of the foyer.

Having been told that their room would not be ready until mid-morning, they left their bags with the concierge and made their way into the dining room for coffee and Kane's long awaited breakfast, ignoring Brian who was on his way to reception. Kane helped himself to the buffet breakfast while Alison settled for a large cup of black coffee.

"So, where do we start?" Alison inquired, her eyes heavy due to lack of sleep and hoping the caffeine in the coffee she was sipping would start to take effect.

"Well, first we'll contact Bill and see if he's got an address for us and if he has, we'll go and check it out."

"I don't think he would be too happy about you calling him, it's only quarter to four in the morning in London."

"Okay smart arse, you know what I meant. I'll phone the central desk for an update."

"And if they haven't got an address?" Alison continued.

"Then we'll just have to turn detective and find it ourselves." Kane replied, dialling in the number as he walked out into a quieter part of the foyer. The call to London proved uneventful in terms of the warehouse address, they did however, come up with an address of a former friend of the assassinated informant Ahmed Hussein which they had obtained from the preliminary investigation notes compiled by Major Henry Morgan shortly after the shooting. Kane scribbled down the address on the back of a beer mat and made his way over to reception to see if they sold any street maps. Brian was hovering just inside the doorway as if he was waiting for someone.

Kane seized the opportunity and as he approached Brian asked in a rather loud voice, "Excuse me, Sir, any idea where this address is?" Holding out the beer mat and ensuring Brian had long enough to read and remember the address.

"No, sorry, I'm just visiting, perhaps reception can help you." Brian replied nodding towards the reception desk.

Kane thanked him and walked across the foyer to the large, marble panelled reception area. A few minutes later he was scanning through the complimentary Islamabad Street Map until he found the street he was looking for. The address was only a few blocks away, maybe two and a half to three kilometres according to the map scale. Kane made his way back to the table and sat down, spreading the open street map on top of the large, red table mat.

"You took your time," Alison remarked. "Did you get the address?"

"No, but we have got the address of one of Ahmed Hussein's friends. It's not far from here so we can walk, it will give Brian chance to keep up."

"Walk, in these shoes!" Alison exclaimed, lifting up her left foot to show a red patent shoe with four inch heels.

"Well, go and change them then, but hurry up I want to get going."

"Patience is a virtue." Alison replied, getting up from the table.

"There's a difference between patience and time wasting which is what you are doing now, so please, get a move on."

"Men." Alison huffed as she turned and walked towards the concierge's room.

Most of Kane's work was sifting through information and looking for the next lead, so he naturally had to have an abundance of patience, but when he had a lead, then he just wanted to crack on with it and disliked being held up, especially for trivial, domestic reasons.

Kane left the table and walked out into the foyer. Brian had started to feel a bit conspicuous hanging around the foyer so had moved outside the main door, occasionally glancing at his watch as if he was waiting for someone who was late. Kane stopped at the large glass doors and turned to scan the opulent foyer and for the next ten minutes subconsciously imitated Brian's checking of his watch.

"Where have you been?" Kane grunted as Alison appeared dressed in knee length white shorts, sandals and a white cotton blouse.

"Well, I just thought this would have been more suitable." Came the curt reply.

"Come on, we're wasting time." Kane retorted, ushering her through the door.

Brian smirked as they went past. If they were 'acting' as a married couple it was a very good act. Kane noticed Brian was tapping a copy of the Islamabad street map against his thigh, indicating that he had picked up on the address and turning to Alison said in a voice loud enough for Brian to hear, "We might as well walk, it's not far." Roughly grabbing Alison's arm, they turned right and began walking down Aga Khan Road.

Brian waited a few more minutes and with one more glance of his watch and emphasised shrug of his shoulders, let out an audible sigh to anybody who was interested, then headed off in the same direction.

Just over twenty minutes later they arrived at their destination. The dirt covered, cracked, white walls of the tired houses were in stark contrast to the grandeur of the Islamabad Marriott.

"Wait here while I have a quick look." Kane whispered and not waiting for a reply, jogged across the road to the other side.

Alison watched him for a few seconds then decided it would look more natural if she pretended to be window shopping so turned abruptly to peer into the nearest shop window. Squinting her eyes and bending to peer through the grime and red, hand painted, window signs, she saw three smiling faces staring back at her. The nearest one was beckoning her to come in and sit next to him in the barber shop's waiting room. She stood upright, went to turn left then changed her mind and turned right to walk in a parallel direction to Kane, occasionally glancing over not to lose sight of him. Kane stopped just short of a house with a flaking, green painted door and next to it a large cracked window which was in dire need of a wash.

Kane pointed his head down at the map but his eyes were lifted to try and focus through the grimy, cracked window into the room beyond, but there were no signs of life. Turning around he began to make his way back to where he had left Alison when he noticed her on the opposite side of the street Her white shorts and blouse did not blend in with the colourful saris or more traditional black coverings with the letter box eye slits of the female population in this area.

"Well, you certainly blend in with the locals," Kane commented out aloud as he walked across the pot holed road towards her. "Why didn't you wait where I left you?"

"Well, I was going to get a haircut but thought I'd keep an eye on you instead. Is that the address?"

"Yes, but it doesn't look as if anybody's home." Kane was about to continue when an old AVM truck, similar to those used for troop carrying in Africa, stuttered to a halt outside the target's door. A large, overweight man shuffled out of the cab and slid awkwardly onto the running board and finally onto the road below. Kane watched as he shuffled around the front of the cab and disappeared through the flaking green door.

"I've got an idea," Kane whispered, looking at the large dent in the front wheel arch on the driver's side of the cab. "How good are you with the local lingo?"

"Good enough, why?"

"If this is our guy then we can make out we dented Ahmed Hussein's truck and agreed that we would pay Ahmed's boss for the repair but didn't get the address, it's worth a try."

"And what do I say if he asks how come we got his address?"

"We'll cross that bridge when we come to it, come on." Kane grabbed her elbow and guided her across the road to the slightly open green door. "Okay, get ready to do your stuff." Kane half whispered as he knocked on the sun dried wooden door.

A few moments later the door opened wide enough to see the large, sweaty figure of the truck driver, his mouth filled with chapatti and the remainder held in a dirty, hair covered fist.

"Over to you." Kane offered emphasising the turn of his head in Alison's direction.

"Do you speak English?" Alison asked.

The driver looked at Alison, then glanced at Kane before returning his gaze to Alison's cleavage and responded, "Yes, I speak English."

Kane stared at Alison for a few seconds involuntarily shaking his head. "Okay, my name's Richmond and I have come to pay for the damage I caused to Ahmed Hussein's truck."

"He not here, gone away." The driver tried to shift his overweight body back far enough to close the door but Kane's outstretched arm held the door open.

"Wait, I just need to see that his boss gets the money and I'll pay you for your time." Kane replied, pulling his wallet out from his trouser pocket.

"You give me money, I pay him. I work in same place." The driver replied staring down at Kane's wallet.

Kane turned to look at the rusting cab, "I thought Ahmed's cab had some sort of palm tree on it?"

"No palm tree, that was Ahmed's truck before..." The driver's conversation trailed off but then came back with "you go now." He said as he quickly closed and bolted the door.

Kane walked back to the truck with Alison in tow. "So much for you knowing the local lingo." Kane smiled at Alison.

"You didn't even tell me his name so I thought I'd see if we could speed things up."

"Okay, we need to get Brian involved." Kane spoke in a soft tone not to be overheard, whilst staring back down the road. As if on cue, Brian emerged from a shop doorway and slowly sauntered across the cracked, tarmac road to the other side. "Tell Brian to get a taxi and follow this truck, I'll make sure our friend does not leave until Brian is ready. Oh and come straight back, I want our friend to be able to see both of us so he will not think he's being followed."

Alison walked at a steady pace down the road, pausing now and then to look up at buildings or the occasional shop front as any normal site-seer would. Kane meanwhile, had taken out his mobile phone and pretended to be talking to someone as he paced up and down past the rusting truck, occasionally glancing towards the large shadowy figure behind the cracked window pane.

As Alison approached the corner of the junction, Brian was stood casually reading the unfolded street map. Alison clipped open her hand bag and as they passed allowed the bag and its' contents to fall to the floor. They both bent down to pick up the scattered articles.

"Thank you." Alison said as she accepted a Chanel eye liner from Brian's outstretched hand, then moving a little closer whispered: "Get a cab and follow that lorry." When all the contents had been returned to Alison's hand bag she again thanked him before turning to re-join Kane. Brian went back to scrutinising his street map and seeing an advert for a taxi firm, pulled out his cell phone and began to key in the number.

Kane ended his pretend call as Alison approached. "Everything okay?"

"Yeah fine," She responded, linking her arm through his and smiling up into his face. "What now?" She whispered.

Kane turned his back to the house and quietly replied "We wait until Brian has his taxi and then we give our guy chance to drive off with us in plain view."

The next few minutes were spent tracing imaginary routes on the street map and another brief, imaginary phone call which was cut short when Kane saw Brian getting into his cab. "Come on." He said, grabbing Alison's hand and slowly walking back down the road, stopping now and then to look at the array of brightly coloured clothing that adorned the spasmodic shop fronts dotted between the dusty dwellings. On the third stop, Kane glanced sideways at the reflection of the road in a surprisingly clean shop front when the driver appeared and walked around the front of the AVG to get into his cab. He paused for a moment and stared up at Kane and Alison who both appeared interested in what that particular shop had to offer, before opening the cab door and beginning the arduous task of getting his bulky frame into the cab and behind the wheel. Kane heard the engine starting and put his arm around Alison's shoulders gently pulling her back and towards him so he could get a better view of the reflection. The driver put his arm out of the window and adjusted his mirror. A few seconds later he pulled away from the kerb slowly accelerating but casting furtive glances back to his mirror before finally accelerating off into the distance with Brian's taxi not far behind.

"Is this your way of being romantic?" Alison purred.

"No," Kane replied, removing his arm, "it's my way of saying let's move, we need to get our own taxi and meet up with Brian. You phone us a cab and I'll phone Brian, see what direction he's heading in."

Alison remembered seeing the taxi advert on the street map and as Kane selected Brian's number from his 'friends' list, she gently eased the map out of his back pocket and unfolded it to display the required number.

Ten minutes later they were climbing into the back of a shiny new, white taxi heading out onto the main highway towards Brian's latest position.

"There's something not right here," Kane mused out aloud. "Why would Ahmed's brother say his lorry had some sort of Palm Tree on it when it hasn't and why did he say this warehouse was near the centre when we are obviously travelling way outside the area."

"Perhaps your friend is not going straight to the warehouse." Alison replied.

“Did you see the frightened look on his face when we said we had to see his boss and he blurted out that the rust bucket used to be Ahmed’s? It was as if the penny had dropped and he realised what happened to Ahmed could happen to him if he gave away any information. So if you were in that situation and didn’t want to get into trouble, what would you do?”

“I’d probably not say anything,” Alison replied, “but then again, I couldn’t take the chance of you turning up and indicating to the boss man that I had spoken to you and hadn’t divulged it. Okay, I’d go straight to the boss and warn him someone was snooping around.”

“Exactly, but even if he isn’t going straight there, he has to end up there at some time, just might be an expensive taxi ride!”

“Well, if it’s going to be that long, I might as well make the most of it.” Alison replied, snuggling down in the seat and resting her head against Kane’s arm. The warm leather upholstery and the even warmer sensation from Kane’s arm lulled her into a sense of total security as she allowed her eye lids to close and her mind to drift off to potentially, more enjoyable times.

8

"Like James Bond, no?" The taxi driver called over his shoulder to Brian who was sat in the back seat just about to update Kane on their whereabouts.

"Eh?" Brian answered, "What are you on about?"

"Follow that lorry, that what James Bond say."

"Oh yeah, him." A wry smile breaking out on Brian's face. "Nothing like that mate, I think that driver's messing around with my wife so I just want to make sure he's not meeting her." The conversation abruptly ended as the lorry pulled into the front yard of an old, dilapidated warehouse. The words Sayed Import and Export were barely visible on the faded white sign. The cab door opened and the driver slowly eased out of his seat to slide unceremoniously down the cab onto the dusty, gravel.

"What, him?" The taxi driver stared in amazement as the lorry driver waddled off into the warehouse.

"Thanks mate," Brian lent over and gave him a handful of notes. "Keep the change," Then he quickly exited the cab and walked into the shadows.

The driver pocketed the money, took one last look at the warehouse and with a shake of his head, accelerated away ready for his next call. Brian quickly scanned the area for a suitable vantage point where he would not look so conspicuous. An old cafe bar with some outside white, tubular, legged tables seemed a good spot, but would be a bit exposed if he was to be there for any length of time, but it was better than where he was now, so decision made, he walked briskly to the farthest table and sat down. Within seconds the shabbily dressed owner appeared and after three attempts, Brian finally managed to order a black coffee. He moved his chair further back into the shadows and pulling out his cell phone, hit the redial button to tell Kane he had reached his destination.

Brian was halfway through his call when two men emerged from the warehouse on the other side of the road. Their white, flowing, hooded Kaftans did little to hide the automatics held by their side. Sliding slowly down in his chair, Brian peered over the top of the upright, drink stained, menu as he watched the two men jog across the road, furtively looking for anything or anyone out of the ordinary, before spreading out and disappearing into the shadowy doorways.

"Looks like our guy told them he'd been paid a visit." Brian whispered into the phone. "Wait a minute, there's two cars and a lorry just emerged from the warehouse…"

"Where are you?" Kane interrupted.

"I'm sat outside a cafe bar on Karachi Road opposite an old Mobil gas station and the warehouse is next to it, but get your driver to stop well before you reach it. There are two very nervous look-outs, with automatics and itchy trigger fingers, lying in wait opposite the warehouse. They might mistake you for the cavalry and re-enact Custer's last stand."

"Too late, we're about to pass you… now."

"Keep going until you're out of sight, you should be passing our nervous friends about now." Brian whispered, as the shiny, white taxi coasted past, keeping his hands behind the menu in an effort to hide the phone from any preying eyes.

"Yeah, just passed one of them, can't see the other one though." Kane replied, scanning the dark doorways with sideways glances without making it obvious.

"Take a wide detour and park up out of sight somewhere. Don't let our lift go though, I've a feeling we might be needing him soon." Brian's attention was now drawn to the vehicles outside the warehouse. People were running back and fore throwing parcels and boxes into the back of the lorry.

"Are you tooled up?" There was a hint of concern in Kane's voice.

"Hunting knife, you?"

"Same, we're just circling around, should be with you in a couple of minutes."

"No probs, I think our friends are about to leave. There's an alleyway opposite the Mobil station you passed. If you can find the other end of it and make your way down to this end, you should just about be able to see the warehouse without giving away your position. Hold it… company…"

Brian pressed the end call button and let the phone rest on the table, pretending to read the time worn menu as the solitary figure in a white, hooded Kaftan sidled slowly past, the bloodshot brown eyes boring into Brian's now tense body. The figure stopped, turned around, paused for several agonising moments before slowly heading back down the road, occasionally glancing back over his shoulder. Car doors slammed, engines revved and the two cars sped away from the warehouse closely followed by the canvass covered lorry. The two black sedans squealed out of the yard and accelerated away down the road whilst the lorry slewed to a halt on the opposite side of the road to pick up the two Kaftans. As the second figure was about to climb into the back of the lorry, he stopped and turned to face down the road to where Brian was seated. Brian instinctively upended the tabled and flattened himself against the floor as a hail of bullets tore through the chairs and table before shattering the window and slamming into the wall behind him.

The lorry trundled off, slowly increasing speed with each change of gear. The broken shards of glass crunched and splintered as Brian rolled over to the cafe doorway and hauled himself upright to see the lorry disappearing from sight. The sound of running footprints alerted his attention in the other direction as first Kane, then Alison ran into view.

"You okay?" Kane asked, looking for any visible signs of injury.

"Yeah, fine…" A squeal of tires stopped the conversation as the new, white taxi sped out of the alleyway and off into the other direction. "There goes our lift, we'll never catch up to them now."

"Anybody left over there?" Kane asked, trying to focus inside the open warehouse door.

"Haven't seen our fat friend yet and his lorry's still there but I don't know who else might be lurking around."

Behind him the cafe owner was shouting down the phone and waving his arms in the air.

"He's called the police, we had better be moving." Alison commented, glad that her translation made her feel useful.

"Just need a quick look before we go." Kane replied, before darting across the dusty, narrow road and through the yard gates.

"Kane… you don't know how many there are?" Brian knew his plea would be in vain so bending down, he unclipped the hunting knife from the inside of his calf and pushing himself off the door frame, headed off in pursuit.

The rough chippings and stone dust of the warehouse yard slowed Kane's advance but his eyes were firmly fixed on the open, sliding doors of the dilapidated building. If anyone appeared now then they could cut him down before he reached any sort of cover. Brian had stopped at the yard entrance, trying to convince himself that the four inch gate post would offer him some sort of cover whilst he kept a look out for any hostiles. Kane meanwhile had reached the corner of the building and flattening himself against the side of the warehouse, inched forward to peer around the corner. Brian could see right into the sparsely lit building and seeing no sign of movement, lifted up his thumb to give Kane the O.K. Scrambling along the front of the warehouse, Kane quickly reached the open door and after a quick look through the gap, slid quietly inside. Brian waited a few seconds then sprinted across the roughly hewn chippings to the open sliding doors. Peering around the rusting framework, Brian could just make out Kane crouched behind a large, wooden container and stooping down to the stone dust floor, began to crawl stealthily towards him.

"See anything?" Brian whispered as he slithered up next to Kane.

"No, but there's a light on in the upstairs office and the door is closed. This place stinks of petrol. Better have a quick look down here first, just in case. I don't want to be caught in the open on the stairway, so you go left and I'll go right."

"Now you decide to be careful." Brian sarcastically whispered back before silently working his way around the wooden cases to the left of the building.

Moments later Kane was quietly climbing the stairs, two at a time, the shiny, new blade of this hunting knife glinting in the reflection of the well-lit office. Kane paused and looked through the corner of the dust covered office window to the large, still figure of the lorry driver lying prone on the floor. Scanning the remainder of the office and finding nothing suspicious, Kane eased open the door and slowly entered. Brian raced up the stairs and barged into the room. Kane was bent over the lifeless body, his fingers pressed against the driver's flabby neck, searching in vain for a pulse.

"Is he dead?" Brian asked but already knowing the answer.

"Yep, looks like a single stab wound… to the heart."

"So, Leidmeister was here."

"Could be, either that or they are all proficient at using a knife." Kane replied, standing upright to take a good look at the remnants of the office. Brian had already begun sifting through the odd bits of paper scattered over the old laminate desk. Their digging for information was brought to an abrupt halt as Alison's warning screamed through the musty air.

"Guys… BOMB!"

They both ran to the office door to see Alison pointing to something attached to the pillar underneath the office floor before turning and running for the open doors.

Bounding down the rickety staircase, Kane paused to look at the flashing red LED display… 9… 8… "Shit!" He shouted, increasing his speed down the remainder of the stairs and across the compacted dust that was the warehouse floor. He was running parallel with Brian and fast catching up with the now staggering Alison. Grabbing an arm each they lifted Alison completely off her feet and through the opening as the muffled boom was soon replaced by an invisible force which catapulted them through the air into the dust and chippings of the warehouse yard.

"Owwww!" Alison let out a slow painful yell as she tried to wipe away the blood splattered stone fragments from both of her palms.

"You alright?" Kane asked, before turning around to see the inside of the warehouse become enveloped in flames. "We'd better get further away in case something else goes up." He continued, struggling to his feet.

"Ouch, my hands… and my knees…" Alison moaned whilst being pulled to her feet by Kane.

"You should have stayed where you were then." Came Kane's unsympathetic response.

"If I had, you would still be in there." Alison replied, looking back into the inferno of the once warehouse.

"That explains the petrol." Brian commented.

"Eh?" Alison queried.

"Doesn't matter," Kane interrupted, "can you walk, because we'd better be out of here before the local law enforcement turns up. We would have a job explaining this one."

"I'll phone us a taxi," Brian coughed through the thickening dust cloud that had now engulfed them. "I'll get them to pick us up at the old Mobil station, can you walk that far."

"I'm not an invalid." Alison retorted, shaking off Kane's arm and doing her best to walk in a controlled, lady like manner.

Every doorway and window seemed to have a pair of eyes staring at the bonfire that was once the dilapidated warehouse, hardly anybody noticed the ragged trio emerging from the dust cloud and casually strolling down the debris covered road to the Mobil station.

Kane stared back over his shoulder to the blazing warehouse before turning back to Brian. “Didn’t see any palm tree logos and this is definitely not near the centre of Islamabad. I think our Mr Abdul Hussein is throwing us a curved ball.”

“What makes you think that?”

“Don’t know really, but the timings seem a bit out. Abdul disappeared from the airport sometime before his brother turned himself in as an informant. I would have expected it to be the other way around. If I was Abdul’s brother and knew my bosses were out to get me, well, I wouldn’t hang around waiting to be picked up.”

Brian thought for a moment, trying to recall the transcripts of the interview. “Didn’t he say something about his brother finding out three days prior to Abdul’s disappearance from the airport?”

“Exactly, if you found out someone was going to abduct or kill a member of your family, would you wait three days before you told them?”

“Depends which member of my family it was… no, you’re right, I’d contact them at the first chance I got, but what could Abdul know that was so important?”

“Guys…” Alison interrupted, “what if everything was true but the other way around? What if it was Abdul that overheard the discussion about the presidential candidate being assassinated and he was the one that had to go into hiding. He would have realised his brother could be used against him and warned him of what was happening, hence the reason he turned informant, to get protection for his own skin.”

Kane pondered over Alison’s theory which fitted in neatly with the complicated, constructive thoughts racing through his mind. “You’re not just a pretty face are you?”

“Well, it took you long enough to notice.”

“If that’s the case,” Brian butted in, re-joining the conversation with his own updated thoughts. “Abdul is more involved in this than we thought.”

“Yep, our friend Abdul did not want us to find this guy Rashid in case it implicated him, hence the red herring, or rather the palm tree logo and a place near the centre."

"But we would have found it sooner or later." Brian replied.

"Yes, but by that time he would have had a new identity, money and freedom to change identity yet again, making it easier to lose himself in any part of the world he took a fancy to. I'm going to give Bill a ring, tell him what we think and ask him to see if he could have a more meaningful conversation with our mate Abdul. Looks like our taxi's here, you two jump in and I'll make the call."

The taxi pulled over onto the forecourt and Brian opened the rear door for Alison to climb in, before jumping in after her and closing the door behind him. It was the same driver Brian had used earlier and having adjusted his mirror, the driver, remembering his fare, turned around and stared at the dishevelled pair, paying particular attention to the grazes on Alison's knees and the thick, grey dust on their crumpled clothing.

"She your wife…?" He asked tentatively.

"No… his." Brian replied, nodding towards Kane.

The driver looked at Brian, then at Alison, before finally looking over to Kane who had now finished his call and was opening the front passenger door.

"Islamabad Marriott Hotel, please." Kane politely ordered.

The driver looked at Kane's dust covered, creased clothes, then glanced back at Brian and Alison and with another shake of his head, accelerated off the forecourt and onto the road heading back to Islamabad.

"Did you speak to the boss?" Brian asked

"Yes, our friend was scheduled to move today so he was going to invite him back to our place for a quick chat."

"Good timing, then?"

"For some of us…"

Alison spent the whole of the journey picking out little pieces of gravel from her grazed knees and checking out the minor cuts in both her palms to ensure all the foreign bodies had been removed. The taxi eventually screamed to a stop outside the opulence of the Islamabad Marriott. Kane paid the driver and climbed out of the cab to join Alison and Brian who were both trying to brush the dust from their clothes before entering the reception area.

"What next?" Brian asked Kane.

"Well, I'm going to have a long shower then get something to eat."

"You had better go and check us in then," Alison suggested, "while I go to the little girl's room and tidy myself up, I won't be long."

Brian watched her glide across the floor in the direction of the Ladies rest room and turning to Kane stated, "She saved both our lives today. We would have been right on top of that bomb when it went off."

"Yes I know and I am grateful… just don't tell her."

"So what do we do now?"

"Wait and see if Bill comes up with anything from our friend Abdul. If he has got anything to hide, Bill's the guy to wheedle it out of him." Kane turned his attention to the young, dark haired receptionist who had walked the full width of the square reception desk to greet him.

"Good afternoon, Sir, may I help you?" Her voice was soft and welcoming but her eyes could not disguise the concern that two, dusty, dishevelled men were standing at her desk looking decidedly out of place compared to the rich furnishings around them.

"Hi, you should have a reservation for Richmond, Mr & Mrs Richmond?"

"Yes, Sir," She replied with a quick glance in Brian's direction, "please wait a moment while I get your details. Ah yes, Mr & Mrs Richmond, twin bedded room for three nights. If you would kindly fill in the registration form and I will need your passports, please."

"Okay, they are in our luggage with the concierge somewhere," Kane replied just as Alison appeared with concierge and luggage in tow. "I thought you'd gone to tidy up?"

"I did, but then all my stuff is in my luggage and I thought I might as well get tidied up properly in the comfort of my own room."

"Don't you mean our room?" Kane smilingly replied.

"Oh yeah, I forgot about that. We need to discuss some ground rules, like I get first dibs at the bathroom and a few more do's and don'ts."

"Okay, but I get first pick of the beds." Kane replied, as he rummaged through the luggage for the passports, which he then offered to the bemused receptionist.

"Thank you, Sir, you are in room 416. If you would kindly sign the registration form and I will get someone to show you to your room."

"No it's okay," Kane replied as he signed the form and picked up the key card. "What floor are we on?"

"You are on the fourth floor Sir; turn left when you get out of the lift."

"Thank you," Turning to Brian he continued, "See you at seven in the bar."

"Okay, I'll probably be there already." Brian replied, before turning to the smiling, welcoming eyes of the waiting receptionist.

Kane and Alison walked across the large, square reception area into the open, waiting lift. The mirrored interior reflected the two, dust covered, travellers who stood in silence as the lift gently sped them to the fourth floor.

"After you." Kane offered as the lift doors quietly opened. Alison walked out of the lift and turned left down the richly decorated corridor, searching out the desired room number.

"Here, it's this one," Kane shouted, placing the key card in the lock and opening the door. The large, well-furnished room appeared cool and relaxing and the two, comfy looking, double beds seemed more than inviting to Kane's tired limbs. "Any preference for which bed you want?"

"I'll have the one furthest from the door." Alison replied, unpacking her bag.

"Okay, I'll have first crack at the shower then."

"Yeah, no problems, have you seen the balcony?"

Kane walked out onto the white painted, flower trimmed, balcony. The warm breeze fanned his face and the soft, scented aroma from the surrounding gardens filled the afternoon air. Kane walked back into the bedroom and headed for the fridge.

"Do you want a drink? Alison…?" Kane called out, realising she was no longer in the room and the sound of a running shower could be heard from behind the closed, bathroom door. "Hey, I thought I had first go at the shower!" He shouted through the locked door.

"Well, you know what they say," Came Alison's muted response. "Possession is nine tenths of the law."

Kane allowed himself a wry smile as he headed back to the fridge and selected a bottle of Budweiser. The cold, crisp drink washed the gritty, warehouse dust away from his mouth and dry, parched throat, sinking almost half a bottle with two large, welcoming swigs. Taking off his shirt and sitting on the edge of the firm but comfortable bed, Kane removed his shoes and picking up the bottle, laid back and allowed the aches and pains of his body to be absorbed into the warm, inviting mattress. His eyes closed and his mind re-lived the events of the last few hours as he slowly allowed his body to relax and for several minutes he was at peace with the world.

"All yours." Alison stated, lifting the tilted bottle out of Kane's hand and taking a large sip.

Kane sat up and rubbed his eyes.

"Sorry, did I wake you?" Alison sounded genuinely concerned as Kane focussed on the white, bath robed figure in front of him. Her freshly washed hair tied up, turban style, in a clean, white, hand towel.

"No, I was just thinking about what happened today… and wondering how much longer you were going to be."

"Well, the bathroom's free now, do you want your drink back?"

"No it's okay, I'll get a fresh one when I'm finished." Kane replied, disappearing into the bathroom and closing the door behind him.

The shower was warm and relaxing. The pine scented shower gel helped to invigorate his aching limbs and he stood for several minutes allowing the pressure shower to bombard his back with numerous needles of water, splashing, probing, massaging away the stresses of the day. Shower ended, the soft, fluffy white bath towel sponged up the droplets of water as with one hand on each end, he dried his back with an almost saw-like action before vigorously rubbing dry his toned chest and bronzed arms. Wrapping the towel around his waist, Kane opened the door and walked out into the bedroom.

"I thought you were never coming out." Remarked Alison as she sat in front of the dressing table putting the finishing touches to her now dry hair.

"I could have stayed there all night," Kane replied heading for the fridge but then stopping to put his hands on Alison's bare shoulders. She was sat in just a white, half cup bra, enhancing her ample breasts and a pair of white, laced trimmed pants. "Can I get you anything to drink?"

"Hey, don't touch what you can't afford and anyway we're meeting Brian at seven so you had better get a move on."

"I thought possession was nine tenths of the law?" Kane smirked.

"You haven't possessed me… yet." The last word trailed off silently as she rose and slipped on the thin, cream, satin blouse that hung by the side of the dressing table.

9

The Interview.

Bill had acted quickly on the information Kane had supplied and was sat in one of the smaller, well equipped, interview rooms in MI6 sifting through the interview transcripts just as Abdul Hussein, accompanied by George Daniels of MI5, entered the warm but sparsely furnished room.

"Ah Mr Hussein, please take a seat." Bill offered Abdul the seat opposite him and turning his attention to George Daniels, nodded to the seat on his right.

"My name is Bill Johnson and I am the section leader for this case."

"Why have I been brought here?" Abdul asked suspiciously. "I must make arrangements for my family, will this take long?"

"How long it takes will depend on you. There have been some developments which we need to go over with you until we are satisfied that the information we have is correct." Bill replied, his stare fixed onto the shifting, nervous eyes that constantly moved between George and Bill.

"I can tell you no more than I have already, there is nothing more to add."

"Well, I think there is," Bill replied in a confident, direct manner which left Abdul Hussein in no doubt that this would not be a straight forward confirmation of facts. "In fact," Bill continued, I think that there is some information that you have supplied us with which may not be correct and that there is also a substantial amount of more, constructive detail that you could furnish us with which could make our jobs one hell of a lot easier."

"Mr Daniels I do not know any more than I have told you already," Abdul blurted, turning his attention to the MI5 section head. "I wish to go now please."

"Mr Daniels has agreed for MI6 to interrogate you until we are satisfied we have all the accurate information that you can give us," Bill interrupted, "so the sooner you give us that information, the sooner you can go."

"No, I have to go now." Abdul shouted, rising from his chair.

"Sit down, Mr Hussein," This time it was George Daniels who snapped the command. "You are going nowhere until Mr Johnson and myself, are satisfied that you have told us everything you know connected with this case."

Abdul Hussein slumped back down onto the red padded chair. "But I… I…" His voice trailed off realising that whatever protest he could utter would fall on deaf ears.

"Right, Mr Hussein," Bill stated in a firm, deliberate, manner. "Let's start at the beginning. First of all, we managed to locate the warehouse where your brother worked, but it was not near the centre of Islamabad as you stated in your first interview. Is there any reason why you should lie about its' location?"

"I did not lie, I… I have only been there couple of times, two maybe three it seemed not far from Islamabad."

"The palm tree logo, it does not exist does it Mr Hussein? Why were you deliberately giving us false information?" Bill purposely lent forward and glared into Abdul's red, watery eyes.

"I didn't, I… I am not sure, what does it matter if there was a palm tree or not?" Abdul blurted out, shifting his eyes from Bill to the table and desperately trying to regain some sort of composure.

"I will repeat the question, but this time I want to hear the truth and no more time wasting. Why did you say the warehouse was near the centre of Islamabad and why did you say there was a palm tree logo on the lorries?"

"I thought I… I… I don't know." Abdul's voice was now calmer, more resigned.

"I know," Bill snapped, "You wanted us to waste time looking for something that didn't exist. To give you time to disappear, isn't that right Abdul?"

"No, no I just want to be safe, you do not understand."

"Then tell me what it is that you are afraid off, help me to understand. The only thing I understand at the moment is that you are deliberately withholding information that could help us move this case forward. If, as you say, you were warned by your brother that these people might use you to get to him, well, without putting too fine a point on it, they have already eliminated your brother, so they have no need to risk getting involved with you. If that is the case, we can inform the media that you have finished helping us with our inquiries and you can be released back to your family home."

"No," Abdul shouted, jumping to his feet. "I'm a dead man if I go back."

"Sit down, Abdul, let's see if we can sort this out," This time Bill's voice was soft, almost caring. He sat back in his chair and for a few seconds studied the quivering figure in front of him. "Is Rashid the real name of the warehouse owner?"

"Yes." Abdul mumbled, still staring at the table.

"Good," Bill stated in a meaningful tone, knowing the response to be true from the background checks carried out on the warehouse address. "We are now starting to get somewhere. After you checked your bags into the airport, where did you go to?"

"I left, I did not go into departure lounge."

"What made you leave so suddenly?"

"I… I had personal reasons."

"You saw someone didn't you Abdul, you admitted it on your first interview, what was his name again?"

"No, it was not… I left for personal reasons."

"Was it Leidmeister or do you know him better as Chantler, the guy with the blonde hair and piercing eyes?"

Abdul physically froze at the description, fear spread across his face.

"When did you phone your brother?"

"… As soon as I got in the taxi outside." Abdul's voice was now calmer and the words started to come a little easier.

"And what did you tell him?"

"I told him I was in trouble and they may come looking for him."

"So why did you say it was the other way around, that your brother was in trouble and they were looking for you?"

"I don't know, I… I panicked."

"Okay," Bill sat forward but not in a menacing way. "If we are going to be able to help you, really help you, then we have to know everything."

George Daniels had been following Bill's train of questioning and now looked at the silent figure in front of him. The confident, almost arrogant air of the first interview had been replaced with a placid, resigned yet nervous facade.

"Abdul," George intervened, "Bill is right, we cannot help you until we know everything, so that nothing and I mean nothing, can come back and bite us on the arse. Or as far as you are concerned, jeopardise your future safety. You were the one who overheard the conversation relating to the assassination of a presidential candidate weren't you?"

"I… yes, I heard them." Abdul Hussein suddenly felt as if a weight had been lifted off his shoulders and could not stop talking. "I had gone back to the office to get some paperwork for my trip to Islamabad and I overheard them say they were going to kill the presidential candidate on the 28th June. They must have realised I was there and came looking for me. They phoned my wife to ask if I was still going to Islamabad. They not very nice people."

"Who did you overhear?"

"Mr Leidmeister and Rashid."

"And where were they when you heard this conversation?"

"In the place where I work, they were in the room my boss uses when he visits."

"You work for Edwards Chemicals, yes?" George interrupted.

"Yes."

"And your boss is Peter Edwards?" Bill asked, an uneasy feeling starting to quell inside him.

"Yes."

"Was he also present at this meeting?" Bill continued.

"Yes." Abdul had been reduced to giving one word responses, not realising the significance of his last answer.

Bill glanced over at George, who had begun to rub his chin with his open hand, his wrinkled brow masking the numerous thoughts and options that now raced through his alert mind. Turning his attention back to Abdul, Bill's voice softened as he asked "Abdul, did they often have these meetings?"

"No… well, yes, but that was the first time that I saw Mr Leidmeister. Rashid has visited the offices several times."

"And where are these offices?"

"On the industrial estate in Chessington."

"What is Peter Edwards' connection with Rashid?" Bill continued.

"I think he is a business contact."

"Can you be a bit more specific, was Peter Edwards supplying him with something or was it Rashid supplying Edwards Chemicals?"

"I don't know, I… this seemed to be more of a personal nature."

"But you visited Rashid several times on behalf of Edwards Chemicals," George could not help butting in, sensing that Abdul was about to close up. "Why were you sent to Islamabad?"

"I did not meet Rashid… well, yes on two occasions when we visited his warehouse. I met with his associate Dr Ashkani."

"And what did you discuss with Dr Ashkani?" George continued.

"I just passed over some files and samples. He would go away and we would meet up the following day and he would give me some files and samples to take back to London."

"What were those samples?" Bill joined in.

"I don't know, the files were all sealed. Now please, I have to see my wife, I have to make arrangements."

"Abdul, when did you last speak to your wife?" George asked, his voice soft and caring but his eyes searching Abdul's for a reaction.

"About three days ago, before I came to see you."

George glanced over to Bill who nodded, knowing what was to be said next.

"Did you visit her at your house or somewhere else?"

"No, I phoned to tell her I was alright and that we would soon be leaving."

"Was that the first time you had contacted her?"

"Yes."

"You phoned your brother as soon as you thought you were in trouble, yet you did not contact your wife?"

"No… I thought they might be waiting for me… I needed time to think…"

"Abdul, where is your wife now?"

"At home, waiting for me to call. You would not let me phone her."

"When you turned yourself in, we visited your house as a matter of routine. Your wife was not at home and our operatives, having looked through the front window, could see that your home had been ransacked so they gained entry via the back door. There was no sign of your wife, is there somewhere else she could have gone, friends, family?"

"No... her family in Pakistan... maybe she will come back?"

"We have had the house under surveillance for the past three days and apart from the postman and a young girl delivering plastic, charity clothes bags, no one else has visited the house." George paused for several seconds to allow that last statement to sink in before continuing. "Abdul, these people are dangerous and the only way we can help you is by knowing everything about them."

Bill picked up on the conversation and suggested they have a break for fifteen minutes whilst Abdul gathered his thoughts to see what other information he had that might be useful. "Mr Daniels and I will leave you for a few moments but I will get an operative to sit with you in case you remember something while we are gone. Can I organise you a tea or coffee?"

"Er... coffee please... black."

Bill and George walked over the thick, red axminster carpet and opened the door. The tall lean figure, alerted by the monitoring team to Bill's request for a 'minder', stepped aside to let them pass before entering the room and closing the door behind him.

"Not much concern for his wife, eh?" Bill commented as they walked towards his office.

"Yeah, mind you, I've got an ex I wouldn't be too concerned about either." George replied, a large smile spreading across his face.

"Have you matched up those blood samples yet?"

"Yes, they probably belong to Abdul's wife, same blood group but there was not much, she could have cut herself on a bread knife or something, it doesn't really prove anything."

"Okay, let's cut to the chase," Bill stated as he stopped walking and turned to look George straight in the eye. "Do you believe everything he said?"

"I take it you mean about Peter Edwards?"

"Yes, we have a file on him that shows nothing untoward and the CIA and FBI have even thicker files, seeing as his son will probably be the next President of the United States. But, as far as I'm aware, nowhere does it give the slightest inkling of anything out of the ordinary."

"I can't see what he would gain by lying at this stage, he knows we will be following up on any information he gives us and earlier on, he buckled fairly quickly when confronted with the truth. I think we have to treat this as being very plausible and go through the usual channels."

"Okay, Edwards Chemicals is based in the UK but this could implicate the next President of the USA so who runs with the ball, MI5 or MI6?"

"Well, a problem shared is a problem halved," George answered, sensing that this could be the tip of the iceberg. "We will start investigating from the UK side and leave you to sort out Pakistan and our friends in the States."

"Well, that's very kind of you," Bill replied, opening the door and ushering George into his office, "just like MI5 to take the easy option."

"So where do we start, this Dr Ashkani guy or do we go straight for the jugular, Peter Edwards himself?"

"Well, if the media got wind that we were investigating the Presidential Candidate's dad, even if it did prove to be totally faultless, it could cause irreparable damage to Dale Edwards's campaign." Bill sat down in his comfy, well-used leather chair and nodded to the seat opposite. "On the other hand, if Peter Edwards is involved, then we need to know sooner rather than later. I'm going to toss the Edwards hot potato over to Chas Wiltson and let them start digging at their end. You check on the dates that Hussein visited Pakistan or anyone else from Edwards Chemicals, especially Peter Edwards and I will ask our central desk to track down Dr Ashkani, that's if he exists."

"I take it you do not believe our Mr Hussein?"

"No, that's just it, I do believe him, it's just that he has a habit of twisting the truth around to point to other people and it could have been him in there on the conversation. Edwards could have been set up to be the opposite, just like his brother and I want to be sure of my facts before starting an international crisis."

"Okay, we'll just have to be a little more delicate with our investigations with Edwards Chemicals. I'll get the ball rolling." George continued, taking his mobile phone out of his jacket pocket and selecting a number from the contacts.

"While you are doing that, I'll get our lot in Pakistan to see what they can dig up on Dr Ashkani, but first..." Bill picked up the internal phone on his desk, "I'll give our central desk a call to see if we already have anything on him."

Both men spent the next fifteen minutes on the phone. Central desk had nothing immediate on Dr Ashkani and Chas Wiltson seemed surprisingly calm about Peter Edwards's possible involvement with Bob Jollinger's assassination, cutting Bill short but promising to phone him back in a little while.

"Kane, it's Bill," The phone had only rung twice before Kane had answered. "I need you to find someone and quick. The guy goes by the name of Dr Ashkani and he has some sort of connection with the warehouse owner Rashid and Abdul Hussein. I need you to find out what that connection is."

"Did you get this information from Hussein?"

"Yes, it turns out he was the one who overheard the conversation about the intended assassination, not his brother. I guess he was just after whatever he could get."

"Any addresses or place of work to go on?"

"No, just that he used to meet with Abdul Hussein when he visited Pakistan, I will try and get some clearer information when we start again with Hussein."

"Dr Ashkani, is he a medical doctor?"

"I don't think so, I am led to believe he is some sort of scientist or laboratory assistant. Sorry Kane, the information we have is minimal at the moment but this guy could be a crucial link to the operation which is why I need you guys to start digging. I'll get central to give you a call if and when they come up with something. Good luck and keep me informed."

Bill ended the call and turned to face George who was replacing his black, government issued iPhone into his inside jacket pocket.

"Well, George, I think we need to assume Hussein is telling the truth and get him to give us as much information as possible about his visits to Pakistan. He must know something of Ashkani's whereabouts but with his track record, we need to confirm anything he gives us as soon as possible. Should he give us anymore duff information then we need to jerk him back on track. My guys will be monitoring the interview and I will get them to follow up anything and everything Hussein gives us. They can interrupt us if they do latch on to anything, especially if it proves to be bogus."

"You really don't trust our Mr Hussein do you?" George commented, rising from the chair.

"I don't trust anybody who lies to me, but let's just say… gut instinct."

The two men walked out of the office down the large, wide corridor to the interview room and opened the oak panelled door.

"Mr Hussein, sorry to have kept you waiting." Bill apologised before settling himself down in the chair opposite. "Did you have your coffee?"

"Yes... thank you. How much longer will I be here?"

"Well, if you carry on where we left off then it should not take too long." Bill turned his attention to the operative stood in the corner of the room. "Did Mr Hussein have anything to add while we were away?"

"No, Sir."

"Okay Mark, you can leave us now."

The 'minder' left the room closing the door quietly behind him.

"Right Mr Hussein," Bill continued, clasping his hands together and allowing them to drop loudly onto the table in front of him before leaning forward just inches from Abdul Hussein's face. "Let's talk some more about Dr Ashkani. How long have you known him?"

Abdul Hussein sat back in his chair, trying to increase the distance between him and Bill. "About a year, maybe less."

"When did you first meet him?"

"It was... about a year ago... maybe this time last year."

Bill knew that it would be relatively easy for the monitoring team to quickly verify when Hussein had visited Pakistan and if anything was amiss he would be informed and change his questioning accordingly.

"Who set up the first meeting?"

"Dr Ashkani."

"So Dr Ashkani contacted you?"

"No... Mr Edwards arranged the meeting."

"Mr Edwards?"

"Yes, Peter Edwards, he owns Edwards Chemicals."

"And where did you meet Dr Ashkani?"

"At his hotel in Cobham."

"Which hotel in Cobham, what was the name?"

"I think it was the... Fairmile... off Portsmouth Road."

"And this would be approximately when?"

"About May or June last year."

"What else do you know about Dr Ashkani, where he came from, where he was going?"

"That's all I know, now can I go, I cannot help you anymore."

"Abdul, you don't seem to realize that this is your security we are talking about. The more we can learn from you, the quicker we can bring this case to an end and the safer you will be. Now, getting back to Dr Ashkani, why did you meet him at his hotel and not in the office?"

"I do not know why, I was just told to meet him and exchange some files."

For the next twenty five minutes Bill bombarded Abdul with questions, hoping that something would materialise that would enable them to move forward. George never spoke a word, he just sat there gauging Abdul Hussein's reaction to the barrage of questions being thrown at him. The questioning was halted briefly by a knock on the door.

"Come in," Bill boomed.

The door opened and a smartly dressed middle aged lady quickly entered the room and handed Bill a folded piece of A4 paper and waited for a response.

Bill unfolded the paper and read the note with interest. The monitoring team had contacted the hotel and managed to get a home address for a Dr Aziri there being no one else registered under the name of Dr Ashkani on the dates in question. The second part of the note showed that Abdul Hussein had been a frequent visitor to Pakistan for the past six years.

"Thank you, Madeleine." Bill smiled as he handed back the note. "Can you give this to central and ask them to pass it to our people in Islamabad please, correcting the information I gave them earlier."

Bill watched her leaving the room and as she closed the door, turned his attention back to Abdul Hussein. "Right Abdul, let's confirm a few things. The first time you met Dr Ashkani was when?"

"In his hotel in Surrey."

"And you had never met him on your previous trips to Pakistan?"

"No… what is this all about?"

"What about Dr Aziri?"

"Who?" Abdul's face was pensive but showed no sign of acknowledgement.

"When did you first begin visiting Pakistan?"

"I was born there, so I often visited my family."

"And when did you first meet Rashid Gazar?"

"I… I don't know, how much longer are you going to keep me here, I cannot tell you anymore. I want to use the toilet and I want to be allowed to go."

"Okay, let's have a break and we will resume again in an hour."

"NO." Abdul shouted, jumping to his feet. "I want to go, now!"

"You will go when I am satisfied you have told us all that you know. Until then, we will carry on the questioning, starting back in an hour's time."

A knock on the door heralded the 'minder' who was to escort Abdul Hussein to the toilet and then to the canteen before returning him back to the interview room and another barrage of questions.

"Did you notice his face when you mentioned Rashid Gazar?" George asked as they disappeared out of the room.

"Yes, he also genuinely appeared not to know the name of Dr Aziri, that is if our Dr Ashkani was using it as a pseudonym, we have a long way to go with this guy yet."

10

Kane, having received Dr Aziri's address from central desk, was easing himself out of the cramped back seat of the taxi which had squealed to a halt halfway down Gomal Road. Alison had tagged along as an interpreter if necessary and was already clambering out behind Kane. The leg room in the back had been greatly reduced due to the driver's seat being pushed back to its' full extent in order to accommodate the driver's large, overly obese frame and Kane was relieved to be stood, stretching his aching legs. He checked the house number and having paid the taxi walked towards the bright, red painted door. The area was in sharp contrast to the lorry driver's abode of yesterday. The crisp, white walls were punctuated with bright red window frames surrounding clean, clear glass windows. White vertical blinds adorned the inside and a gleaming brass knocker beckoned on the large red door.

"You let our lift go again, what if he's not here?"

"Then we'll just have to ask around." Kane responded, as he knocked three times on the door in quick succession.

A few moments later an elderly lady dressed in a predominantly blue Sari opened the door and squinted in the sunlight.

"Is Dr Amiri available?" Kane asked.

"Eh." Came the response, as she held her hand behind her ear.

Kane tried again, then Alison tried in Urdu but she still could not understand. Finally, Alison went into her bag and pulled out a pen and some paper and having written a brief line showed it to her.

گے کریں بات سے aziri ڈاکٹر میں

The old lady looked at the writing, nodded and turned back inside the house, partially closing the door behind her.

"So what was the note?" Kane asked, slightly impressed with her language skills.

"I told her you were a wanker but you would pay her 100,000 rupees if she could tell us where Dr Aziri was."

"Funny. Now what did it really say?"

"I just asked to speak to Dr Aziri."

The door suddenly opened and a very smartly dressed lady in her late thirties, early forties, stood pensively in the doorway.

"Can I help you, I'm Dr Aziri?"

"Oh sorry, we were looking for a Mr Aziri; we must have the wrong address."

"That would be my brother, Ali, but he no longer lives here. He has a house just up the road, but he will be in work now. Can I help in any way?" The doctor softly asked, her eyes scanning Kane's rugged features and taut torso.

"Does he work locally?"

"Yes, but what do you want with Ali?"

"My name's Kane Richmond and this is my assistant. A mutual friend of ours gave us his name and suggested we may be able to do business together. So where did you say he worked?"

"I didn't, what sort of business did you say you were in?"

"I didn't… okay, we could fence with one another all day and as much as I'd like the challenge, I really do need to speak with Dr Aziri, I mean Ali, as soon as possible if we are to do business with one another."

"Challenge?" The lady posed, casting her eye over Alison before returning her attention to the bronzed figure in front of her. "We might even enjoy it."

"We might at that. Perhaps we ought to take a rain check. Does Ali work nearby?"

"He works at Punjab Pharmaceuticals, just past the zoo and off Margalla Road."

"Has he got a telephone number we can contact him on?"

"Just a minute," She flashed Kane a beaming white smile before turning and re-entering the house. A minute later she reappeared with a scribbled note in her hand. "This is his number at work, but if you cannot get through to him then my number is underneath."

Kane noticed the bottom number had the name Safia clearly written next to it

"Thank you, we'll be in touch."

"I will look forward to it."

Kane gave a brief nod of the head and turned to walk briskly down the street with Alison trying to catch up.

"And I thought it was only men that undressed with their eyes and what's this assistant business? I thought I was supposed to be your wife?"

"You're not jealous again are you?"

"What, of Doctor flipping nymphomaniac? No chance."

"Well, she has got curves in all the right places…"

"Yeah, including her skin. She must be fifty odd if she's a day. Anyway, what do you mean again? You should be so lucky… not."

"Okay, let's give our Dr Aziri a ring." Kane responded, keying in the top number and bringing the banter to a close.

On the fourth ring a voice answered, "Dr Aziri speaking, how may I help you?"

"Sorry, I misdialled, wrong number."

"What was all that about?" Alison asked, looking rather perplexed.

"Just checking to see the number was genuine. We need to get Brian down here and meet up with this guy as soon as possible. Give him a ring and ask him to meet us… um… outside the main zoo entrance, it's as good a place as any. I'll give Bill a ring to update him and see if we have anything else to go on."

Alison finished making the arrangements with Brian and ending the call, strained to pick up on the conversation Kane was having with Bill.

"Anything new?" Alison asked.

"Nothing we did not know already. Bill's going to see what he can dig up on Punjab Pharmaceuticals and he wants us to reign in this Dr Aziri as soon as possible. No time for juggling, Bill wants us to confirm Dr Aziri is the guy Abdul Hussein is supposed to have met up with in London. Is Brian on his way?"

"Yes, he should be waiting for us by the time we get there, I take it we're walking?"

"Of course."

"Great, my feet will never be the same. What happens if this guy is the one we are looking for?"

"Then we need to pump him for as much information as possible. He's some sort of messenger or go between, but if he is our guy and we put the frighteners on him, there's a good chance he will tell us all we want to know."

Ali Aziri replaced the handset and shrugged his shoulders before rising from his chair and walking over to the water cooler in the corner of his well-appointed office. A large clear window overlooked a patch of brown, barren wasteland, stretching to the edge of the zoo gardens beyond.

Dr Ali Aziri was thirty four years of age, with light brown eyes, light brown complexion and jet black hair. A thin moustache covered his top lip and a faded, three inch scar stretched from the corner of his mouth towards the bottom of his left ear. As he gazed over the sun dried wasteland his fingers gently traced the length of his facial scar while his mind travelled back thirteen years to the fateful day when he had taken his family to visit his mother. An American Cruise missile had exploded in the building next to his mother's home in Afghanistan and the resulting falling debris was responsible for killing his mother, brother, wife and two year old daughter, as well as his friend's wife. He was later dug out of the wreckage with a fractured jaw, broken arm and a burning hatred for the killers of his family.

His sister Safia, was in her final year at medical college in Pakistan and he was in his third year, studying Chemistry at the University of Punjab in Lahore. He was the youngest of three children but had a different father to Safia and his oldest brother, Devalda. When Devalda was just seven years old, to escape the wrath of his biological father, he climbed up onto the roof of the small, breeze block building he shared with his parents and baby sister Safia. His father Mohamed, had a very short temper and would often beat Ali or his mother Sinitta for the slightest reason. The roof gave way and they both tumbled three metres to the floor, Mohamed's fall being cushioned by Devalda's back and neck as they both crashed to the concrete base below. Mohamed got to his feet and began kicking the lifeless form on the floor in front of him. Sinitta screamed that he was not moving and ran to cover Devalda's prone torso with her body, absorbing the painful kicks that still vented Mohamed's temper. Eventually, the kicking stopped and Mohamed sloped off into the market place. Sinitta enlisted the help of her neighbour and together they carried Devalda to the local health centre. A five minute examination concluded with Devalda being taken to the Allied

Hospital in Punjab where he was diagnosed with a broken vertebrae and broken neck. The only thing Devalda could move was his eyes but Sinitta vowed to look after him for the rest of his life and when Mohammed's body was found floating in the river Indus two weeks later, Sinitta took Devalda and Safia to live with her cousin in Afghanistan.

Sinitta was a very pretty twenty six year old devoted mother to her two children Devalda and Safia. Her long jet black hair reached down to her trim waist and her hour glass figure could not conceal her ample breasts which drew the attention of many an admirer. Her cousin encouraged her to go out to work and lovingly helped out caring for Devalda and Safia. Sinitta was grateful for the break but still rushed home from her part time job as a receptionist in a local office block. A year later she started an affair with a married man who regularly visited the offices and soon after, Ali was born. The affair ended but Ali's father supported the family financially until the day she died and even then made sure that Ali and Safia had enough money to see them through college.

Ali's thoughts were interrupted with the phone ringing again. "Hello," He uttered without his usual courteous approach.

"Dr Aziri?" A female voice inquired.

"Yes, this is Dr Aziri. How may I help you?"

"My name's Alison Richmond, a mutual friend of ours suggested we may be able to do some reciprocal business."

"Friend? What friend?"

"Abdul Hussein."

Ali Aziri paused and looked at his office door expecting it to be thrown open at any time. "Who are you?" He continued, his eyes still focussed on the door.

"We are friends and need to speak to you straight away, it's urgent."

"What is this all about? Why do you need to speak with me?"

"Dr Aziri, we can either come to your offices or meet you locally but it is imperative that we meet as soon as possible?"

"Where are you now?"

"We are just down the road from your offices. Would you like us to come over and see you there?"

"Who is we?" Aziri's mind was asking questions his brain could not answer. How did they know where to find him? What could they want? How much did they know?

"Myself and my colleague." Alison replied, smirking at Kane thinking two can play at that game.

"And if we were to meet locally, away from the office, where do you suggest we meet?" Ali had now regained his control and thought he would find out if they really did know the whereabouts of his office.

"Well, we are outside the zoo at the moment, you could walk here in ten minutes."

"No, I am too busy, we will have to make it another day."

"I'm afraid it's a case of today or too late. We are leaving this afternoon and really need to speak to you before we go."

Ali thought for a moment, he was sure he had not left any clues to his whereabouts, certainly not with Abdul Hussein. If they knew where his offices were, which apparently they did and it was the government or other intelligence sources, then they would have just barged in and gone through all his files. On the other hand, they would have not broken their cover and would have put him under surveillance, or had he been under surveillance all along?

"Okay, I will meet you in front of the zoo entrance in fifteen minutes. How will I recognise you?"

"I will be wearing dark blue slacks and a light blue blouse carrying a white handbag," Alison replied. "How will I recognise you?"

Good, Ali thought to himself. He would have been concerned if they knew what he looked like because it would have meant that they probably did have him under surveillance. "I will be wearing a light cream jacket and trousers." Ali replied, the almost white, light suits were a popular choice with the local business men for both comfort during the hot summer days and appearance and there were bound to be several similarly dressed men around the zoo area.

"Okay we will see you in ten minutes."

"No, fifteen." Ali repeated before terminating the call.

"He's our man then?" Kane asked, it was more of a statement than a question as he already knew the answer. "I'll let Bill know and see if he can find out anymore for us."

Dr Aziri spent the next ten minutes checking that nothing was immediately evident that would suggest Punjab Pharmaceuticals was anything other than a manufacturer of pharmaceutical drugs, which, on the face of it, it was. Satisfied that there were was nothing incriminating in his office, Ali left the building and began the five minute walk to the zoo's main entrance.

Brian watched the white suited figure leave the building and head off in the direction of the zoo. Waiting until Dr Aziri was almost out of sight, Brian folded his newspaper and set off at a brisk pace, slowly decreasing the gap between them. Alison meanwhile, was trying to find a prominent position in front of the zoo entrance.

"What did Bill have to say?"

"He's already contacted our guys at the Embassy but he is going to put a bit of pressure on. Sounds like he has the bit between his teeth and wants this resolved as soon as possible, so we've got, virtually, a free hand."

Dr Ali Aziri stopped by a street lamp on the opposite side of the zoo entrance. A young lady in dark blue slacks and a light blue blouse smiled at an ageing gent in a white suit who stopped, looked her up and down and then moved on, not giving her a second glance.

"That's the third one in the last five minutes, I don't think he's going to come." Alison whispered to Kane who was a couple of feet behind her pretending to read his street map. Kane was about to make a sarky comment when his phone rang.

"Don't look now but our friend is on the opposite side of the road behind a silver Kia Sorrento." Came the sound of Brian's voice.

"Is he on his own?"

"Looks like it, he came out on his own and nobody followed him. Wait a sec. He's clocked you on the phone and is looking around to see if anyone else looks like their talking to you. He's a pretty shrewd guy by the looks of it. What do you want to do next?"

"We'll give him another couple of minutes and if he does not approach us, then we'll approach him."

Kane ended the call and walked over to Alison pretending to look at his watch. "Our guy's here but don't look up. Phone his office number and act as if we are about to leave."

Alison selected the number from her previous call list and let it ring for about twenty rings before ending the call, somewhat surprised that an answer phone had not kicked in. With an over emphasised shrug of her shoulders she made ready to leave as Kane walked up to her side.

Feeling both confident and curious, Ali stepped from behind the Sorrento and walked towards the pair. Alison saw him approach and smiled her now well-practiced welcoming smile. Ali Aziri smiled back and as he approached her asked in a loud confident manner "Alison?"

"Yes, Dr Aziri I presume."

"And you are?" Ali had turned his attention to Kane who was standing about a metre away.

"Kane Richmond, Alison's husband and associate."

"So, Mr And Mrs Richmond, how can I help you?"

"Well, it's more of a case of how we can help you." Kane replied, moving to stand directly in front of Dr Aziri.

Ali Aziri studied Kane's face for several seconds. The chiselled features and confident stare started to trigger off little alarm bells in Ali's mind. There was something about this man that put Ali instantly on his guard, so turning his attention to Alison he rephrased his question, "So how can you help me?"

"We believe you have certain information which could help us and in return, we will help you." Alison replied in a soft but confident tone.

"Help me in which way?"

"To stay alive for a start." Kane interjected.

"Who are you people? British, American? Who or what do you represent?"

"It doesn't matter who we are," Kane continued, "What matters is how you can help us and how we can help you."

"Mr Richmond, I do not do business with anyone I do not know. I think this meeting is now concluded." Ali Aziri had been weighing up the situation from the time he left the office. He was meticulous about his privacy and decided that now was the time to force them to reveal what they were really after. "Good day Mr And Mrs Richmond." Ali gave them one more glance each and turned to walk back across the busy, tarmac road.

Kane had completely underestimated Ali Aziri. He was not the simple 'messenger boy' he had assumed from the data they had been given. Assume, he thought to himself, making an Ass out of u and me, how many times had he been in this position? Anyway, he continued unravelling his thoughts, Aziri is walking away and I have to stop him.

"And what about Mr Edwards?" Alison shouted out, causing Kane to stop his advance.

Dr Aziri stopped and turned slowly around. "Which Mr Edwards?"

"Both." Alison suddenly felt a surge of confidence. Her interrogation training had instilled in her the importance of using key words or phrases whilst not giving anything away. All she had to do then was look for the buying signals, the signs that whatever was said had created some sort of interest from the other party. Aziri's body language and the concerned frown on his face, gave her the buying signal at the first attempt.

"All we want is ten minutes of your time then you are free to go." Alison continued, "Shall we take a seat?" Alison's outstretched arm and open palm pointing to a newly painted green bench some three metres away.

Ali looked into Alison's clear green, blue eyes, but they gave nothing away. He needed to know how much they knew but also did not want to put himself in a position, both physically and verbally, where it would be difficult to extricate himself from. He walked slowly over to the bench and sat down, Alison came and sat next to him.

Kane remained where he was, the bulldozer approach had not worked and Alison appeared to be breaking down barriers.

"So," Ali continued, "Before we continue, who do you represent?"

Alison glanced up at Kane but his concentrated expression gave her no pointers as to what to do next. "Okay I'll level with you," There was another glance in Kane's direction, but no intervention. "We are with British National Security…"

"MI6?" Ali interrupted.

"Yes," Alison replied, this time not bothering to glance at Kane, "We think that you have information from your dealings with certain colleagues that would help us speed up our investigations."

"Investigations into what?"

"That doesn't matter at the moment, what does matter is that just by being here you have put your life in danger."

A thin smile spread across Kane's lips as his admiration for Alison's handling of the situation started to grow. Ali Aziri on the other hand, was interested to find out what they knew, or more importantly, what they thought they knew.

"And who am I in danger from?"

"What is your involvement with Rashid Gazar?"

"I supply him with certain pharmaceuticals which he sells on the internet," The response was instant and he suddenly thought perhaps he should not have divulged the pre-planned response so soon. It was a response which Kane had already noted. “But why would Rashid Gazar want to harm me?” He continued.

“Rashid Gazar has been associated with several different terrorist activities, but anyone in his circle of business acquaintances who has spoken to us or our colleagues, has ended up being eliminated. You don’t want that to happen to you, do you?”

Ali looked into Alison’s confident eyes, which still gave nothing away. He gradually started piecing together the different bits of information to try and determine what they knew and how they thought he was involved, before deciding to go for the forthright approach. “How do I fit into all this?”

“What sort of pharmaceuticals do you supply Rashid with?” Kane asked, not being able to subdue his input for any longer.

“The usual internet drugs. Viagra, Ciallis I can get you some free samples if you need them.” Ali responded, turning his attention to Kane.

This time it was Alison’s turn to have a thin smile spread across her lips. “And Edwards Chemicals, what is your involvement with them?” Alison continued.

“There are certain chemicals required to make up the various formulas which I purchase from them.”

“My understanding was that Edwards Chemicals was a Research and Development company and not a supplier.”

“Yes, we collaborated on various formulas to try and get our products to match the branded names as closely as possible.” Ali’s response was slow and deliberate. He felt he was being put on the back foot and needed to get back in control. “But they have other manufacturing plants, which, if you have investigated them, you must surely know.”

Kane studied Ali’s confident body language. This was one switched on guy. He was shrewd, confident but like all of us mortals vulnerable and there had been at least two occasions when his defensive wall had been rattled. He cursed himself for totally misjudging his pre conceived assessment of Dr Aziri but at the same time, allowed himself to form a growing admiration for the way Alison was repairing his mistake.

“How well do you know Rashid Gazar?” Alison asked, this time her tone was softer and not so direct.

“I’ve known him for a couple of years, but I have only met him on about three occasions. His business is, how shall we say, not one that I would like to advertise my involvement in. We produce standard everyday drugs, Paracetamol, Aspirin under licence, but the licence fees are extortionate so copy drugs provide me with the income to keep the company going."

"What about his associates, what do you know of them?"

"I'm afraid I do not know any of his associates, I have only ever met with him, as I said, about three times."

"A tall fair haired man, did you ever meet with him." Alison asked, leaning slightly forward.

"No, I do not recall meeting with anyone else. Why do you ask, should I know him?"

"Not necessarily, but we are interested in any of Rashid's associates, so any information you can give us will be extremely useful."

"And what is in it for me?" Ali asked, sensing the conversation would soon be coming to an end.

"That depends on what information you can get for us."

"Get? What do you mean by get?"

"Well, you have told us nothing that we did not already know. We are prepared to pay handsomely for any information that would help us progress with this case, with the emphasis on progress, so you need to come up with something useful."

"Can I go now?"

Alison looked over to Kane, "Anything you want to ask?"

"No, Dr Aziri has been very helpful."

"Then I bid you both good day." Ali replied, rising from his seat to turn and walk briskly across the road in the direction of his office.

"What do you think?" Alison asked looking up into Kane's face.

"Well, I think he got more out of us than we got out of him."

"Well, I didn't hear you asking many questions."

"Down girl, I'm not having a dig, you did okay. We haven't got time to beat about the bush so we had little option other than take the direct approach. I'll give Brian a ring and ask him to shadow our friend for the rest of the day. But anyway, you were the lead on this one what did you think?"

"He seemed to run hot and cold. I think he knows more than he is letting on, so how do we push him?"

"When you explained about his involvement with Rashid he answered straight away, as if it had been rehearsed. Then, when you pointed out that any of Rashid's associates that had spoken to us had been eliminated there was no sign of concern. If it had been me I would have wanted to know what happened, who they were and how we could prevent that from happening again. No, I think our Dr Aziri is in this deeper than we thought. I'll make the call to Brian."

11

Bill Johnson studied the written notes in front of him, pausing every now and then to highlight certain words or phrases and then drawing connecting arrow lines linking particular sentences together. The ongoing interview with Abdul Hussein was puzzling to say the least. The facts, in the main, were proving to be correct but each had a twist in the tale. The majority of the information was, on the face of it, true, so why did he have this feeling, this gut instinct that he was missing out on something?

The direct line on his desk rang into life, pulling him away from his nagging thoughts.

"Bill Johnson." He answered, his eyes still searching the scribbled notes for inspiration.

"Hi Bill, it's Chas."

"Hi Chas, how are things your end?"

"Fine thanks, I just thought I'd update you on your Mr Edwards."

"Okay, what have you got?"

"Well, Jollinger's staff has been digging around to see what dirt they could come up with on Dale Edwards. In a nutshell they came up with zilch, so they started digging on his family, particularly Mr Edwards Senior. Apparently, Bob Jollinger uncovered something which he thought would be well worth a pop shot at Dale Edwards and intended announcing it on one of his campaign platforms. We have yet to uncover what it was but, if it had been serious he would not have waited, he would have leaked it to the media at the very least."

"I take it this was just before he was assassinated?"

"Well, from what we can gather, this was a week or two before, so, as I said, it appears it was nothing earth shattering."

"Does any of his staff know what he was working on, or who he was working with?"

"All they know was that a week or two before his proposed visit to Memphis Bob Jollinger phoned Dale Edwards to try and rattle him with whatever he had found out so far. We spoke with Edwards but it was his personal assistant, David Butane that fended off the call and according to Mr Butane, all Jollinger said was that his speech at the Promotional Dinner in Memphis would be a memorable one, the usual sparring rhetoric you would expect from competing candidates."

"So us having a quiet word with Mr Edwards Senior would not harm any of your inquiries?"

"Nope, not at all, I'm just as interested in finding out if he's involved as you are, but I doubt it. Have you got anything more to go on?"

"It seems he was, or is alleged to have supplied, formulas and ingredients to a pharmaceutical company for making drugs, so we need to confirm that."

"Drugs… interesting, but you emphasised the alleged bit, I take it you're not convinced?"

"Well, let's just say our informant's information has been fairly accurate, but somewhat twisted, so I need to hear it from the horse's mouth before I jump to any conclusions. Why the drugs interest, it seems to have struck a chord with you?"

"Same old Bill, sharp as ever. When we questioned Jollinger's aides about what Bob Jollinger intended saying at the Promotional Dinner, one of them mentioned they thought it was something to do with Peter Edwards' promiscuity or taking drugs, but all our investigations have proved negative."

"Well, I'll let you know if we come up with anything." Bill began ending the call with the usual formalities and as he returned the handset to the cradle glanced over to where George Daniels was sat, scribbling down his own notes.

"I heard," George uttered without looking up from his notes, "you must be getting deaf in your old age, I could hear nearly everything Chas said."

"I suppose you want the Edwards interview then?"

"Home ground, Bill, home ground, that's where MI5 take over, but we'll keep you up to date. I'll get a couple of operatives around there straight away."

"He might still be in the States."

"No, he has been here for the last three days. Got into his office at 8am this morning and been there ever since."

"You crafty bugger. You've been expecting this all along."

"Yes, as if you haven't. Now, anything in particular you would like my boys to ask?"

"No, just to see what he says about Abdul and his connection with Dr Aziri or what was the other name… Ashkani."

"Okay Bill, I am going to head back to my office but I will let you know the outcome of our meeting." George rose from the plush, but well-worn leather arm chair and strode towards the door. "Can you hang on to Mr Hussein for me while I'm away?"

"Don't worry, he's going nowhere."

Brian followed Dr Aziri back to his office, being careful not to be noticed on each of the seven times Ali stopped to turn around and scan the people around him for any signs of being followed. He strode on past his office for three hundred metres before turning and heading back and when he was completely satisfied that he had not been followed, entered the building and climbed the stairs to his office.

Sitting in the blue swivel chair, he tilted back, staring up at the white painted ceiling, his mind going over the events of the past hour. It was obvious they thought Rashid to be the main man and a broad grin spread across his face. But how did they know where to find him? Ali picked up the phone and keyed in a memory number.

"Safia," Ali spoke softly as the call was answered. "Has anybody been asking after me recently?"

"Yes, this morning, but they said they wanted to do business with you. There's nothing wrong Ali, is there?"

"No Safia, all's fine, did they say how they got the address?"

"No, I thought they could be customers for you, did I do wrong?"

"No Safia, everything is good, in fact, how would you like to go out for dinner tonight? I'll pick you up about 7pm, okay?"

"Okay Ali, I will be ready, bye."

"Bye Safia, see you later."

Ali put down the phone and smiled. Since their mother's death Safia and Ali had become very close and Ali enjoyed the 'motherly' love she poured on him, always looking out for his best interests, always wanting him to succeed, just like his mother would have done if she had been allowed to live. Ali picked up the phone and keyed in another number which answered on the third ring.

"It's me, Ali, has the shipment arrived at its destination?"

"Yes Ali, just as you ordered."

"Good, then we need to change our plans and bring them forward."

"How much forward?"

"This week, four days' time would be ideal."

"Four days! How will we get access?"

"I'm afraid I am going to have to leave the how bit to you, but can you still get the plan of the plant and do you know exactly where I want the shipment deposited?"

"Yes, the main pipeline after the purifiers. The visit is not scheduled for another two weeks but I should be able to get a copy of the plans by saying I want to prepare for the visit and select key points of interest for media coverage. Osama will be avenged."

"So will Sinitta." Ali whispered as he put down the phone.

Ali turned to look out of the large, rectangular window into the serene, light blue sky. It did not matter now if he was taken, events would still take place, just a bit sooner than expected, but he needed at least one more day with his sister. He picked up the phone and keyed in another number, which answered after several rings.

"Yes, Ali."

"Are you local?"

"Yes, I'm in the Blue Quarter, is there a problem?" Rashid replied.

"Not one you can't handle. I have brought things forward a bit. Washington will be this week so I need the zoo to be the day before, I want them to panic, I want them to know we do not make idle threats. Will you be ready the day after tomorrow?"

"We could do it tonight if you want?"

"No, I do not want to give them too much time; just enough to know it is coming. One more thing, I have another job for you and our fair haired friend. There are two agents from British intelligence snooping around. They gave their names as Mr And Mrs Richmond and they are probably staying in one of the local hotels. It is likely that they have been here for a few days already, but I would appreciate it if their visit was cut short."

"I will get my men on it straight away, but for the zoo, I will need to know the mixing quantities and the tank location which is in your office, shall I come over?"

"No, just in case our friends are watching us. I will meet you in the Monal in an hour's time. That should give me enough time to make sure I am not being followed."

"Okay, shall I bring the fair haired one?"

"Will you have located our friends by then? They did say they were going this afternoon so it may be worth checking the airport, have you any contacts there?"

"Ali, I have contacts everywhere. If they are still here, I will find them and punish them. What if they are booked to leave today?"

"Then they are very lucky people, but if not, I trust you will make sure their luck has run out."

"Your wish is my command. I will see you in an hour."

Ali ended the call and walked over to an old, grey Smithson safe stood in the corner of the room. Turning the tumbler several times clockwise and anticlockwise, he eventually pulled the heavy door open. Inside were three shelves with various bundles of insurance papers, stock certificates and other sundry documents. On the top shelf was a large, blue cash box sat on top of a blue wallet file. Ali opened the cash box and selected a bundle of notes, held together with a narrow, paper collar strip. Lifting the box he removed the blue wallet and closed the heavy, steel door. Ali took the wallet file to his desk and pulled out a folded A3 plan. Picking up his red Parker pen he scribbled down some mixing quantities before returning the plan to the wallet file. Ali took one last look around the office then picked up the phone and ordered a taxi.

As the taxi arrived, Ali Aziri jogged out of the main building and clambered into the back. "Pir Sohawa Road please."

"Pir Sohawa?"

"No, the start of the road, go please."

As the taxi drove out into the traffic, towards Saidpur, Ali turned around to look through the back window, but there were no obvious signs of being followed.

"How far into Pir Sohawa Road?" The driver asked. The road to Pir Sohawa was long, desolate, narrow and twisted back on itself in several areas. If this was to be a long journey then he would need to be paid up front.

"Not far, just outside Saidpur." Ali replied, again turning to look out of the window.

Brian watched the taxi pull up and saw Ali Aziri climb into the back. His surveillance training kept him just out of sight but his instincts wanted to dash out and hail down the next taxi that passed, not that this was an area that taxis frequented. He quickly wrote down the registration and dialled his now familiar taxi number, just as the taxi pulled out into the traffic.

"How long?" Brian asked.

"Ten minutes."

"Can't you do it sooner?"

"No sorry, Sir, ten minutes."

"Okay, forget it, thanks." Brian begrudgingly ended the call, the taxi was already out of sight and could be headed anywhere. Better update Kane, he thought to himself, keying in his number from the contacts list.

The taxi driver drove through Saidpur and onto the desolate Pir Sohawa Road. After three miles the driver asked Ali how much further he wanted to go.

Ali glanced around and seeing that there were no other vehicles in sight turned back to the driver. "Okay, we can go back now."

"Back?"

"Yes, drop me off in the Blue Quarter, please."

The puzzled taxi driver turned the car around on the narrow road and headed back in the direction he had come from. Ali watched the road ahead but the only vehicle that came into view was an old red Nissan, travelling in the opposite direction. The parents in the front were obviously arguing with the two young children trying to put their heads out of the open back windows. Ali smiled to himself; it would be a long journey to Pir Sohawa.

Bill Johnson drank the remainder of his tea and stood up to brush the crumbs off his neatly pressed dark blue flannel trousers. Chelsea buns were one of his favourite snacks but the sugar and cake crumbs seemed to go everywhere. Satisfied that the last remaining remnants had been brushed off, Bill straightened himself up and began to walk briskly out of the canteen towards his office when his mobile sprung into life.

"Bill, it's George. We are with Mr Edwards at the moment, but on the dates in question he was in the States."

"Which dates are you talking about?"

"All of the ones Abdul Hussein gave us. He came back to the UK three days ago having spent six weeks in the States helping his son with his campaign so he could not have been here a few weeks ago when Abdul said he overheard Leidmeister and the other guy in the office where Peter Edwards was also supposed to be present. Also, this time last year Mr Edwards was in New York from April to August overseeing the takeover of a rival company. But there's more. Mr Edwards remembers a Dr Ashkani who wanted to re-develop a formula that he had misplaced and asked if he could use their resources to try and accomplish it but when Mr Edwards found out that one of the carrier components was to be Hepatitis A he terminated their discussions. Apparently you need special licences for each drug and as it was not something he used, or would ever use, he told Dr Ashkani or Aziri as we know him, that he could not help him."

"So our Mr Hussein has been lying to us all along?"

"Not about everything, just Mr Edwards's involvement. On May 19th the General Manager at Edwards Chemicals found Abdul Hussein in a training room with a tall guy with fair hair and another who fits the description of Rashid Gazar. When he questioned Abdul later he was not satisfied with the very vague reasons given and spent the following day investigating what Abdul had been working on. There were large gaps in his documented research notes and some of the chemicals he was evaluating had nothing to do with the research and development tasks he had been set. In addition, he would book a couple of days off every now and again, at short notice and when he returned, according to his colleagues, seemed to be splashing his money about. So the manager deduced he was moonlighting on the side and started preparing disciplinary procedures. That is why he is so sure of the dates and also why they were not unduly surprised when he did not report back to work."

"I think it's time for another talk with Mr Hussein," Bill stated, his gut instinct now stronger than ever. "Anything else?"

"No, we are still checking on his holiday dates to see if they match his visits to Pakistan and we will check his financial status, but Edwards looks clean."

"Okay George, catch you later."

Bill had barely finished the call when the phone rang again. This time it was Major Henry Morgan, anxious to relay his information and get back into MI6's good books. Bill listened as the Major explained that as soon as he had received the request for information on Dr Ali Aziri, he had organised a phone tap on the doctor's business number and had requested usage details on his mobile phone. Bill screwed up his face as he listened to the fast talking Major. It would take a Judge's order to get a phone tap over here and then there had to be a good reason.

"Whoa, slow down a bit, what was that last part?"

"He had made several calls this morning, but we could only tape the last two."

"What were the calls?"

"One was to a taxi firm and the other to a mobile in Islamabad. That one referred to something in Washington and the zoo, but it also mentioned Mr and Mrs Richmond and wanting to cut short their visit."

"Can you send me a copy of the tapes?"

"Already done, they should be with your central desk as we speak."

"Okay Major, well done. Keep me informed if anything else happens." Bill hurried down the corridor to the offices of central Desk. "Anything for me from Islamabad?" He shouted as he was halfway through the door.

"Yes, it has just been deciphered. There's some written text and a sound clip. Would you like to hear that now?" The operator asked, holding out a headset.

"Yes, have you got it set up?"

"Take a seat and give me two seconds."

Bill put on the headset and began listening to the conversation between Aziri and Rashid. Halfway through he shouted to the operator, somewhat louder than intended, to get Kane on the line, then resumed listing to the sound clip. The taped telephone call concluded, Bill removed the headset. "Got hold of Kane yet?"

"No, it's going straight to voicemail."

"And Alison?"

"Same thing, must be poor reception in their area."

"Try Brian." Bill snapped curtly, before sifting through the printed transcripts.

"Got Brian Sir, you can take it through the headset if you want."

"Yeah fine, put him through." Bill barked, struggling to get the headset lined up on his head so the small, thin mike tube nestled by his cheek.

"Brian, you with Kane?"

"No Bill, they went back to the hotel, I'm sat in a cafe having a coffee and keeping an eye out to see if Dr Aziri returns."

"Well, he just made a call from his office phone, it seems Kane and Alison have upset him and looks like he intends paying them a visit, well not personally, but get them out of their hotel pronto and wait for my phone call."

"Are you sure it was his office phone? I have been watching his office all afternoon and I am sure he has not returned whilst I have been here. When did you say Aziri made the call?"

Bill sifted through the transcripts and read out the printed time at the top of the page. "13.15pm"

"That's our time or yours?"

"Shit, what's the time there?"

"Nearly 6.30pm."

"This call is over five hours old, get them out of that hotel now."

Bill cancelled the call and barked out the order to keep ringing Kane until they had a response. Brian strode out of the cafe, dialling his favourite taxi company as he went.

Brian waited impatiently for the taxi, altering his calls between Kane and Alison. He had already left a voicemail asking them to contact him urgently and phoned the hotel to be put through to their room, but still no answer. He began to fear the worst even if they were playing at the physical side of man and wife they would pause to answer the phone.

On the ninth attempt Kane answered. "Where have you been? Is Alison with you?" Brian blurted, relieved to hear his voice.

"I've been following our Dr Aziri and his mate. They sauntered out of a restaurant just in front of us so we decided to see where they were going."

"Where are you now?"

"In the car park just across from the hotel. They met a couple of guys, chatted for a few minutes then walked into the car park and got into in a black Mitsubishi Shogun. It was you that phoned earlier then? It echoed around the car park so we put our phones on silent."

"It was either me or Bill. Listen, don't go back to the hotel, they intend paying you a visit and have had a five hour start on tracking you down."

"How do you know this?" Kane quickly responded, with seemingly more concern than usual.

"Bill had his phone tapped and it looks like he's setting up a couple of guys to pay you a visit."

"Brian, Alison has gone back to change," Kane shouted, breaking into a steady jog. "I'm going to get her out."

"I'll be with you in about five minutes, I'll keep trying her mobile but take care, don't do anything stupid."

Brian called her number several times, but each time it ended up going to voicemail. As the taxi pulled up to the Marriott Hotel, he removed the hunting knife from the strap on his leg and slipped it under his shirt, tucked into his waistband. Kane should be there by now he thought to himself.

Alison stood in the bathroom admiring her naked, slender form in the mirror. How could he resist me on our last night? She thought to herself, a seductive smile breaking out at the corners of her mouth.

Turning on the shower she stood back to wait for the water to warm up before entering. A gentle, barely audible knock at the door brought her back from her dreams. She quickly glanced in the mirror and buffed up her hair before wrapping herself in a bath towel and heading for the door.

"Christ, I haven't even had a shower yet." She shouted, opening the door. The smiling face and cold grey blue eyes of Henryk Leidmeister greeted her. Instinctively she tried to slam the door shut just as the flash from the end of a silencer sent the bullet skimming past the end of the door to bury deep in her chest. Alison's mouth fell open as she bounced back against the wall then fell forward against the opening door, partially closing it. She collapsed onto the floor, her body resting against the part opened door, only to be shoved backwards with each surge of the heaving bodies that finally forced the door open enough for Leidmeister to step over Alison's blood soaked semi naked body and into the bedroom, whilst his associate burst into the steam filled bathroom. Henryk Leidmeister scanned the well-furnished room. He carefully pointed his pistol at the far side of the bedroom as he slowly walked around the foot of the bed. A muffled sound made him turn around just in time to see his colleague crumple to the floor, the handle of a hunting knife clearly visible in the centre of his back and Kane frantically trying to ease the semi-automatic from his right hand.

Leidmeister let off two quick shots, forcing Kane to fall back into the bathroom dropping the gun onto the wet slippery floor.

"Kane you alright?"

Brian's voice came from just outside in the hallway.

"Yes, Alison's been hit, he's in the bedroom."

"I'm coming in." Brian shouted, pushing the door open then retreating back behind the hall wall. The expected volley of shots did not come, so crouching down he moved to peer through the gap and slowly pushed open the door which had bounced back off Alison's crumpled body. He inched forward, gun held out in front of him ready to target anything that moved.

"I'm in, where are you?" Once again Brian expected to be peppered with bullets but nothing.

"I'm in the bathroom to your right, I heard the balcony door open, but be careful."

Brian slowly inched his way forward and stopped at Alison's motionless form. Kane eased into the doorway of the steamed up bathroom stretching his neck to see the dressing table mirror that reflected back into the bedroom. Brian reached down and felt Alison's neck for a pulse.

"She's alive." Brian whispered, "it's weak but it's a pulse."

"Let's get this bastard and get her out of here." Kane hissed through gritted teeth as he slid out of the bathroom and moved silently down the wall into the large, well lit, empty bedroom. A scream from the outside made Kane look in the direction of the open balcony door. "He's got out." Kane shouted moving quickly across the floor, both hands holding the gun in front of him whilst his eyes scanned all corners of the room.

Brian entered the bedroom just behind Kane and satisfied the room was clear, picked up the phone and dialled reception. Kane carefully exited through the doors onto the white, pillared balcony. The screams came from below. Kane looked at the pillars and guessed that Leidmeister had climbed down them, albeit with difficulty, to the floor beneath. Kane turned and ran back through the room just as Brian was replacing the receiver.

"You stay with Alison, I'm going after him."

Kane stood on the prone assailant and paused for a moment to look down at Alison's still and twisted torso before gently stepping over her and running out into the hall. Another body lay in a foetal shape on the floor. That's where Brian got his gun from he thought to himself, running past and out onto the stairway. Kane thundered down the stairs two at a time and burst out onto the hallway, gun at the ready. Alerted by the screams and seeing Kane walking purposely down the corridor, gun in front, held in a double handed grip, a grey haired lady with small, gold rimmed spectacles ducked her head back into the room and closed the door, before making a bee line for the telephone. Kane slowed as he reached the open door which he estimated to be directly under his room. In one movement he lurched into the open doorway, squatting down to make himself a smaller target and levelling his gun at a half dressed lady, now speechless with shock and clutching a pillow in front of her, partly to hide her modesty partly for comfort.

"Where is he?" Kane snapped, his eyes searching out the nooks and crannies of the room.

She did not speak but slowly raised her arm to point in the direction of the doorway. Kane turned and ran back down the corridor to the stairs. Bounding down the remaining two flights of stairs he burst out into the reception area, startling some of the hotel guests on their way to dinner. The receptionist put her hand to her mouth as she saw the gun in Kane's hand which he had now relaxed and let drop to his side. He strode through reception and out through the large glass doors frantically scanning the area outside. He was oblivious to the two police cars that had screamed to a halt on the Aga Khan Road, the occupants of which were now running towards Kane, weapons drawn and levelling them in his direction.

"Drop the gun." The command from the stocky police sergeant slowly filtered through to Kane, his mind set on finding Leidmeister amongst the ornamental shrubs and flower beds. A second louder command to drop his gun finally attracted his attention to the four men bearing down on him. Kane bent his knees and slowly lowered the gun to the ground before standing upright, his hands above his head. The nearest policeman walked behind Kane and roughly grabbing his right hand, pulled it down, snapping a handcuff on it before repeating the operation with the other hand. Satisfied his hands were secured, he pushed Kane down, forcing him to sit on the cold, marble steps. Kane just stared in front, his eyes continuing the search.

Two hours of interrogation later, Kane was taken to a holding room and offered a cup of coffee. It was fifteen minutes before it arrived and it was Brian who entered the room with a cup in each hand, closely followed by the sullen looking Police sergeant.

"You are free to go as soon as your lift gets here." The sergeant boomed, before leaving, closing the door behind him.

"How's Alison?" Kane asked, accepting the plastic cup of vended coffee from Brian

"I don't know, I was waiting for the ambulance when these guys turned up, cuffed me and brought me here. Did you catch up with Leidmeister?"

"No, he gave me the slip; I must have missed him by seconds."

The door of the sparsely furnished holding room swung open and a fresh faced young police constable entered followed by Major Henry Morgan.

"Right gentlemen, if you gather your belongings, I'll take you back to the Embassy." Henry Morgan's brash manner made it sound like he had found two schoolboys playing truant and was taking them back to school.

"How's Alison?" Kane asked, "Can we see her?"

"She's been taken to hospital and her condition was said to be serious but she's in the best place and will be well looked after. You have been released into my custody while they work out what they can do about the two bodies you left behind. The other lady had slight concussion and should be released tomorrow."

"So can we see Alison?"

"No, sorry, the terms of your release state that you have to remain at the Embassy and they can have access to you if and when needed. You two are still in serious trouble. It is only because our guys and the Americans think you can help with some on-going investigation that they have put pressure on the Pakistan Government to release you into my custody. But, technically, you are still under arrest."

Kane and Brian picked up the remainder of their belongings and followed the Major out to the gleaming, black Jaguar XJS parked outside. The Major got into the front passenger seat and Kane and Brian slid into the back. The 4.2 litre engine purred into life and eased out into the evening traffic towards the Embassy.

"You mentioned about the other lady, with concussion. What happened to her?" Kane asked, suddenly recalling the conversation.

"Don't know yet," The Major replied, "She was found unconscious in the room under yours."

"Bastard, he was there all the time," Kane turned his attention to Brian. "I should have known I would have seen or heard him on the stairs or corridor."

"But if you had stopped to clear the room and he had already legged it, then you would have lost precious seconds, minutes even," Brian responded, seeing the anger in Kane's face. "Don't beat yourself up over it, we'll get him."

"You boys will not be getting anyone," The Major interrupted. "If and when you two are released, officially, you are to be sent straight back home."

The conversation was interrupted by the ringing of the Major's phone. "Hello… yes… when was this? … Okay, thank you."

The Major ended the call and turned to face the two weary passengers. "Your colleague passed away ten minutes ago… I'm sorry."

Brian lowered his head to stare unconsciously into his lap, while Kane looked aimlessly out of the window into the darkening, cold night sky. Neither spoke for the remainder of the journey.

12

"Right Mr Hussein," Bill glared into Abdul's cold and frightened eyes. "I'm in no mood for any more of your lies. I have just lost a good operator and if you had been more honest with us then it might have prevented her from getting killed."

"But I have told you the truth." Abdul protested.

"Like your brother overhearing the conversation with Rashid and Leidmeister… like Peter Edwards setting up your meetings with Dr Aziri or Ashanti or whatever it is you call him. They were lies, so what else have you told us that is untrue?" Bill paused, waiting for a reaction but Abdul Hussein sat there, staring at the table in front of him.

"You have one last chance," Bill continued, "but if I think for one minute that you are telling me lies, or worse that you are holding back information from me, then I can assure you, the fear of these guys catching up to you will be the least of your worries. Now let's start at the beginning, when did you first meet Aziri or Ashanti whatever name you know him by?"

Abdul lifted his head but seeing Bill's stern stare lowered his eyes back to the table and mumbled, "Ashkani, Dr Ashkani."

"Go on." Bill coaxed after a few seconds of silence.

"I was present at the meeting with Peter Edwards and afterwards took Dr Ashkani back to reception. We started talking about his work and he made it sound like he had discovered a prevention formula for Hepatitis A but had somehow lost it and needed to re-develop the formula. It was then that he suggested I could maybe assist him after working hours and left me his telephone number, saying I would be well rewarded."

"Okay, carry on." Bill was keen to keep the conversation flowing without having to be forceful.

"I met him at his hotel and we discussed his theories, in fact, he admitted he had successfully cultivated the formula but had not been able to reproduce it since. He wanted to split the research in two. Whilst he worked on one part of the formula, someone else would work on the other part. He offered me money… and I took it."

"What does this formula do?"

"It was supposed to attack the Hepatitis A bug carried in water systems but…" Abdul's conversation trailed off.

"But…? Go on." Bill again coaxed.

"But the work I was given was to make it a carrier, a piggy back cell."

"Piggy back cell?" Bill looked sideways at Mark who was helping him to conduct the interview and wondering if he needed the aid of someone with some sort of chemistry knowledge. "What do you mean by piggy back cell?"

"It is something that is used to safely carry another cell in circumstances where it would not survive on its own, in this case water."

"Let me test my understanding of this. You were working on something which could be carried by Hepatitis A in water. Is that correct?"

"Yes."

"What was it?"

"I… don't know."

"Abdul," Bill lent forward in his chair, "let me remind you of something. If I find out you are withholding information, I will treat that more serious than telling lies. Now, what was it?"

"I don't know… all I know is that it was more powerful than Hepatitis A but in its natural state it is destroyed by water but, when linked with the Hepatitis virus, it takes on some of its characteristics and apart from making it immune, it grows at a tremendous rate, like bacteria, it splits and doubles every twenty minutes. If you start off with one, in twenty minutes you have two, forty minutes four, an hour you have eight and in four hours you have over four thousand. This keeps on doubling every twenty minutes, so in another hour you could have over thirty two thousand… and still doubling."

"So how do you stop it?"

"Normally it would need room temperature and moisture to grow, but this grows in most temperatures."

"Were you working on this in Edwards Chemicals?"

"Yes."

"So why hasn't Edwards Chemicals been overrun with these bugs?"

"The samples are frozen, they do not die, merely go into a type of hibernation until the temperature is increased."

"Is this harmful to humans, some sort of master bug?"

"I'm not sure." Abdul hesitantly replied.

"You are a chemist, you know what is harmful and what isn't, so don't tell me you're not sure, spit it out man."

"It… it affects the nervous system, shuts it down, like sleeping sickness. One minute you are wide awake, the next fast asleep."

"So it's not a killer as such?"

"Well, yes, having shut down the nervous system the rest of the vital organs will start to shut down."

"Do you know what Aziri, Ashkani, whatever his name was going to do with it?"

"No, but as the formula was being perfected I tried to pull out but he threatened to tell Mr Edwards, or worse. Then, at the end, he sent Rashid and Leidmeister to collect all the samples and everything I was working on. I was to go with them back to Pakistan, it was then I heard them say about killing that man, I thought it was going to be me."

"What about your wife, do you know where she is?"

"She is safe, in a house in Bromsgrove which I bought with the money from Dr Ashkani… sorry, Aziri."

"Anything else you think we should know?"

"No, that is all I know. Can I go now?"

"No, we will need to question you further, but I will need the address of the house in Bromsgrove so that we can confirm your story and make sure you are both kept safe until this is resolved."

Abdul gave a resigned sigh and went back to staring at the table.

Bill returned to his office and flopped down in the comfy swivel chair. The worn, leather upholstery signified it needed a change years ago, but Bill opted for comfort rather than looks and flatly refused any suggestions to change it. He had noticed, however, that George always made a bee line for the comfy seat. Perhaps he should move it behind his side of the desk.

He rubbed his tired face and eyes with the open palm of his right hand. He had been interviewing Abdul Hussein, on and off, since the early hours and it was now well into the evening. Bill slowly sifted through the scribbled notes he had taken from the pile on his desk, comparing key points from Abdul's interview with the transcripts of Aziri's telephone Rashid.

Tank… mixing quantities… America… Bill circled the words on the transcript, then circled water… sleeping sickness… on the notes from Abdul's interview. Picking up the phone transcript Bill read through it twice before dialling the direct line to Chas Wiltson.

"Chas, I think you have a problem." Which was the start of a thirty five minute conversation with his counterpart in Texas.

Almost an hour after Bill started the call with Chas, he then selected Kane's number. Five rings later a subdued voice answered the call "Yeah?"

"Did I wake you?"

"Jeez Bill, it's half past two in the morning, what's up?"

"Are you still at the Embassy?"

"Where else would I be? I had to give my word of honour not to leave."

"Well, break it. I need you and Brian to find this Dr Aziri and bring him in. Oh and sorry about Alison. She was a good operative."

"Yeah, what about Major Morgan?" Brian quickly moved on, not wanting to dwell on the subject of Alison's death.

"I'll handle him, but I need to speak to the Ambassador first, so get ready to go in about ten minutes."

"Any idea where we are going to?"

"I mean go to work, phones, files. You're the experts, it's what you do best, but this time it has to be your best and quickest. I've sent you over the transcripts of the interview with Hussein and you already have the one on Aziri's phone call. If our deductions are right, It looks like they are going to contaminate the water supply in Washington, but first they are going to do something to the zoo. They want to make some sort of statement or just prove that they are capable of doing what they say they will do."

"Ransom?"

"No, I think it is worse than that. They may ask for a ransom, but I think they are hell bent on going through with it."

"What sort of contamination is it?"

"Some sort of bug that grows quickly in water and I mean quickly. I worked it out and the rate this thing grows it could go from one to over two million in just seven hours."

"What, creepy crawly bugs?"

"No, viruses," Bill tried to work out if Kane was joking or being serious, but decided there was no time for jokes. "Listen, as I said earlier, it looks like they are going to try some of this stuff in the zoo the day after tomorrow, no wait a minute, it will be your tomorrow. Anyway, you have the transcripts you can work it out for yourself. This bug, virus, whatever they call it is probably already in the States. At the rate it grows, it has the possibility of killing millions, so I need you to find out when it left there and where it went, it was probably sometime in the last two weeks."

"Okay, I'll go wake up Brian." Kane yawned as he ended the call and swung his legs out to sit on the edge of the bed. How much of this chemical are we looking for? How is it packed? These were questions that started flowing through his mind as he gradually became more and more awake.

Fifteen minutes later Brian and Kane were sat at two of the hot desks, normally reserved for visiting journalists, in one of the administration offices. He read through the interview and phone transcripts and then looked at the list of recent calls from Aziri's business line. Taxi company, the recorded call, mobile number and a local call whose number looked familiar. Kane pulled a crumpled bit of paper from his pocket and compared it to the numbers scribbled down. Well, that was his sister, what about the mobile? He looked at the clock, nearly 3.00am. What the heck, he thought to himself as he keyed in the number.

The phone answered within a few rings "Hello?"

"Hi, is that Brian?"

"No you have the wrong number pal."

"What number is this?"

"It's the one you just dialled and it's not Brian." The call abruptly ended.

Kane pondered over the voice, it was definitely an American accent. He keyed in Bill's number on the grey, hot desk phone.

"Hi Bill, it's Kane. Did you run a check on the mobile number from Aziri's office?"

"Yes, it's a pay as you go so there's no registered information. Chas is running location checks using the phone's ISN signal."

"I take it the phone is in the States then?"

"Yes and it appears to be mirroring Dale Edwards' travelling pattern."

"Do you think him and his old man are involved?"

"So far, everything Peter Edwards has told us has rung true and I can't see how Dale Edwards would benefit if he was involved. Chas is rechecking his campaign staff and travelling journalists and if and when he narrows it down, he will probably get the number dialled and see who answers."

"I've just dialled it, don't worry, it was a wrong number call and brief. I'd put the guy in his late thirties, definitely American, but it was too brief to detect any regional accent."

"Okay, well, ease off that one for the time being, how are you getting on with tracking down the shipment to the States?"

"Well, it would help if we knew what sort of quantities we are looking for. Just as important, how is it packed?"

"This thing spreads like wildfire when the different parts of the formula are mixed together so I would have thought we are looking at a small quantity, probably several small quantities. Talking to our friend Abdul, two million of these little buggers would fit on a pin head."

"How safe is it? Is there an antidote?"

"It can be transported the same as vaccines, it is only when they are mixed and placed in water that it becomes lethal. As for an antidote, I don't think so, but maybe Mr Hussein could come up with something, seeing as he helped develop it. While you are on, I have spoken to the Ambassador and to the Police commissioner in Islamabad. He was not a happy chappie being woken up at quarter to three in the morning. Anyway, they are going to raid Aziri's offices and both his and his sister's houses. They have agreed to keep a low key on the Zoo part of it, if we draw a blank at Aziri's then we need to catch them in the act at the Zoo so that we know exactly what we are dealing with. I have got them to agree to let you and Brian take part in any stake out at the Zoo, should their early morning raids prove unfruitful, but we need them alive Kane. Now get it done son."

"Okay Bill, goodnight." Kane replaced the receiver, it was obvious that Bill knew of his desire for vengeance and was gently trying to get him back into line, but once they had the information they needed...

Kane's mobile phone vibrated loudly in silent mode as it gently bounced across the polished, laminated desk top.

"Hello." Kane answered as he snatched up the Nokia before it bounced off the desk.

"I forgot to tell you," Bill stated, "the police commissioner is concerned about the zoo. It has its own water supply but is topped up by the mains. If any of this stuff gets into the mains supply, well... As a result, he wants all the help he can get, so he has agreed to give you two free reign. The Ambassador has spoken to the Master at Arms so you can collect whatever weapons you need from him, but damage limitation Kane, damage limitation."

"We're up and running Brian." Kane commented eagerly as he ended the call.

"Where we going?"

"Anywhere but here, I hate being sat behind a desk twiddling my thumbs. How about we start with the warehouse?"

"The fire would have taken care of most of it and the locals would have made off with anything left standing. Are you looking for anything in particular?"

"Not really, but it's as good a place as any to start. We need to find the duty officer and sort out a pool car, collect some weapons and then find something to eat." Kane's adrenaline was pumping, at last he felt he was doing something and Leidmeister would not escape this time.

The headlights of the dark blue Toyota Avensis lit up the charred remains of the warehouse as they slowly drove into the yard, the tires crunching on the patchy chippings spread thinly over the dry cracked earth. They alighted from the car and switched on their black LED Lenser torches, courtesy of the duty officer and stand in Master at Arms, before heading into the remains of the blackened building, ducking under the obligatory Police do not cross tape. The stench of burnt, charcoaled wood filled their nostrils as they trod, carefully, through the rubble piled on the floor.

Brian picked up the charred remains of an invoice but it was written in Urdu. "We could have done with Alison on this." He commented, then pulled a grimaced face as he realised what he had said.

"We could do with Alison full stop," Kane replied, trying to push the thoughts of her from his mind. "That's where the office used to be." Kane's torch light shone on a large pile of rubble to one side of what was the warehouse building, three half-height, blackened walls and several piles of rubble were all that remained.

After forty five minutes of fruitless digging around they moved back out into the yard. "What about the lorry?" Brian asked, flashing his light at the cab, both doors left wide open. Closer examination revealed the radio and any other bit of electrical equipment had been cannibalised. All that remained were some discarded empty food cartons and the local rats would eventually move those too.

"What about his house?" Kane wanted something positive to work on and was searching for links. "There may be something there we can go on."

"Did he live on his own?"

"Don't know, but there's one way of finding out." Kane replied, striding back to the car.

The tired, green door creaked open with the aid of the tire lever from the Avensis. Kane eased himself inside into the barren hallway and Brian followed close on his heels, carefully closing the paint flaked door behind him.

Gently placing one foot on the old, wooden stairs, Kane waved Brian past him into the downstairs area while he carefully and quietly crept up the ageing staircase to the top landing. His eyes had adjusted to the lack of light, three rooms led off the bare wooden landing and each door had been left wide open. Kane passed the first small room, which he had already identified as the toilet from the stench of old urine that greeted him on the staircase. He peered into the second, larger bedroom, the acrid smell of stale sweat replacing that of the urine. Glancing to the third, smaller room he could see that it was full of what looked like boxes and general household bric a bracs. He slowly switched on the torch and shone it in the direction of the bed. Crumpled blankets were partly spread over a bare mattress and a brown stained pillow hung half way over the edge. A small, double wardrobe stood in the corner of the room, the door wide open to reveal an array of creased and faded clothing. Satisfied that no-one was in the upstairs part of the house, Kane retraced his steps down the stairs to join Brian.

"Find anything?" Brian asked in a loud whisper.

"Yeah, a mess. You?"

"There are papers everywhere, mostly bills by the look of it, but they are all in Urdu."

"Let's have a better look." Kane replied, finding the light switch and turning it on.

It took a few seconds for their eyes to adjust to the light. A large coffee and food stained Formica topped table sat in the middle of the room, with two white plastic, garden chairs, one placed either side. Various condiments had been herded to the centre of the table and a large, white plate with what looked like the remnants of a curry lay was lined up in front of one of the plastic chairs. A pile of odd bits of paper was precariously stacked on the far corner of the sticky, grime covered table. Brian continued to carefully sift through the pile while Kane walked back down the hall into the front room. Drawing the thin, blue faded curtains, he flicked on the light switch.

The worn, floral patterned two seated sofa was perched against the wall and an ageing Sony television sat on a rickety metal stand in the centre of the room. Around the rest of the room, old cardboard boxes, filled with clothes and household junk, were piled on top of one another. Kane lifted off the top box and gingerly poked through the contents.

An old, fading, address label showed Sayed Import & Export, Karachi Road. Kane guessed he had been taking the discarded boxes to hoard the rubbish he had obviously been collecting for a long time. On the fourth box Kane noticed the address was different. The typeface was identical but the address read Siddique Transport, Rawal Road. Kane unclipped the biro from his shirt pocket and pulling out the crumpled piece of paper from his trouser pocket, scribbled down the address before carrying on with his prodding and poking, not really wanting to delve his hands into the boxes. Losing patience he decided to up end the boxes onto the two seated sofa. He was just emptying the last box, the contents of which were spilling onto the threadbare rug, when Brian walked in.

"I'm done in there." Brian stated. "Apart from bills and rubbish there's nothing worth clocking, how about you?"

"Have you got your map on you?"

"Never go anywhere without it." Brian smiled, reaching into his back pocket to pull out the creased and well-thumbed street map.

"See if you can find Rawal Road and how far away it is." Kane asked, using his foot to spread the contents of the final box across the floor.

"I've found it, it's not far but it's a long road, got a number?"

"No, but I've got a name. C'mon, let's get going; switch the lights off behind you eh."

Barely fifteen minutes later they were cruising down the length of Rawal Road searching for Siddique Transport, but to no avail.

"Right, let's try again. They obviously don't like advertising so… if it's a transport company they need a yard for the lorries to get in and out of, keep your eyes peeled, the sun's starting to rise so the daylight will make it easier."

"What's that place there?" Brian pointed to a building with a large, open space in the front. Kane slowed and parked outside.

"No, it's a house."

"Could be working from home." Brian suggested.

"I don't think so, he had several boxes with this address on them and so they must need some sort of warehouse."

Kane drove off but kept his speed as low as possible but the traffic was already starting to build up. They passed several more houses, then a lane and a large double fronted house. Kane suddenly pulled to a halt at the side of the road. Checking his mirror, Kane reversed the car back along the road and stopped in front of the lane. "What's that up there?"

"It's some sort of building and there's a light on." The blackness of night had already given way to the greyness of dawn, the rising sun imminent. "We can't drive up there without being seen and there's not much cover."

"Well, in that case," Kane responded, putting the car into first and accelerating across the road onto a small open patch of land, "We had better park up and leg it up the lane before it gets any lighter."

The double beep and flash of the indicator lights confirmed the fob had locked the blue Avensis as they both jogged across the road into the mouth of the lane. Stopping at the start of the hedge lined entrance for a quick check of their Glock hand guns they returned them to their leather shoulder holsters secluded beneath their thin, Embassy issued, grey windcheaters. Taking a side each, they made their way quickly up the old tarmac lane, crouching low and skimming past the thorny, leaf free hedgerow on either side.

"Wait!" Kane whispered, as a white Kaftanned figure opened the main door of the large, aluminium clad, building at the top of the lane and walked towards a black, dust covered Mitsubushi Shogun. Opening the driver's door he lent in and retrieved a small packet of what looked like cigarettes, but it was too far off to tell. Closing the door he turned and headed back into the building.

"I think that's my friend from the other warehouse, the one that re-arranged the cafe I was sat in." Brian scanned the outside of the green, cladded building as he spoke. "Do you think they have CCTV?"

"Can't see any, but keep your eyes peeled, just in case." Kane inched forward a few feet then paused and repeated the process until they were in front of the large, steel framed, wire mesh gates.

"How's your lock picking skills?" Brian asked, noticing the heavy chain and padlock that secured the gates together.

"No time for that." Kane replied, satisfied that there were no visible cameras or obvious prying eyes. He ran forward and quickly but quietly, climbed up and over the old mesh gates with Brian close behind. They hit the dusty ground with a soft thud and ran stealthily over the rough earth to the cover of the black Shogun.

"How many can you see?" Brian asked, straining to see through the front office window. The light was on but the rising sun was starting to display the yard and building in all its' glory. "I make it two."

"Are you sure that guy was the one from the warehouse?" Kane whispered, taking the safety off his Glock and flexing his grip on the handle.

"When someone is staring at you with a Kalashnikov in their hands and all you have in yours is a cup of cold coffee, you tend to remember what they looked like. It certainly looked like him, but I'd need a closer look to be sure."

"Okay, you cover me, I'm going to have a quick look around." Kane crouched low and ran over to the edge of the window. He carefully peered through the red dust, covered glass into the large, well lit room before ducking down, under the window and crawling to the other side, where he repeated the process. Laying back against the cold, aluminium cladding he faced Brian and held up three fingers, then he crept silently, past the front door and around to the side of the building before disappearing out of sight.

Three minutes later, Kane reappeared at the same side of the building and beckoned Brian to join him. Easing himself around the black Shogun, Brian crouched low and darted across the yard, keeping his attention on the window and door.

"What's up?" He breathed, noticing the look of concern in Kane's tired face.

"No windows apart from the front office, can't see anything inside the main building. So do we take them and have a good look around or do we wait and watch, see who comes and goes? You'd better have a quick squint through the window and confirm they are the guys from the warehouse before we decide what we are going to do."

Brian crawled silently, on his hands and knees, across the front of the building and he had just passed the main steel door when it eased open. A large framed guard in a white Kaftan emerged into the dawning light, almost stepping on the soles of Brian's shoes. The guard shouted out as he unslung the Kalashnikov from his shoulder, Brian rolled onto his back and frantically reached under his jacket for the Glock just as the guard's finger slipped onto the trigger.

Brian heard the loud thud as the butt of Kane's hand gun crashed into the guard's head just above the temple. "Decision made." He stated, as the guard crashed to the floor. Kane stepped over the body and into the office firing two shots at one of the guards whose automatic was being levelled in his direction. A hail of bullets, from the third guard, peppered the doorframe above him as he ducked back out into the yard. A muffled crack, the sound of breaking glass followed by the loud thud of the third guard hitting the floor, caused Kane to spin around as Brian, hand gun still aimed through the shattered window, prepared to fire a second shot if needed.

"I don't think he's dead, but I'll keep him covered from here if you'd like to check." Brian suggested, the two handed grip on the gun held out in front of him relaxing slightly.

Kane peered inside then quickly jumped over the body of the second guard, kicking away both fallen weapons as he bent down to feel for a pulse on the third guard.

"Nope, he's dead," Kane announced, feeling no pulse in his neck or wrist before moving back to the second guard and repeating the test. "So is this one."

"That makes three then," Brian added, raising himself up from the body of the third guard. "Better sweep the rest of the building, but I think if there were someone else here we would have known it by now."

Cautiously opening the rear door of the office they slipped into a narrow hallway where two open doors displayed vacant, but very smelly, toilets. They proceeded down the hallway through the third door and into the dark, cool warehouse. Kane searched the nearby walls and eventually found the light switches, flicking them on as quickly as possible while Brian stayed alert, watching for any signs of movement, but none came.

Ten minutes later, satisfied the building was clear, they re-entered the front office. The early morning sun started to track across the yard and highlight the front of the building, including the body outside, Kane walked over to the window and looked outside. Several faces, alerted by the sound of the gunfire, were peering out of the windows of nearby houses and Kane could see two or three people jostling back and fore across the mouth of the lane but not daring to enter.

"Better call this in and get this place secured before the local police get here." Kane thought out aloud dialling Bill's number. Brian nodded and stood by the side of the window, staring down the lane while Kane finished off his telephone call.

"Well, there must be something here otherwise they would not have left three people to guard it. Bill's going to get a team over here to secure the building and arrange for some technical guys to sift through the warehouse."

"Well, they had better be quick," Brian answered, "We've got company."

Kane ran over to the window just as two police cars, lights flashing and sirens blazing screeched to a halt outside the chained gates. A third police car pulled across the entrance to the lane as one of the agitated police men retrieved something from the trunk of the first car and proceeded to cut through the chains securing the gates. The gates flung open and the police car cruised slowly through the open gates into the barren yard, closely followed by the several police officers who had alighted from their vehicles and were now using the car as a mobile shield. The second police car followed at a slightly safer distance.

"Looks like we had better give ourselves up before they get too nervous," Kane remarked moving towards the door. "We're coming out." He shouted as he was opening the door and walking out, hands above his head, with Brian following suit.

"On the floor." Barked a familiar sounding voice. Kane and Brian lay prone on the rough, dusty, floor, arms still outstretched.

Whilst two of the officers roughly handcuffed first Kane then Brian, the stocky Police sergeant bent down and moving closer to Kane, turned him over onto his back and proceeded a body search, finding and removing the holstered Glock with his first touch. "Why are you here? You were released into the custody of your Embassy."

"Your government asked us to help out." Kane answered, shifting onto his side to relieve the discomfort of lying on his arms.

“Put them in the car.” He growled, as he rose to his feet and strode across the yard into the devastation of the office.

“How come we’re always the ones being arrested?” Brian moaned as he was pushed, unceremoniously, into the back of the first police car. Kane went to follow him but was quickly ushered towards the second car and deposited onto the rear seat. Kane stared back through the open office door, wondering if what they were looking for would be found inside.

Ten minutes later the sergeant appeared and bent down to have a closer look at the corpse outside. He glanced over to the two police cars and then back to the corpse before rising to his feet and with his eyes firmly fixed on Kane, who was still sat in the rear of the second car, strode purposefully over, his eyes never wavering from the object of his glare.

A large black sedan skidded through the gates and past the police car before screeching to a halt in front of the sergeant.

“Are you in charge?” The passenger shouted, as he clambered out of the car, flashing a shiny I.D. badge.

Kane watched intently as the sergeant’s face got redder and redder. Every now and then he would stretch his arm out to indicate the damaged office and the crumpled corpse outside. The driver had now joined the arguing pair as a black transit van slid into the yard and four men and a woman climbed out and headed for the building. The sergeant threw his arms in the air and stormed back to the first police car as two of the men from the Transit stretched out the crumpled corpse then lifted him, one either end, to carry him back to the waiting van.

As Brian was ushered out of the first car, the sergeant climbed into the front passenger seat and as soon as the rear door closed, the engine started up and the now revving police car turned a half circle in the tight confines of the small yard and out through the gates,

Kane caught the sergeant’s glowering stare as they drove past, before it was his turn to be ushered out of the car and have the handcuffs removed.

“Our weapons?” Kane asked the police officer removing his handcuffs. He looked nervously around, the sergeant had gone and the other police officers were all leaving. “They’re in your trunk, man, I saw them being put there.”

The officer walked around to the trunk, opened it and took out the two hand guns. Pausing for a couple of seconds, he turned and walked back to hand both weapons to Kane. Brian came over and taking the offered gun from Kane, replaced it in the brown, leather shoulder holster.

“What now?” Brian asked, looking over to the crew who had just arrived.

“We say our goodbyes and leave them to it. I could do with a couple of hour’s kip while they see what they can find.”

“Me too, are we going back to the Embassy or a hotel?”

“I think it had better be the Embassy, don’t want to push our luck too far.” Kane replied, as they walked over to the black sedan.

13

Peter Edwards sat back in his large, comfortable, black leather executive chair. He had been asked to allow Abdul Hussein to work, under supervision, in his extensive laboratories and had further agreed to supply all the labour and resources to try and develop an antidote for the unknown 'killer bug' about to be unleashed in Washington. Abdul had mixed the formula he had helped to develop with the Hepatitis A strain but could not produce the same devastating effect, there was something missing. Even if this missing ingredient were to be found, forty eight hours would not be long enough to develop an antidote, but Peter knew that Washington could be just the start.

Peter picked up the phone and selected a number from the short dial list. "Dale, is that you?" The background noise was making it difficult to hear the response. "Where are you?"

"I'm in Los Angeles, we're in the middle of a campaign party, I thought you were coming back out?"

"No, something cropped up, which is why I'm calling. I want you and the family to come over here for a bit, like an extended vacation."

"What, now? Dad this is my opportunity to pick up some of the floating votes. The campaign may have been suspended until they can find another candidate to oppose me, but I have to be here to keep the momentum going. I'm off to Washington tomorrow and New York next week. Depending on who they put up against me, I should be able to take a few days off after that."

"Washington! I don't…"

"I know dad, the FBI have kept me fully up to date with what's going on. They haven't gone public for obvious reasons, can you imagine the chaos of a mass exodus from the Capital? If it makes you any happier I promise just to drink bottled water."

"It's not just drinking Dale, it's food preparation, washing, even brushing your teeth. If this virus does get into the water system… well, you know the rest."

"That's exactly why I have to go to Washington dad. There's a good chance this will leak out and we need to show them that we are confident we can prevent this from happening. Yes, me being in the thick of it will hold me in good stead when it all blows over, but it's not just about the voters' perception of me. I have some excellent, experienced people supporting my campaign. Jimmy Lawson, my campaign manager is a qualified engineer, my personal assistant, David Butane is a qualified Chemist and we have been actively working with the water companies and City Hall studying all the plans of the main water supplies and trying to work out the best way of continuous testing and segregation so that should they be successful in getting it into the mains supply we can quickly isolate and destroy it."

"How are you going to do that? You sound confident."

"I am, otherwise I would not be going to Washington, I'm not that stupid dad. We know that boiling water will kill it from the notes you sent over from that Hussein fella and freezing it is an option, though both are not very practical in the short period of time we have, but we are looking at other options. I have the plans of the entire Washington water system and we are working to segregate the mains supply into as many secondary units as possible. With constant monitoring, if the virus is detected we just isolate that section."

"How many people would one section affect?" Peter asked, trying to work out how many sections they may logically be able to construct in the next forty eight hours.

"Alright dad, it will still be probably in excess of a few thousand, but it is better than the potentially hundreds of thousands, if not more, at the moment. You are forgetting the heightened security as well. The whole system has been locked down tight, only specially cleared personnel are allowed anywhere near the water supply."

"Dale, you mentioned that you were working on other options, anything we can help you with?"

"You can help by coming up with an antidote. That will be more effective than anything else, but in the meantime, one of the options we are looking at is placing a dual lighting system into every segment we can construct. At present, the water system is controlled by a series of valves which are primarily there to turn off the water in any particular area if there has been a burst or large leak, but these would be too slow in the event of contamination taking place. We are looking to insert slider seals that can be dropped instantly as soon as the virus is detected, isolating not only that area but also the adjoining segments. The dual lighting system will hopefully do the rest. The first is infrared, which apparently will speed up the growth rate and the second is Ultra Violet which, according to David, should instantly kill off the now larger cells."

"Well, give me a call if you need any help, but take care of yourself son, if this stuff does get into the system it will cost lives and I don't want yours being one of them."

"I will dad, stop worrying, catch up with you and mom soon." Dale finished saying his goodbyes and ended the call. He smiled as he looked down at the now silent cell phone. That was the first time his father had openly stated any form of affection for him.

"Kane, it's Bill, what kept you?" Kane rubbed his eyes and tried to drag his mind back to reality.

"I was asleep, you wouldn't let me get any last night, remember?"

"Well, wake up, they found the stuff at that warehouse you visited this morning. There were three briefcases, each containing two carefully strapped, small, sealed, chemical bottles, together with a larger empty one, along with instructions on how to mix them and where to put the resulting mixture. They were going to do it that day. Those guys at the warehouse would have just walked into the Zoo, found somewhere quiet to mix the solution and then deposited it in the designated places. Anyone who visited the Zoo the following day would have been affected and as for the animals, well… Anyway you and Brian are booked on a flight to Washington in two hours' time so you better get your arses in gear. You have special clearance to deliver one of these briefcases to the guys over there. Chas is making arrangements for you to be met at the airport and will then have the briefcase and you guys, whisked away to some local laboratory for analysis. One of the briefcases is already on its way to London for Peter Edwards and his crew to look at."

"And the third?" Kane inquired.

"The Pakistani authorities are evaluating that one, so hopefully, between the three of us we can come up with something. But there's more, last week a sealed medical shipment was sent to Washington and collected by a private medical company. Initial checks cannot find them registered on any records, so we have to accept that the virus is already in the States. Now get going and call me when you get there."

Kane noted the time on the small travel clock by the side of his bed. Ten past three in the afternoon, he had been asleep for about four hours but it only felt like four minutes. He ruffled his short cropped hair, phoned Brian to give him the glad news, had a quick shower, dressed and having bundled his meagre belongings into his blue, travelling bag and jogged downstairs to meet up with Brian at the front desk. Brian was already sat in the back of the black Jaguar XJS purring away outside the Embassy entrance and he smiled as he watched Kane being escorted down the steps by two burly marines.

"Anybody would think they can't wait to get rid of us." Brian laughed as Kane clambered into the back.

"What about the briefcase? Who's got it?"

"We're meeting someone at the airport." Brian replied, trying to rub the sleep from his eyes. "Apparently, they have our tickets and a parcel for us, so I assume the briefcase is the parcel."

Kane eased back in the soft, leather seat as the Jaguar coasted out into the afternoon traffic en route to Islamabad International airport, not relishing the prospect of yet another long haul flight ahead of him.

On arrival at the airport Kane and Brian were greeted by two government agents and a senior customs officer. A cheap, vinyl covered, black briefcase was produced and promptly handcuffed to Kane's wrist. They were each given a key to the handcuffs, together with a sealed plastic pouch containing documents and a key to the briefcase itself, but were also informed that at no time should the briefcase be opened. Knowing what was inside, Kane and Brian had no intention of looking at it anyway.

Their afternoon nap had satisfied their need for sleep and as a result, the fifteen hour flight proved to be long and boring, despite the updated in-flight entertainment. They took it in turns to look after the briefcase and relieve the constant restrictions of their additional piece of hand luggage, which two stewards had already asked if they could put it away in the overhead lockers before realising it was 'attached'.

Rashid looked up into the clear, blue, Islamabad sky. The white, vapour trails of a plane started to thin and fade and for a moment he let himself wonder where it was heading, Europe? America? He pressed the button to raise the driver's window of the metallic blue Mercedes E270 cdi automatic as he turned off Rawal Road into the hedge lined lane.

"Someone coming up the lane." Shouted the first member of the Pakistani anti-terrorist squad to his three companions, sat around a desk, playing cards.

"How many?" One of them asked, drawing his weapon from beneath his coat.

"Just the one I think," He replied, keying the button on his hand held Motorola two way radio. "Unit one to unit two… we have a visitor."

"We got him unit one… moving into position." The static reply.

Rashid stopped the car at the chain link gates and waited for a few moments before switching off the engine and removing the bunch of keys from the ignition. Climbing out of the driver's seat he ambled over to the gates, selecting a key as he went and wondering why no-one had rushed out to open it for him… as they normally would have. He slowed as he approached the thick, chain linked gates and noticed that the heavy, padlocked chain was no longer in place. He reached instinctively for his mobile phone, then stopped, remembering the battery had gone dead earlier that afternoon and he had not had the chance to recharge it. He pushed open the first gate on the right until it lined up with the entrance door giving him ample opportunity to peer in through the distant window but there was no sign of life. He went back to the second gate and started to push it open but was only half way when he noticed the clean cut, link lying on the dusty floor. He stopped and walked calmly back to his car.

"I think he's rumbled us." The lookout whispered out aloud, straining his neck for a better view out of the window.

Rashid got back into the car and started the engine. He had just caught a glimpse of the unknown face in the bottom right, corner of the office window, confirming his rising fears. Rashid slammed the now revving motor into reverse as two suited figures burst out of the reception door, guns aimed and shouting "STOP" in both Urdu and English.

The Mercedes hastily reversed back down the lane as Rashid stretched his head over his shoulder to look out of the narrow, black tinted, rear window. A black Honda Accord skidded to a halt at the mouth of the lane's entrance, blocking his escape. Rashid pressed the accelerator hard to the floor and waited for the impact. The crunch of metal on metal was quickly followed by the thud of Rashid's head hitting the inside roof of the E270, as the sudden impact lifted him out of the seat. He pressed his foot hard on the accelerator but the car barely moved. The trunk had burst open with the force of the impact and he could not see what was happening behind him. He had to escape, his route to the road was blocked, perhaps he could drive up the lane and through the back gardens of one of the nearby houses, but his options were running out. As he paused to look out of the windscreen he could see three armed men slowly making their way down the lane. He was left with no choice, slamming the car into drive he accelerated up the lane, trying to keep his head as low as he could. The first officer opened fire and several shots smashed through the windscreen, the last also entered Rashid's forehead, just above his left eye. The Mercedes swerved into the hedge, the driver's limp and lifeless body slumped back into the cream, now red speckled seat as the first agent slowly crept up to the car. With the gun still aimed at Rashid's bloodied head, he opened the door, turned off the engine and felt for a pulse… it was very weak, barely detectable.

The Dreamliner landed with a gentle bump followed by the rushing sound of reverse engines as it rapidly slowed and began the short taxi to the designated terminal. Kane and Brian exited the plane and walked through the busy baggage area, their small holdalls accompanied them onto the plane, being classed as hand luggage so, having no need to wait for any additional luggage, they made their way straight through to customs. On production of their passports, they were directed over to two smartly dressed, rather young looking men who proudly flashed their CIA badges and introduced themselves as the agents sent to escort them downtown. Kane wondered whether agents were getting younger, or he was getting older, but opted for the first observation.

A short drive later, through the bustling, Washington traffic, Kane and Brian found themselves being escorted through a very active security block into some old, tired offices beyond. Kane was introduced to Dr Martin, a small diminutive man in his late forties, the white, grey hair almost matching his well washed, but faded lab coat. A pair of reading glasses perched on top of his nose as he carefully scanned through the documents from the plastic pouch.

Kane undid the handcuffs from his wrist and placed the briefcase in the centre of the table, then gently rubbed his wrist while he patiently waited for the doctor to finish his reading.

"Thank you gentlemen," He eventually uttered. "I'll take care of this now." Leaning forward and slowly picking up the briefcase to lay it gently on top of what could only be described as a tall hospital instrument trolley. The doctor moved to the other end of the trolley and slowly pushed it towards the door which was immediately opened by one of the fresh faced agents. Kane watched the trolley being carefully manoeuvred out through the door into the hallway, thinking perhaps he should have been a bit more careful with it.

"Okay guys," One of the young agents croaked before clearing his throat and carrying on. "We're going to take you to your hotel so you can get some rest, you've a meeting with the Firewall team tomorrow so it's an early start."

"Firewall?" Kane spoke his thoughts out aloud. "What's that when it's at home?"

They briefly looked at one another before the second agent broke the silence.

"It's a team set up to prevent whatever it is that may be happening. Some section leader in Texas thought you might be useful, so you're in."

Kane allowed himself a half smile as he realised these agents were merely gophers for the time being, go for this, go for that, may even have been their first official assignment. "Okay guys," Kane continued, rising from his chair, "We're with you, lead the way."

The Regency Hotel was not as opulent as the Islamabad Marriott, but far better than the basic guest rooms of the British Embassy. Kane stretched out on the bed, allowing his tired, stiff muscles to relax. His body needed to get back into some sort of normal routine, but then, this was becoming normal for him. His eyelids started to close and sleep finally took over.

"Kane, where are you?" Bill's opening greeting as he answered the call on his cell phone.

"I'm just about to go into a meeting that you guys apparently got us involved in, why?"

"If that's the Firewall meeting I didn't think it was due to start for another hour?"

"So I gather, but our chaperones were keen to get us here on time."

"Listen, that cell phone number on Aziri's phone list, the ESN was transmitting albeit briefly from the same location as yours. What's more disconcerting is that it appears to be wherever Dale Edwards is."

"So do you really think he's involved?"

"No... well, I don't know is the short answer. He could have another phone, but his sheet's clean."

"Have you tried dialling it?"

"No, the ESN comes and goes, so whoever it is, only has it on for short periods of time. That's one of the reasons we've wangled you onto the Firewall Team. The phone is tapped now but I think he knows we are onto him because he is not using it for voice calls only text messages and they are brief and very general. Edwards proposed this Firewall Team and some of his guys are heading it up, along with a couple of guys from the water company and City Hall. They want to split the water system into different groups or something"

"But during the meeting, won't they have a 'switch off mobile phones' policy?"

"Probably, but then the meeting is going to be delayed; they'll be told they can put their phones on and make personal calls, etcetera, so in about an hour's time, as soon as that ESN starts transmitting, we'll be dialling the number. You and Brian need to stick close to Edwards' group, if the phone's on, it might be on silent mode, so I hope your ears are good enough to pick up on vibration, mine certainly wouldn't!"

"Okay, I'll tell Brian. What if it is Edwards or one of his group, what do you want us to do?"

"Nothing, just tell me whose phone rang, our friends in the FBI have everything set up ready to go. There's just one other thing Kane. The text messages were to and from two unregistered cell phones in Pakistan, but they are no longer in Pakistan, they're ESN signal puts them in Washington"

No sooner had Bill ended the call than his phone rang. It was George Daniels.

"Bill, we did some digging and guess what?"

"You broke your spade...!"

"Funny, our Mr Edwards is not as squeaky clean as we thought."

"Which one? Dale or Peter?"

"Peter Edwards, apparently he had an affair some time ago and ended up with an illegitimate son."

"Well, it must have been a while ago, the guy must be in his seventies."

"It was thirty five years ago to be precise. He became friendly with an employee of a company he was considering buying but the price was too high or something. They had a collaborative agreement for a couple of years, during which time he started this affair and his son was born. The records show Peter Edwards was sending regular amounts of money out to her, including what looks like being a hefty final payment some twelve years ago."

"Where's the woman now?"

"Dead, she and her other son were killed in Afghanistan where she was living, along with her daughter-in-law and grand-daughter, oh and a friend of the daughter-in-law also died."

"What about the son, was he killed?"

"No, he and his college friend were pulled from the wreckage, but both their wives perished in the incident. Edwards' son had a very close bond with his family and apparently was very distraught that he did not die with them."

"What was the incident?"

"A Cruise missile which was targeted at some safe house nearby, aren't you going to ask me the name of the son?"

"I take it I'm supposed to know him?"

"Try Ali… Ali Aziri."

"You're joking, so Edwards is mixed up in this after all?"

"That's what we're going to find out, we're on our way there now."

It had been ten minutes since George's call and Bill was still sat twiddling his pencil, staring out of the tinted, glass window and trying to find a reason why Peter Edwards, a successful, well respected businessman with apparently close family ties, would want to wreak untold havoc on thousands, if not millions, of innocent people. If Peter Edwards was involved then Dale Edwards might be their prime target after all.

The attendees were informed that the meeting was going to be delayed for about half an hour while they sorted out a technical problem with the overhead projector but they could feel free to use their phones or any other amenities until it was resolved. Dale Edwards wanted to carry on without it but the security advisor held firm, insisting it was necessary to clarify what they were trying to achieve.

Kane glanced at his watch. Both he and Kane had managed to get in amongst Edwards and his staff and were now straining their ears to pick up the faintest ring which should be imminent.

The faint hum and buzz of a vibrating phone drew Kane's attention to the other side of the table. Brian raised his eyebrows, picked up his phone from the highly polished walnut table and switched it off, noticing Kane's slow shake of the head as he did so. For the next five minutes the pair studied the faces around them, but there were no ring tones, no audible vibrations and no indication that any of them were the suspect.

Twenty minutes later the meeting started, chaired by a senior member of the security staff who spent over half an hour of his introduction stating how tight security was around the entire Washington Water system. Kane settled back to what looked like being a long meeting. Dale Edwards was one of the first to speak and Kane was impressed with his 'take charge' attitude but at the same time, he realised the amount of information he had relating to the entire Washington water network system. This, together with the access granted him in his current position, would make it relatively easy for him to gain entry into any of the key installations. Sure, he would still have to get the chemicals past security, but then, if they were shipped out last week, they could already be inside one of the many key areas now locked down tight.

Brian was sat on the opposite side of the table to Kane, trying to work out who was who. He had met most of the participants in the preamble prior to the meeting starting but there had been no customary introductions and as far as he could work out, there were only three people in Dale Edwards' immediate group, one of which was Edwards himself and another was a young lady, obviously taking the minutes. Eventually Dale Edwards introduced the other male member of his team as his Campaign manager, a very experience engineer who was working 'hand in glove' with the Water companies to minimise the spread of any virus. He also mentioned his personal assistant who was a qualified chemist and who was working closely with chemists and technicians to try and nullify the virus, but made no reference to anyone sat around the table.

George and Neil arrived at Edwards Chemicals and briefly flashed their badges at a startled receptionist before marching down the corridor to the room where they last interviewed Peter Edwards. They courteously knocked on the door before opening it and entered into the well-furnished office.

Peter Edwards looked up, somewhat surprised to see them. "Mr Daniels, was there something you forgot to ask?" Edwards' sharp business brain and years studying the body language of his competitors could see from their demeanour that they needed answers.

"Not so much ask, Mr Edwards," George replied. "More like a confirmation."

"Fire away, I'm willing to help in any way I can." Peter Edwards stood up and offered them the two chairs on the opposite side of the desk.

"Prior to the meeting you had with Dr Ashkani, which you informed us about, have you ever met with him before?"

"No that was the first time, why?"

"What about Dr Aziri? Does the name Ali Aziri have any meaning for you?"

Peter Edwards slowly sat down into the black leather, executive chair. "It's him isn't it?"

"Whom do you mean by him?" George quizzed.

"My... son?"

"Tell me about your son, where was he born?"

"Afghanistan, I... I met his mother and he was born about two years later."

"Have you been in contact since?"

"No, my business involvement in that area came to an end and I had a family here and I suppose I could come up with loads of excuses... but I made sure they were looked after financially."

"Who would they be Mr Edwards?"

"His mother, Sinitta and her other two children."

"Do you know where your son is now?"

"No, I didn't even know he was my son. There was something about Ashkani that made me meet with him, but his attitude was as if I... owed him something, that I should be helping him, working together, in fact he actually commented that we would all be together one day, but as soon as I found out he wanted to use a strain of Hepatitis in his research, well... it just would not have been feasible."

"So when did you know he was your son?"

"His mother's maiden name was Aziri and although our relationship ended before the boy was born, I still kept in contact by phone. She told me that she had called him Ali and yes, for a moment when I heard that Ashkani was really Ali Aziri, I did think he could be my son, but only for a moment."

"Are you still in contact with his mother?"

"No, as I said, I used to speak to her by phone several times a year. She accepted that I had a family over here and that the boy we had together would always give her fond memories of our relationship. If I had not already been married… well, she really was a treasure." Peter Edwards' eyes moistened and his face saddened as he continued his story. "She was killed in Afghanistan, along with her elder son and other members of her family. Her cousin wrote to me and told me about it."

"I believe Ali Aziri was visiting at the time?"

"If you already know all this, why are you asking me?" The guilt of the years was starting to catch up with Peter and he could feel the anger building up inside.

"Who survived with him? There were two people pulled from the wreckage."

"I think he was one of his university friends, an American I believe, but it was some time ago, I cannot recall much else."

"Do you know his name?"

"No, I only remember her cousin's letter saying something about his new wife being killed and inferring how poignant it was that Americans were responsible."

"Can you tell us what University your son attended and the years?"

"It was the University of Punjab in Lahore, but I need to check on the years."

"A rough guess would do for now Mr Edwards."

"It would be around the year two thousand, maybe two thousand and one, somewhere around there."

"Okay, Mr Edwards, just a few more questions." George carried on asking probing, sometimes intimate, questions to determine the depth of Peter Edwards' involvement whilst Neil Bishop walked to the corner of the room and passed the information already uncovered onto the central desks of both MI5 and MI6 as agreed.

The Firewall meeting lasted for just over two hours and as they funnelled out of the large, well furnished, meeting room, Brian tugged on Kane's arm.

"Edwards' personal assistant, Dave Butane, he's not here."

"I guessed as much. I've been trying to work out who's who too! Might as well find out straight from the horse's mouth… Mr Edwards." Kane shouted to the figure three metres in front of him.

Dale Edwards turned to face the direction of the call. "Ah, Mr Rhodes isn't it. I understand that you have been responsible for uncovering most of what we have learnt so far. Well done."

"Thanks, but I think it is what you guys come up with from here on in that will count. Saying that, I haven't seen your chemist guy, David Butane, is he here?"

"No, when the meeting was delayed he had to leave and visit some of the sites we have been working on. There's quite a bit of work to be done in the next twenty four hours."

"What are your plans during that time?"

"You said that with an air of a British bobby, is there something I should know?" Dale Edwards was a shrewd lawyer and could sense from the tone and the line of questioning that something was not right.

Kane's response was halted by the ringing of his cell phone. "Excuse me a minute, Mr Edwards."

Kane quickly finished the call and realised that the time scale and urgency of this case was making him rush things far quicker than normal, but he had no choice, time was of the essence.

"Did you ever go to University in Pakistan?" Kane asked.

"No, I went to Princeton in New Jersey, why?"

"Did any of your immediate staff go to University in Pakistan?"

"I don't know, I would have to dig out their personnel files to find that out, but why do you want to know? I am afraid I have to insist on an explanation before I answer any more of your questions."

Kane glanced briefly at Brian before continuing. "Someone close to your campaign may be involved in this threat. We have an unregistered mobile phone number which is linked to a known terrorist. The problem is that the Electronic Serial Number emitted by the phone when it is switched on, always emulates from the vicinity you happen to be in at the time. So, simple deduction means it is either you or one of your close travelling companions."

"And you think it could be me?"

"No, my gut instinct tells me otherwise, though we will be stuck to you like leeches for the next twenty four hours."

Dale stared into Kane's clear, blue but unwavering eyes. "So assuming it's not me… you think it's David?"

"That's what we are here to find out. How long have you known him and your campaign manager?"

"I've known both of them since I started my campaign, fourteen months ago. They applied for the advertised positions and have done very well since they came on board… although David was the second choice. The first candidate had more experience but then, having been offered the job, phoned up to decline the position, so it went to David, who has, by the way, proved to be equally capable. We need to sort this out… bear with me a minute… Harry," Dale Edwards called over to the Security chief. "Is there a room we can use for about fifteen minutes?"

"Well… you can use the room we were just in if you like. There's nothing booked until this afternoon. Do you need anything else?"

"No that's fine thanks Harry. After you, gentlemen."

George Daniels sat across from Peter Edwards, studying his now silent, resigned features. "Is there anything else you think we should know Mr Edwards?"

"No, but I would like to tell my son Dale personally. He has no idea about my affair… and it should come from me. In fact, I was going to phone him about something else. They are going to use infrared and Ultra Violet rays to try and combat this virus, but when I mentioned it to Abdul he was adamant that from the research he has already done on this, the infrared will make the virus harder to control. As it is, in its' normal state, you would need a slow throughput and very large lamp for Ultra Violet rays to have any effect, but if it was multiplied… well…"

"And who came up with the idea to use these rays?"

"Dale… well, his staff anyway, but I just need to check that this has been thought through properly. If this does happen, he's right in the thick of it."

"Okay, give him a ring, but I would appreciate it if you did not say anything relating to your other son at this moment in time."

Peter Edwards nodded once then picked up the phone and dialled Dale's number.

The meeting room seemed considerably larger with just the three of them in it. As Kane sat down next to Dale Edwards, he turned to face him and asked, "David Butane, where did you say he went?"

"It was something to do with the water plant, but he didn't say where."

"Didn't you find it strange that, knowing he had this important meeting, he would arrange another one so close, time wise?"

"Well time is not on our side so we do have to squeeze in…" Dale's cell phone rang, stopping him in mid-sentence. "Excuse me gentlemen."

Dale answered the call and it was obvious from the responses that it was his father on the other end of the line. His face became pensive and he looked up to catch Kane's inquisitive stare. Ending the call, he looked Kane squarely in the eyes. "I've just remembered, on David's C.V. it showed that he got his Chemistry degree in Lahore. I remember thinking it was a place I had never been to but would like to visit one day. My father phoned to tell me that one of his researchers did not think that what we have planned to do would be effective, in fact the opposite. One of the Water Board's technicians also challenged it and I can remember David taking him to one side to explain the options while we carried on with the tour."

"Mr Edwards, this is important, we need a list of everywhere David Butane has been over the last week or so, especially any water installations."

"He's been to loads, but why would he get involved with something like this. He's American, for God's sake!"

"Only he can answer that, but the facts are that because of his association with you, he now has the plans and entry access to any and all water sites in Washington State."

Dale Edwards looked down pensively at the rich, walnut table top. "Right," He exclaimed, picking up his phone. "I'm going to start getting his site access revoked, but it means the Water Board will have to phone all their plants, it will take a while. My father also said there was no way they could develop an antidote in time so it's down to us to make sure this never happens. While I'm sorting this out, haven't you two got something you could be doing?"

Brian looked across the table and half smiled at Kane. They had gone from grilling a suspect to virtually taking orders from him. It was easy to see why he was potentially, the next President of the United States.

14

Kane asked for and received a list of all the water sites David Butane had visited. Both he and Brian were carefully sifting through the data and highlighting areas that were visited more than once, paying particular attention to those he had visited during the last week.

"I make that six sites that he has re-visited during the last week and... two... no three new sites." Kane finished writing the last address and turned to speak to Dale Edwards, passing him the list of addresses as he spoke. "Mr Edwards, if you can get these sites contacted, Brian and I will see if we can get our chaperones to show us where these sites are."

"Chaperones?"

"Yes, sorry, personal joke. We have two young CIA agents at our disposal. I think they've been assigned to baby sit us."

"So I take it I am no longer a suspect then?"

"Everybody's a suspect at the moment Mr Edwards, just some more than most."

Bill Johnson had just begun to read through the thin, photocopied file that had been delivered from central desk. The first page of information confirmed that David Butane did attend Punjab College in Lahore at the same time as Ali Aziri. It also showed that he had obtained a degree in Chemistry but had not stayed on to do his masters as previously planned. The second piece of paper was a copy of a marriage certificate between David Butane and Zahra Jafuzai dated 18th April, 2000. The final document showed a list of his recent employment history but there was no information relating from the time he left university to his first job some three years later.

“Is that the file on Butane?” George Daniels asked as he stood in the doorway of Bill’s office.

“Yes, but it’s just what our guys have dug up.”

“Yeah, they phoned me on the way over here and gave me an update.” Bill responded as he walked across the floor and plonked himself down into Bill’s very comfortable armchair.

“Make yourself at home.” Bill uttered sarcastically. “What are you doing here anyway? I thought you would have been home by now.”

“I’m doing the same as you, looking for a way to prevent this disaster from happening.”

“And I always thought you were a glass half full man. You don’t seem very confident that we can stop this.”

“I’ll feel confident when we have the mixture or virus, whatever you want to call it and the perpetrators, whoever they may be, safely in our hands, or the FBI’s, CIA’s… whatever.”

“How have you left it with Peter Edwards? Is he involved?”

“I don’t believe so, but I have two of our guys keeping him company just in case. He has his team working with Abdul to try and create an antidote but is not very hopeful of finding one in time. Talking of time…”

“I know, I’ve been thinking of that all afternoon. They know we are onto them so it’s only logical that they bring the event forward, but hopefully, that will be their downfall.”

“How’s that?”

“Well, up until now everything’s been part of a bigger set up. I think it is safe to say that David Butane is the American connection. He must know we are onto him so he has two choices. He either runs, or he brings the plans forward and tries to get the job done before he is caught.”

“Well, my money’s on the latter. But how will that be their downfall?”

“Up until now, he has been able to camouflage where and when he intends to strike by visiting numerous sites and installations all over Washington. The stuff was sent to the States a week ago so with our inquiries getting closer and closer it’s a safe bet the chemicals are already in-situ, just waiting to be mixed and added to the water supply. He knows it is only a matter of time before we catch up with him so he’s going to make a bee line for wherever the stuff is and we will be ready and waiting for him.”

“Sounds like you know where it is.”

"No, our boys have narrowed it down a bit and there are local police and FBI agents being sent to every site, especially the one's visited in the last week. Dale Edwards has used his influence to get the entire water supply primed ready for an immediate shutdown if necessary. It will cause havoc with the manufacturing industry but if it means saving thousands of lives then there's no contest."

"So, what do we do now?"

"We wait." Bill's frustrating reply.

The four men cruised through the heavy, afternoon traffic to the first water station on the list. As their black, Lincoln Navigator pulled level with the security box, two suit clad figures emerged from the far side and asked to see their I.D., displaying their own FBI badges at the same time. Kane also noticed two uniformed police officers to the rear of the car. Dale Edwards had worked fast. A smartly dressed Apex security guard, wearing a white shirt, company tie, black logoed pullover, stay creased trousers and highly polished black safety shoes, also checked the I.D.s and when he was finally satisfied asked all four of them to sign the visitors book. Kane and Brian got out of the Navigator and quizzed the security guard on who was allowed access to the site and confirmed that he had been informed the FBI would be detaining David Butane if he turned up on site. Satisfied that the site was relatively secure, Kane asked the babysitters to take them to the next site on the list. The second site proved to be a duplicate of the first. Two FBI officers, two uniformed police officers and a smartly dressed Apex guard who smelt of garlic and reminded Kane he had not eaten yet today.

They pressed on to the third site, a large water treatment site which processed and treated water gathered from a large underground reservoir before being released into the main water supply system. The site was fully automated and only manned by a Shift controller, two engineers, two security men and a cleaner come odd job man. The Lincoln pulled onto the long tree lined access ramp and coasted down to the blue security box, stopping in front of the lowered security barrier. It was a couple of minutes before the guard eventually came out to inform them that no-one was allowed access to the plant. Kane could see the two figures peering out of the security box but there was no sign of any uniformed police officers. Kane opened the door and climbed out to be immediately challenged by the guard, a young Asian guy wearing a checked shirt, an oversized black, logoed pullover and sneakers.

"No get out of car, the site is closed, you leave now please."

"Okay, pal." Kane replied as he glanced over to the two figures that had now moved to the shadows at the side of the security box. "When will this be open?"

"Tomorrow." The guard replied, moving slightly to his left so that the two figures by the security box had a good view of Kane.

"Tomorrow it is then," Kane stated, climbing back into the vehicle. "Okay guys, get us out of here."

The driver turned around to speak to Kane. "Something's wrong, he…" A burst of gunfire smashed through the windscreen as he instinctively put the stick into reverse and slammed on the accelerator. Another burst of gunfire riddled the front grill, causing geysers of white, hot steam to spurt from the shattered radiator. The Navigator skidded to a halt and all four clambered out to seek cover behind the trunk. The two chaperones had now drawn their standard issue Glock 22's and were popping off single shots in the direction of the security box.

"Got anything for us?" Brian shouted as another hail of automatic fire pebble dashed the Lincoln's roof. The young, but surprisingly composed agent, bent low and shuffled to the front of the car using the open driver's door as cover and leaning in popped the trunk before returning to the comparative safety of the Lincoln's rear. Reaching into the trunk he unclipped and removed two pump action shotguns and handed one each to Kane and Brian.

"Do you want to swap?" Kane asked, holding out the shotgun to the first agent. The babysitters looked at one another briefly before both handed over their Glocks for the offered shotguns. "Left or right?" Kane shouted to Brian as another burst shattered the Navigator's side windows.

"I'll take the left, seeing as I'm here already. Are you good to go?"

"Yep, after the next burst." Kane had just finished talking when a stream of bullets ricocheted off the concrete access road. "Cover us guys." Kane shouted as he broke from the cover of the now battered Lincoln and darted for the nearby shrubbery.

The two shotguns fired simultaneously with the spread shot peppering the security box and the ground in front. They were too far away to be effective but at least it had temporarily halted the bursts of gunfire long enough for both Kane and Brian to disappear into the undergrowth.

The chain link fence behind the tall shrubs restricted their movements, especially Brian's who twice had to break cover from the thick branched, tree like shrubs to move further down the access ramp, attracting short bursts of fire each time. Kane, fortunately, had a little more room to work in and squeezing himself between the tree like shrubs and chain link fence he quickly made his way down to the end of the tree line to peer out some ten metres from the silent, shot riddled security box. As Kane watched, a short, stocky figure jumped out from behind the far end of the security box and fired a short burst into the tall, thick branched shrubs four or five metres behind where Kane was crouching, then quickly disappeared back behind the corner of the unit.

Kane raised the Glock 22 and aimed just to the left of the building's corner. Moments later the figure jumped into view again but as he raised his weapon, Kane gently squeezed the trigger of the Glock, sending the .40 calibre bullet crashing into his assailant's chest, forcing him to stagger backwards, then stumble forward a few paces to land on his knees before eventually collapsing on to his back.

The Asian guard in the black, oversized, pullover ran from behind the security box towards a large, white painted, concrete flower box. He had almost reached it when a single shot from Brian's hand gun sent him spinning to the ground, dropping his weapon and grabbing his shoulder in pain. Kane watched as he painfully dragged himself to the cover of the concrete box. The green, red tipped leaves of the exotic palms obscuring any further view, but Kane was more interested in the third assailant. With his weapon levelled in front of him Kane slowly emerged from the cover of the foliage and seeing no obvious signs of the remaining target, jumped to his feet and started running for the front of the security box. The third man jumped up and fired a short burst through the glass fronted window in the direction of the fast approaching footsteps, forcing Kane to dive to the hard, concrete floor. No sooner had the glass been shattered from the inside than a well-aimed shotgun blast sent shards of glass streaming into the square shaped room, ripping flesh and piercing the attacker's left eye. He stood bolt upright, shouting in agony as Kane's finger squeezed once more on the trigger and his pain was over.

Brian broke cover and ran over to the second man who was softly whimpering in pain behind the flower box. "None of these are Butane." He shouted to Kane, before crouching back down and scanning the box and the main building beyond.

Kane was already up and running and flattened himself against the front corner of the security box before carefully peering around the side. Four bodies were lined up on the floor, out of view. Two were in uniform, two were in suits. He carefully stepped over the bodies and walked around the back, pausing only to look into the small, square shaped room and the prone, lifeless body, a neat dark red hole in the centre of his glass ripped, forehead and a large, slither of glass sticking out of his left eye. In the far corner was the crumpled body of a larger white shirted figure, probably the owner of the oversized, Apex logoed pullover, he thought to himself.

"Clear." Kane shouted as he rounded the corner and glanced down at the twisted body of the second man. "How's your guy, we need to know if there are anymore."

"How many more?" Brian shouted as his captive sobbed in pain, but no answer. Using the gun to move away his blood soaked hand Brian jabbed the end of the barrel deep into the wound causing him to scream out in agony.

"Two… two." He shouted.

"Where are they?" Brian demanded, his Glock hovering over the open wound which was now bleeding profusely.

"There… in there." The injured man gestured with a movement of his head. Brian looked over to the building and the open reception door.

"Shit, Kane, they're in."

Brian and Kane were soon joined by the now experienced FBI agents, shotguns at the ready, adrenaline flowing and eager for more action.

"You'd better call this in." Kane suggested and then taking out his own cell phone called Dale Edwards and asked him to get this area's water supply sealed off. Then he called Bill Johnson and asked him to do the same… just in case his gut instinct about Dale Edwards was wrong.

"Got anymore ammo guys?" Brian asked, checking the handgun.

"I think two of the bodies behind security are your guys," Kane added, taking two offered ammo clips and tucking them into his trousers. "You wait for the cavalry and we'll check out the building."

The mention of bodies linked with your guys brought the two raw but blooded, recruits back to reality and with the adrenaline starting to wane, offered little protest at being left behind.

"Do you know what those guys' names are?" Kane asked as they jogged quickly down to the open reception door.

"They just answer to guys, so I didn't bother to ask their names."

Stopping either side of the open, glass door they both peered into the small, neat reception area. Four blue reception chairs lined one wall and a tall pine reception counter took pride of place in the centre of the room. Two black trousered legs with highly polished, black safety boots were poking out from the right side of the unit. Kane crouched low and made his way across the grey tiled, floor to the body of the second security guard. Turning him over to lie on his back, he notice the light blue Apex logo on his black pullover was tinged with red. He gently pulled down the top of the jumper to reveal a patch of blood on his shirt, in the middle of which was a small tear, just over his heart.

"Leidmeister?" Brian whispered, looking over Kane's shoulder.

"Could be," Kane replied, "we'd better get going, don't know how long they've been in here."

Brian looked through the glass panels of the large, blue, double doors in the corner of the reception area. He could see a small corridor with a white door on either side and another pair of large, blue, doors at the other end. Satisfied it was safe to enter, Brian slid in between the partially opened doors, closely followed by Kane. They moved quickly down the corridor and peered through the small, glass squares of the second pair of blue doors, into the massive water purifying plant beyond. Cylindrical, wide diameter pipes traversed the inside of the building and periodically dropped through tall, odd-shaped pieces of machinery before carrying on through the floor into the huge holding tanks underneath. Kane strained his neck to see the foetal shaped body of a man just to the left of the blue doors, the nozzle of a large industrial vacuum cleaner still held firmly in his hand. Kane slowly pushed the door open and slid into the start of the spacious, main floor area.

Stooping down, Kane indicated to Brian to go right and then, still crouching low, quickly made his way down the left side of the room area, passing the body of the hapless cleaner and only slowing down when he reached the open corner. As he turned to make his way down the other side, he noticed a large, glass fronted room looking out onto the myriad of equipment sparsely dotted around the expanse of the large floor. Two figures could be seen walking around inside. One was dressed in a white round necked t-shirt and white trousers and the other was holding a gun, he was tall with close cropped, fair hair… Leidmeister!

Brian reached the corner on the right side of the doors and worked his way quickly down the whole length of the building before having to turn left to meet up with Kane. As he made his way down the third side he noticed three people in the far corner of the water plant. Two were kneeling on the floor apparently working on something whilst the third was standing over them with his back to Brian.

Using the machinery to hide his approach, Brian leap-frogged from one to the other until he was almost upon them. Two men in dark blue overalls and white hard hats were kneeling on the floor undoing the bolts securing the inspection cover for the outgoing mains supply, at least, he hoped they were undoing them and not doing them up. Next to them was a large, lamp case which had been taken apart and Brian rightly assumed they had got the virus in by smuggling it inside one of the several Ultra Violet light units they had proposed to install in the outlet systems. As he made one final check of his gun, Brian moved out from behind a large down pipe just as one of the engineers looked up and his startled expression was enough to make David Butane spin around, firing off a shot as soon as he turned. The bullet went inches over Brian's head as he darted behind a large, cylindrical tank. Levelling his gun Brian peered out to see the two engineers diving behind a very large, orange painted motor. David Butane had disappeared but as Brian instinctively ducked, a second bullet thudded into the tank just inches from his nose, causing a fountain of water to arc out of the tank and spread across the floor. A third bullet ricocheted off the large metal support stand that held the cylindrical tank in place as Brian sought out the direction of the attack.

The first shot fired alerted Henryk Leidmeister and Kane could do nothing to stop him from bringing the butt of his gun down on the shift controller's head, twice, before turning to look out of the large glass fronted window in the direction of the second and now third gunshot. Kane was already racing down the side of the building as Leidmeister emerged from the control room and seeing Kane fast approaching, dived behind a large, steel downpipe just as Kane's first shot skipped off the white, concrete floor behind him. Leidmeister fired off two quick shots then darted behind a small, square, sampling station. Ducking low he strained to see where Kane had got to, when another .40 calibre tore through the pipe behind him. The resulting stream of water cascaded over his head and down his back forcing him to seek better cover.

Brian heard the other gunfire and guessed that Kane had caught up with Leidmeister, but was too busy trying to work out where Butane was. He saw the gun flash, but too late, as the searing pain in his left arm started to trickle blood through his blue, denim shirt. Brian fired off a shot in the direction of the gun flash and dragged himself back, behind a large, hour shaped valve, the large, locking wheel protruding out above his head, his left arm now limp and useless.

Kane darted from one piece of equipment to another trying to outflank Leidmeister and give him a clear shot. Reaching one of the many concrete support pillars, Kane stood up and carefully looked around the pillar to where he expected Leidmeister to be. The pillar exploded just below his left ear as the bullet tore into the concrete, sending small chunks of cement and stone in all directions. Kane dropped to the floor and rolled away as another bullet whistled inches above his head. Not that he could hear it, the loud ringing in his head muffled all other sounds as he poked his finger in his ear and frantically wriggled it around trying to clear the pressure building up inside his head. Kane cursed himself for allowing the assassin to outflank him

Brian inched further into the centre of the plant, he had to gain a good vantage point but there were too many open spaces and his arm was slowing him down. The tables had turned; he was the one now being stalked.

Kane shook his head in a futile effort to get rid of the buzzing sensation. He glanced behind him and then visually swept in front before darting across to the next concrete pillar. This time he did not stand up but carefully peered around the base of the pillar occasionally scanning behind, to the sides and then back in front of him. It was then that he saw Brian, crouched low and with his back to him, his left arm hanging loose. The shadowy figure of David Butane loomed to Brian's left as Kane instinctively raised the Glock 22 and fired two shots in quick succession. The figure staggered backwards and collapsed in a heap on the floor.

Brian spun around and levelling his gun, fired off a round in the direction the shots had come from, then taking careful aim, he gently squeezed the trigger and fired the second, fateful shot.

The first bullet had gone deep into Leidmeister's shoulder as he lay on top of a purifier, levelling the gun at Kane's head. The pain and surprise of the first bullet caused him to lift himself up onto his knees and give Brian ample opportunity to place the second shot square in the middle of his forehead, sending him crashing off the unit onto the cold, concrete floor.

Kane got to his feet and ran over to the twisted body, kicking away the automatic that had fallen from the assassin's hand. Staring down he wished he could see some sort of movement that would give him the justifiable reason for emptying his magazine into the prostrate body, but the cold, blue eyes now really were lifeless.

"You alright?" Kane shouted over to Brian, again noticing his bloodied, limp arm.

"Why is it always me that has to get shot? I think my arm is broken, the bullet must have cracked the bone on the way through. How about you?" Brian asked, noticing the blood trickling down the side of Kane's grazed cheek.

"I'm fine, just stood too close to a pillar he was using for firing practice."

"Is that all of them?"

"I think so… hey guys," Kane shouted to the two engineers curled up behind one of the units. "We're here with the FBI, how many of them were there?"

There was a long pause before a quiet, frightened voice responded "Two… I think."

"Freeze." The shout came from the back of the building as Kane turned to see a mixture of suits and uniforms pour in through the large double blue doors and fan out through the assortment of well-spaced, machinery dotted over the expanse of the water treatment plant.

"It's okay, they're the Brits we told you about."

Brian turned around to see the two baby sitters darting in and out of the spaces between the units and heading straight towards them, smiles of relief written all over their faces.

"Boy, are we glad to see you two." Sighed the first as he looked down at Leidmeister's body.

"Are you two hurt bad?" The second blurted, seeing the blood trickling down Kane's face and Brian's bloodied, dangling left arm.

"No we'll be fine after a bit of attention guys. While we're on the subject, what are your names? We can't keep calling you 'guys' all the time." Brian winced as the pain in his arm started to come to life.

"I'm Krzysztof and he's Wienczyslaw, our parents were Polish."

Responded the first proud agent.

Brian looked across to Kane who smiled and shook his head before turning to them both. “Okay, guys, lead us to your medics and let’s get out of here.”

Kane and Brian handed back the Glock 22’s to their rightful owners who gratefully accepted them, shouldering them as quickly as possible before any of the other agents could see they had lent out their weapons.

“Wait a minute,” Krzysztof thought out aloud. “We’ve got to fill out gun discharge reports about these two.” He was pointing to the two blood soaked bodies on the floor.

“They’re your guns,” Kane smiled back, “You’d better fill them out.” Then he turned and walked out, with Brian, to the waiting paramedics.

“So that’s Leidmeister and Butane out of the equation, what about Dr Aziri and the middleman Rashid?” Brian asked as they walked, holding his arm to prevent any unnecessary movement and pain.

“We’ll leave those for someone else to tidy up. Anyway, from the looks of you, you’ll be on sick leave for a while.”

“Hold up there guys, let me get that for you.” A tall, suited, well groomed man in his mid-thirties pushed open both of the large, blue doors and held them while they walked through. “I’m agent Morrison, get yourself some treatment and then I’m gonna need to take some reports from you. Did you find the viruses and are they intact?”

“I believe they’re over in the far corner, with the two guys in blue overalls.” Kane replied, not relishing the thought of paperwork.

“What two guys? Where?” The agent had obviously missed them on his sweep.

“Those two with Kris and Winey,” Kane nodded towards the two former chaperones now guiding the two hapless engineers into the control room. “They must have still been behind that big orange motor; those two did well to find them.”

“Well, get yourself some treatment and I’ll catch up with you later.” The agent turned on his heels, without waiting for a response and headed back into the plant towards the control room.

“Do you think this was the only plant they intended to hit?” Brian asked Kane as they were about to be descended upon by a team of paramedics.

“From what Bill told me, the growth rate of this stuff is quite phenomenal, they would only need one good insertion point and I guess this was it."

"Hold on guys, I can walk, I don't need that." Brian tried to push away the wheelchair that had been placed in front of him by the paramedics.

"Sorry, Sir, it's the rules. Let's get you back to the wagon and sort you out, it will be more comfortable for your arm too."

Brian reluctantly sat down in the wheelchair and cradled his arm in front of him. "I guess all the other sites will be locked down tight by now." He continued.

"You're thinking of Aziri aren't you?"

"Well, aren't you? This is the guy that started it all, so you think he'd be there at the end."

Kane shared Brian's concern but did not realise how much until that last statement.

15

George Daniels stood in his modest office staring out of the large, triple glazed window at the various, mesmerising, assortment of boats and cabin cruisers that constantly chugged up and down through the grey, murky waters of the river Thames. He had just finished a telephone call with Bill Johnson who had updated him on the events of the last twenty four hours.

The attack on the zoo had been prevented, stored stock of the virus recovered and the planned attack on the Washington water system had been thwarted. Everybody at the States end was patting themselves on the back, but George knew there were still a few loose ends to tie up.

It turns out that David Butane and Ali Aziri spent three years in Afghanistan involved with a special religious sect. Firstly, it was to relieve their grief over the loss of their loved ones but as the weeks and months passed, they were slowly and clinically indoctrinated, brainwashed into thinking that America was the world's aggressor, a cancer that had to be stopped.

George had seen and heard it all before, but this was slightly different. Ali Aziri had come from a background that, whilst it was not what you might call stable, it was definitely not one associated with religion or fanaticism. David Butane had a strong American background and when he went to study in Pakistan, he had fallen in love with a fellow student and married her against her parents' wishes. If they knew she was pregnant at the time it might have been even worse. But whatever happened during the three years in Afghanistan, they had both led virtually, unblemished lives since then being until now, model citizens in their respective countries.

He trudged across to his double pedestal desk and bent down, tapping the keyboard to wake his system from sleep mode. George concluded a brief email to Bill Johnson asking for any and all information on the Religious sect in Afghanistan and then he put on his coat and headed for the door. It had been a long twenty four hours and for him; tomorrow would be just as demanding.

Having had initial treatment for their injuries, Kane and Brian went through an on-site debrief with agent Morrison where it was confirmed that the virus vials were still intact and safely on their way back to the labs. Brian was released to be taken off to hospital for x-rays and Kane was deposited back to the hotel with a caution that he may be requested to give a fuller account later in the day.

Kane sat on the edge of his freshly made bed, using his cellular phone to update Bill Johnson with the finer points of the day's events. He was well pleased with the recovery of the virus but jokingly rebuked Kane for not taking Leidmeister or Butane alive so that they could be questioned about Dr Aziri's whereabouts. Bill had been updated by his Washington contacts at various points throughout the day and was the first to call Brian having been told he was being treated for a gunshot wound.

"How is Brian? Is he back from hospital yet?" Bill's concern was genuine, which was another reason why Kane admired him.

"No not yet, but he doesn't like hospitals at the best of times, so he won't be there for long."

Three loud taps on the door briefly halted the conversation. "Hold on a sec, Bill."

Kane got up from the bed and walked over to open the door. "Talk of the devil and he appears…come in, mate."

"I take it he's got back then?" Bill asked, listening to the conversation on the other end of the phone.

"Yeah, arm's in a sling but he's still bouncing about."

"Good, well you two catch up and I'll speak to you in the morning."

Kane ended the call, suddenly realising that it must be late evening over there and Bill was still on the case.

"So what did they say then? Are you being pensioned out of the service or what?" Kane jokingly inquired.

"It went right through and just nicked the bone on the way out. Have to rest it for a couple of days then plenty of physiotherapy to get the full feeling back, but it should be fine. What did Bill have to say?"

"He was obviously chuffed that we recovered the vials and stopped Leidmeister and Butane, but like us, he still wants Aziri tracked down."

"Don't forget his mate Rashid."

"That was the other thing. Rashid turned up at the warehouse while we were on our way to the states. He tried to make a run for it when he realised the warehouse had been turned over and one of the local agents shot him. He died the following morning without recovering consciousness."

"And then there was one… do you fancy going out to a bar for a drink?"

"Sure, any particular bar in mind?"

"Yes, the first one we come to."

George Daniels had a restless night. He had spent the whole of the evening going over and over the updated files on Peter Edwards, Abdul Hussein and Ali Aziri. Sleep had been fitful, his over active mind searched for answers, even for questions that had not yet been asked. Rising early he showered, dressed and settled for an early start at the office. He was ninety nine per cent sure that Peter Edwards had not been in contact with Ali Aziri since his birth, apart from the meeting at Chessington where he posed as Dr Ashkani and his reactions did not portray him as someone who needed to make amends for his past misdemeanours. Abdul Hussein was just a greedy, selfish man and having been faced with the possibility of spending the rest of his life in hiding, now basked in the importance of the work he had been given to accomplish.

Dr Aziri was more complicated. He had a secure childhood, good education, Peter Edwards had seen to it that the family were financially secure and he had settled down, married with a child of his own. The death of his family would have had an enormous impact on him, but taking into account his upbringing, any idea of revenge would have been sought immediately, that is, if he truly felt that way. For it to be shelved away for over twelve years, to be developed into a calculated, cold blooded, attack on a civilian population, it just did not make sense. Or did it? When you analyse it from that perspective, that's exactly what happened to him. His family and friends, part of a civilian population, were killed by a clinical attack. George pushed the fleeting thought of Ali's justification right out of his mind as he realised how someone with that sort of grief could easily be manipulated by trained, sadistic, brainwashers. But there was something… something that he had heard or seen that kept drawing him back to Aziri, Edwards, London or Hussein?

The phone on his desk burst into life as he jumped from his thoughts and picked up the handset and answered, "George Daniels."

"What's the matter, can't you sleep?" Bill Johnson sniggered.

"I was just about to ask you the same question."

"Well, I left it until 7.00am and if you had not answered your office phone I would have rung your mobile. I have some more information on that religious sect Aziri and Butane linked up with. They are tied in with Al Qaeda but, from what we have been able to determine so far, do their own thing to a certain degree. Al Qaeda are happy to fund them when necessary but, like most religious cults, they tend to indoctrinate their disciples and brainwash them to their way of thinking."

"Which is?" George interrupted.

"Hang on George, we haven't got that far yet. All we know is that they select prominent people, who have lost several close family members in the, as they put it, battle against evil and enforcing the belief that to be complete a family should always be together… George, you still there?"

"Yes Bill, I'm still here. What about Aziri, have you tracked him down yet?"

"No, he's gone completely off the radar. No trace of him in Pakistan, no sign of entry into the States… haven't got a clue where he is."

"I may have," George remarked thoughtfully. "Something you just said struck a chord."

"What was that? Losing close family members?"

"No, it was when you said to be complete a family should always be together."

"So where do you think he is now?"

"Where his father is… here in London."

"Have you still got guys babysitting him?"

"No, they were taken off last night."

"But I cannot see Edwards, blood relation or not, harbouring a known terrorist, not with his first born son aiming to be the next President of the United States. He would have no chance of having a life with him now."

"I was not thinking of life," Bill responded, still pulling things together in his mind. "Peter Edwards said that Ali Aziri, or rather his alter ego

Ashkanti, gave him the impression that he owed him something and that they would all be together one day. Edwards thought he meant working together, but I think Aziri meant as a complete family."

"Well, he would have a hard job making that happen, his mother and brother are already dead."

"Exactly."

It had been forty five minutes since Bill's telephone conversation with George. Most of that time had been spent trying to get updates on where Aziri could be now, but he had also received some further information which troubled him even more. Three recent suicide bombers had been traced back to the same religious sect that Aziri and Butane had spent three years with and all three were at the sect at around the same time as Butane and Aziri.

Bill spent the next forty five minutes shuffling papers and going through the brief file he had started on the Religious sect known as al-Jahid. Finally, he picked up the phone and dialled his Department Head, Tom Flannery.

"Tom it's me, Bill. Sorry to trouble you so early but we could have a situation here which goes further than the Washington water threat."

"I'm about half an hour away, will it wait?"

"Well, yes, I'll wait until you get here."

"Hold on a second," Tom heard the hint of disappointment in Bill's voice as he slipped the phone into the car kit cradle. "That's better, I'm on hands free now so fire away."

"Have you managed to read the report on the Washington virus case?"

"I've scanned through it, seems like your guys deserve a pat on the back. How's the one that got shot?"

"Yeah, he'll be okay, but did you read the background on Aziri and Butane?"

"Well, as I said, I scanned through it, but are you referring to the fact that they both lost their wives?"

"Yes… in a way. After that incident they both spent three years in a religious sect."

"Al-Jahid?"

"Yes, I see you are quite up to date with our information. Well, this sect has also been linked to three recent suicide bombers and they were all there at the same time as Aziri and Butane."

"And your point is?"

"I think this may be the tip of the iceberg. My concern is that there may be more sleepers out there with possibly bigger threats to pose than the Washington virus and all originating from al-Jahid."

"Okay… well, Bill, as you know, I always trust your judgement and by the way, congratulations on the Washington job. You and your guys Kane and Brian did well, considering this also started out as a hunch. Set up a meeting for… let's say 9am. Invite some of the intelligence people who have been collating this information and see if Interpol or any of the Intelligence Agencies in the States can add any more leverage to this. I'll wake up a few people in the Foreign Office and see who we can lean on in Afghanistan to help speed things up. I suggest you get your best team together ready to send out there. If your hunch is right, we could have disasters springing up everywhere. But Aziri is still alive isn't he? And Butane was shot dead, so they don't seem like suicide fanatics to me."

Butane did not give himself up, or try to escape and we also believe Aziri may be going to kill himself and take the Presidential candidate's father with him.

"So what are we doing about that little Chestnut?"

"George Daniels and his firm are looking after the London end of it. As far as I'm aware, Peter Edwards is still in the UK If he goes back to America, well… it will be down to the FBI or CIA to look out for him. My best team are still in Washington, I was going to give them a few days off but I think I had better prepare them for a trip out East."

"What about the one that got shot?"

"He'll be okay, nicked a bone but apart from that it was a clean shot, right through. Just needs a couple of days to heal and he will be as right as rain."

"Have you got a couple of days?"

"I'll tell you that after we've had our meeting."

Kane had just finished his phone conversation with Bill Johnson and was still trying to fully open his eyelids. The digital clock at the side of his bed shone out 6.05am, whilst the dull ache in his head urged him to go back to sleep. A few Buds, a steak, a few more Buds, then an assortment of 'house specials' concocted by a friendly bartender with a wicked sense of humour, had rounded off a 'release' evening with Brian and his damaged wing. The last few days had been hectic and last night was a good excuse to unwind, just a pity Alison was not there to share it with them. This morning was a different story. He smiled as he thought about phoning Brian and waking him up to tell him they would shortly be on their way to Afghanistan and how his head should be thumping worse than his own, but then relented when his pounding headache forced him to lie gently back and drift off into blissful slumber.

Just over an hour later Kane was woken up by loud knocking on his bedroom door. He pulled back the light-weight duvet and swung his legs out of the bed until he was sat upright, rubbing his face back to consciousness.

"Alright, I'm coming." Kane shouted as another rap on the door echoed throughout the neat but compact bedroom.

Using the wall for support, Kane fumbled around the bedroom until he found the bedroom door and peered out through the round, magnified, spy hole. Brian was stood the other side, just about to beat another drum roll on his door.

"Aren't you up yet?" Brian laughed as he strode through the now opened door.

"Well, I am now. How come you are so chirpy? I thought you would have slept for a week the amount you drank last night."

"Bill phoned me about half an hour ago so, as I was then wide awake, I thought I would shower, dress and go down for breakfast. I take it he phoned you?"

"Yes, just after six this morning. They had some sort of meeting earlier and it looks like we will be off to Afghanistan, is that what he told you?"

"More or less, except I've got to go back to London first for a medical, see if I'm fit for duty."

"Lucky bugger! That's about six weeks for a start."

"I don't think so, I think I am being set up as bait for something or other, I thought you might know more about it."

"No, he never mentioned anything like that to me, just that we may be doing some digging around in Afghanistan. The other thing he was on about was Aziri, they think he may be in London, or the UK at least. He seems to have gone to ground, no sightings anywhere."

"Have they asked his sister?"

"She's disappeared too; nobody's seen her for a couple of days."

"Have you still got her phone number? Give her a ring and ask her where she is, from what I heard, I'm sure she'll tell you."

"I think her brother would have probably filled her in on who we really are by now, so I don't think she would be very cooperative and anyway, if they are on the run, she would have probably ditched the phone by now."

"So what are you looking for then?" He asked, noticing Kane rummaging through the pockets of both pairs of his trousers.

"If I have still got it and if she is still using it, then perhaps they can get her location and if her brother is with her, then they can get him as well."

"That's a lot of ifs Kane, but it would be nice to put Aziri away and finish the job."

"Well, if we are off to Afghanistan, it looks as if we are going to have to leave that to someone else to finish. Got it!" Kane exclaimed as he unravelled a piece of very creased paper. "Here, you give this number to Bill, if it is still on they should be able to trace the ESN and find out where she is. I'm going to have a shower while you're doing that and then we'll try some breakfast?"

Tom Flannery was not a happy man. His nine o'clock meeting had left him with more potential problems than he cared to think about. The rest of the morning had been spent contacting various intelligence agencies around the world, trying to gather as much information as possible about al-Jahid. The CIA had come up trumps with a list of people known to be connected with the sect, but they seemed to have gone to ground and only reappear on very rare occasions. They have, however, an operative already working in Kabul, though they do admit to be coming up against a brick wall. Tom had discussed various options with Bill Johnson, of how they may possibly infiltrate the sect but, apart from one, none of the others looked feasible.

"So what about Alison Jenkins' family, have they been informed of her death?" Tom continued his conversation with Bill Johnson.

"Her listed next of kin is an aunt living in New York. The father was killed in a motor bike accident when she was seven and the mother died of cancer five years ago. We were going to contact the aunt when the body was brought home to be repatriated."

"So nobody in her family knows yet?"

"No, are we still looking to go down this route?"

"Is it because you don't think it will work or because you feel guilty about using a dead agent's body as bait?"

"That's below the belt Tom. Yes, it would have a good chance of working, well, as good as anything else we could have come up with, but it's going to be very raw for the same team she was killed with to accept this. I don't know how I would feel if I were in their shoes."

"Have you told Brian about this yet?"

"Not exactly, I have told him he may have to work under cover and his injured arm would help improve his case, but I have not mentioned anything about Alison Jenkins yet and I need to know that this Aziri guy is not going to pop up and compromise our efforts."

"What is the latest on him?"

"We are keeping tabs on a telephone number belonging to his sister. Our information shows she was with Aziri having a meal, just before they both disappeared. If she still has the phone and switches it on, then we should be able to find out which part of the world she is in and if we are due for any luck, he might be with her."

"Bill, if your hunch is right and the more I think about it, the more convinced I am, then this sect has to be sought out and destroyed and the sooner the better. But before it is eliminated, we need to find out who, how many and where they are. If you cannot think of a better alternative, Alison Jenkins has to be our only option."

"Okay Tom, it will take a day or two to set up the background details and find a suitable incident to relate it to. It will also give those two an extra day of relaxation before I hit them with the glad news. I have given George Daniels the details of that mobile phone number Brian passed us earlier. I will feel a darn sight happier about this if we had this Aziri guy in our hands though. Right, I had better start making the arrangements." Bill finished off, rising to leave.

"I know this is not a very pleasant option Bill, but it is our best shot at getting on the inside, that is, if they take the bait."

Bill nodded once, turned and walked out the door back to his office. He did not relish having to explain the proposed plan to Kane and Brian, but at least he had another twenty four hours before that conversation would take place.

Peter Edwards pulled off the M4 at Junction 33 and cruised down the dual carriageway, past the entrance to St Fagans parklands and on to Barry to meet up with his brother Kevin. The two and a half hour drive from Chessington had gone surprisingly quickly, maybe it was the relief that Dale was alright and the danger, hopefully, had been removed or maybe it was the relief of a thirty six year old secret coming out into the open. It was going to be hard to tell Dale and his mother Catherine, which is why he thought he would practice on his brother first. He selected a memory number from his Nokia cellular phone and waited for the call to answer.

"Good afternoon, Edwards Chemicals, how may I help you?" The voice echoed from the car's hands free speakers.

"Hi Marge, it's Peter. Any messages?"

"Yes there's a couple here for you. A Mr George Daniels phoned and would like you to phone him back as soon as you get the message, I have the number here or have you already got it?"

"No, but I'll phone him later, what else have you got?"

"A lady phoned for you and asked if you were here. I told her you were out of the office for the day and she said she would phone back later. The final message was from Kevin just checking you were on your way, which was about half an hour ago."

"Where was the woman from?"

"She did not say, I thought she was Welsh at first but I think it was more of an Indian accent. I did ask if I could pass on a message but she just asked if you would be in tomorrow and said she would phone then. You are in tomorrow Peter?"

"Yes, I'll be there first thing. Okay Marge, have a good afternoon and I'll see you in the morning."

Peter ended the call and remembered he did not get George Daniel's number but after the last couple of days he was not that keen to talk to him anyway. If it was important then he would phone again. Manoeuvring around the busy Culverhouse Cross roundabout, Peter drove past the familiar HTV Television Studios and onto Port Road heading into Barry and his hastily arranged meeting with Kevin.

"He is not there?"

"No Ali, he will not be back until tomorrow, he will have such a shock when you tell him who you are. I hope he can help you sort out your problems, I worry about you."

"I think he already has an idea who I am and yes, all our problems will be sorted out, there is no need to worry about me, Safia, everything will be alright."

"I still think we should have gone to the authorities, they will track down these people and put them away and why do we have to use false names in this country? Surely they would not follow us here."

"The authorities are corrupt; they are the last people we should be speaking to. Tomorrow everything will be finalised and we can all be happy again. You will need a hotel for tonight; I will sort one out for you."

"What about you? Where are you going to stay?"

"I have something to do tonight and I need those sample vials you carried for me in your medical case, but I will meet you in the morning," Ali answered whilst scrolling through the internet on his mobile phone, looking for address and post code details in areas outside London. "I will book you in to the hotel and you can tell them you live in... Bristol... you can say you are a Doctor there."

"Why do I have to say I live in Bristol? And what is this sample? Is this why they are after you?"

"If you say you live in Pakistan they will ask for your passport, which we do not have. Please Safia, just do as I ask, tomorrow we will all be back together."

Special agent Dean Morrison was reading through the background reports on the Washington water incident, highlighting the paragraphs which mentioned information received from MI6 or other British Intelligence agencies. He quickly scanned all the highlighted areas once more before selecting a number from the contact list and keying it into the phone handset.

"Hi, is that Chas Wiltson?"

"Yes, who is this?"

"Special agent Dean Morrison, I would like to talk to you about Kane Rhodes if you have a minute."

"Kane... oh yes, the Brit. What do you want to know and why?"

"His name keeps coming up on a case I am working on, but now we look as if we are overlapping one another, so I either need him to butt out or we pool some of our resources."

"He's a good guy to have on board. The Brits were one step ahead of us with the Washington issue and things may have worked out differently if they hadn't been around."

"Well, we're one step ahead of them on another issue they are getting involved in and I don't want them compromising our agent in the field."

"In that case you had better take it up with Bill Johnson."

"Who is Bill Johnson, one of ours or theirs?"

"He's Kane's boss. If you are working on the same case then he is the man to talk to. Hold on a minute and I will dig out his number."

Chas Wiltson pulled up the number from the memory contact list and read it out to special agent Morrison before ending the call. He was still adding the finishing touches to his final report before sending it off to the Bureau head. The final paragraph had concluded that The Dallas assassin, Henri Devaux, was a decoy away from the real target, Bob Jollinger. With the risk of their plans being compromised, they had to stall any general investigations, especially as Edwards' popularity had peaked and was starting to fall and Jollinger's was starting to rise. They needed to quickly eliminate Jollinger before he could tarnish Dale Edwards' march along the Presidential Trail by connecting his father with an illegitimate child in Pakistan. If Edwards did take the Presidency then David Butane would have had access to water companies all over the United States. As it was, the access he already had could have been catastrophic. All in all, the Dallas involvement was portrayed as being successfully managed. The Memphis shooting would take one hell of a lot of explaining and Chas was glad he did not have to write that report.

"Bill Johnson." The sharp, introduction as he picked up the phone.

"Hi, my name is special agent Dean Morrison. Chas Wiltson gave me your number with reference to a case we are working on."

"Okay, agent Morrison, how can I help you?"

"You have some of your operatives infringing on one of my operations and I do not want my agent or our work compromised."

"Well, agent Morrison, it would help if you told me what you are working on and I will tell you whether we are compromising you or not."

"Your agents Kane Rhodes and Brian Jones; they helped out with the Washington operation and I believe they are investigating a situation in Afghanistan."

"Situation? You are going to have to be more informative than that agent Morrison. As you are aware, there are numerous situations in Afghanistan, would you care to be more specific?"

“I understand you are enquiring about a certain religious sect and my concern is that we trip over one another.”

“So what do you suggest?”

“Well, you back off and we will keep you up to date, or we work together on this.”

“I take it you have spoken to your superiors then?”

“Well, yes… they have informed me you want in.”

“It is not a case of wanting in, as you put it agent Morrison, more a case of what we have here could be the tip of the iceberg and we need to pool our resources. I suggest you meet up with our guys while they are over there and bring each other up to date. I will update your people and mine within the next twenty four hours and together we will determine a way forward, but we all need to progress and quickly if we are to get to the bottom of this. Good day, agent Morrison.”

Dean Morrison replaced the handset with a mumbled ‘dick head’; he did not like losing out on control but also knew that their present efforts were starting to dry up. It was time to try something different.

16

The early morning, summer sun hung low in the damp, Welsh sky as the silver, Bentley Mullinger's 6.75 litre engine increased the revs to coast off the slip road and glide into the first lane of the east bound M4 motorway. Traffic was light but Peter Edwards wanted to make an early start and get back to the Chessington office and clear up a few outstanding work issues before heading back to his home in Esher and explaining his secret past to his wife, Catherine.

The meeting with his brother Kevin had gone better than expected and his confession of an affair over thirty years ago apparently came as no surprise. Kevin knew by his mannerisms that something was going on at that time, but made no reference to it as to him, what his brother did, was his business. They decided not to say anything to Kevin's wife until Peter had told Catherine and Dale, settling instead for an Indian take away and a few glasses of wine before Peter retired for an early night in Kevin's spare room.

Several hours earlier, a cold and determined Ali Aziri skirted around Grosvenor Square and paused to look at the brightly lit American Embassy. The outstretched wings of the golden eagle statue symbolised to Ali the flights of destruction from planes, missiles and other weapons that devastated families in their own homes.

He gently patted the bubble wrapped vials held firmly in his hand and smiled at the thought that he would actually be personally avenging American sins. He turned and worked his way through the gardens towards Park Lane and the pumping house.

It had taken Ali Aziri three attempts to find the pumping house which was only recognisable by a small sign showing the Thames Water trademark and the initials TWRM (Thames Water Ring Main). The building blended in with the other large city houses and a small fence ran around the rear of the unit with most of the works being underground. He stood looking at the door, then to the grey metal fence and the surrounding buildings on either side. The only research he had done was to find out the nearest pumping station to Grosvenor Square, how he was going to induce the vials into the water system was another matter. It was just before two o'clock on a cold, damp, dewy morning. The streets were still active with late night revellers and alcohol filled, tourists, taking in the more elegant parts of Central London. Ali Aziri left Park Lane behind him to work his way down the cold, grey steel fence, looking for a means of access. Aziri was not what you would call a physical man, preferring to use his brains not his brawn. He had no idea what he was going to do when he got inside the pumping house; all he knew was that this was his opportunity to get his own revenge personally, before he carried out the final step of his plans. There was obviously some sort of access into the mains water supply; he just had to find it. The lethal concoction in the vials would do the rest.

The events of the last forty eight hours and the trawling through the numerous reports, data files and case histories had taken its' toll on George Daniels' mental agility. Apart from two brief 'wake ups' he had slept solidly from the time he went to bed at 11.40pm to the time he opened his eyes to look at the bedside clock.

"7.50 am!" He exclaimed, turning to his wife Joan who was sat up in bed reading with the help of a dimly lit, bedside lamp. "Why didn't you wake me?"

"Well, you obviously needed the rest," She replied sympathetically, "and besides, I knew your snoring would wake you up sooner or later. You go and have your shower and I'll make you some breakfast."

"I haven't got time for breakfast, there's too much to do." George replied, leaping out of bed.

"By the time you have showered and dressed your breakfast will be on the table ready and waiting. Five minutes will not make any difference to what you have to do today."

George scratched his head through his thinning grey hair as he watched Joan put on her dressing gown and glide out the door to make her way downstairs to the kitchen. 'Five minutes could be a long time with Aziri still on the loose' he thought to himself. But then consoled himself with the fact that half of his office would have been working through the night to track down the whereabouts of Dr Ali Aziri. As if on cue his cellular phone rang.

"George, it's Neil, there's been a suspicious chemical find in the south leg of the Thames Water Ring Main."

"Good God, has it got into the system?"

"Don't know, Thames Water informed the Police and they have just informed us."

"Okay, Neil, make sure the area is sealed off and get a chemical response team down there straight away. What's the address?"

"It's in Park Lane and the local police have already sealed off the area. Apparently two of the night shift staff has been taken to hospital, one with respiratory problems, so they are evacuating the surrounding area."

"Right, meet me there in about forty, make it forty five minutes."

George finished the call and hurried in to the bathroom to brush his teeth whilst turning on the shower. 'No time to shave' he thought to himself as he climbed into the shower for a quick lather and rinse before climbing back out and towelling himself dry as he walked back into the bedroom to get dressed. He sat on the large, king sized bed, struggling to put a clean pair of black, cotton socks over his damp, water wrinkled feet and noticed the wet footprints in the thick piled, beige, wool carpet. Joan would have a hissy fit when she saw that, but he would be long gone by then.

The cold, morning air helped to stave off the desire for sleep as Ali Aziri judged the distance to the top of the fence. The tips of each metal slat were slightly bent over and pointed in alternate directions. He looked up and down the fence for something to stand on then remembered seeing a green wheelie bin on the edge of the road. Scrambling back up the narrow alleyway he came out onto Park Lane and walked the few paces to where the bin was tucked away behind the ornate railings of a large, double fronted city house. Ali went through the black painted, wrought iron gate which creaked loudly on its hinges. He paused and looked up at the windows, ready to run at the first sign of movement, but none came. He gently tugged at the front of the bin which moved about half a metre before the clinking of a chain halted its travels. He bent down, cursing his luck but in the dim light of a distant street lamp he could see that the chain was not padlocked, merely wrapped around the railings and tied in one loose knot. He carefully undid the knot and slowly unravelled the clinking chain, keep a constant eye on the windows for any sudden appearances. The bin now freed, he slowly pulled it out through the gate along the paved road and into the cramped, dark alley. There was just enough room for the width of the bin as he finally brought it to rest near one of the fence's support poles. Ali gently pushed the bubble wrapped vials through the gap between the metal slats then began tucking the bottoms of his trousers into his light brown, socks before clambering up on top of the wobbling, plastic bin. Carefully grabbing hold of the bent slat tops he lifted his left leg onto the row of twisted tips and pulled himself up to balance for several precarious seconds on the top of the metal slatted fence before toppling over, to land with a thud on the dew tipped, grass below. A security light, sensing the motion, lit up an array of pipes and culverts that spread out in front of him. Ali smiled inwardly; one of these would surely give him the access he craved for. The light went out and his hand stretched back to the fence to retrieve the packaged vials. His fingers wrapped around half of a house brick which he released and stretched further back until his probing fingers found the soft, squeaky, bubble wrap covering. With the parcel safely in his grasp, Ali started to move forward when the light came on again. He stayed perfectly still, trying to determine the detection range of the security light and work out a way around it. He was halfway through his mental calculations when the backdoor of the pump house opened and a dark uniformed figure strode out onto the grass.

"Bloody cats." The security guard mumbled as he shone his torch through the unlit parts of the area. The beam of light skipped through the darkened shadows before travelling over Aziri's tucked up body only to return and shine brightly in Ali's startled face. "Oi, what you up to?" The guard shouted making his way between the pipes to the cringing form.

Ali reached out behind him and found the old, half house brick which he quickly grasped and pulled up behind his back, slowly rising to his feet as he did so.

"Right sunshine, what's your game then?" The elderly guard shouted with just a hint of quiver in his voice. He kept the torch pointed squarely in Ali's face and did not see his right hand swinging around until just before the brick smacked into the side of his head, knocking off his peaked, black security hat. He staggered then tried to stand upright as a second blow brought him crashing to his knees before falling forward onto his face.

Aziri pulled out the two vials and carefully undid the top of the larger one before placing it to stand upright against a large, dark green, pipe. Then he undid the top of the second vial which had a long conical, tapered neck before placing that one against the pipe also. Picking up the first vial, he gently rolled up the rubber collar until it protruded over the top lip then picking up the second vial, quickly inserted the tapered tip into the mouth of the first one until the tapered width prevented it from going any further. Then he quickly rolled up the rubber collar to form a perfect airtight seal. The liquid from the second vial began to slowly drip into the first and the deadly process had begun.

"Fred… Fred… where are you?" The shout came from the open back door.

A tall figure in a white lab coat walked out of the building, setting off the security light once more.

"Hey…" He shouted, as Ali stood up looking for an escape route. The newcomer was soon on him, grabbing the front of his jacket as he frantically tried to get away. The conjoined vials flew out of his hand and smashed on a metal culvert cover.

"What was that, what have you…" The startled captor momentarily slackened his grip as he heard the glass break and saw the prone body of the security guard. It was long enough for Aziri to break free and dash into the back of the house, slamming the door shut behind him. The man in the lab coat looked down at the still figure of the security guard and then over to the shattered glass and glistening liquid before running over to bang loudly on the door.

Ali Aziri ran to the front of the building without making any further contact and finding the large, dark blue painted front door, unlocked it, easing it open just wide enough to slip out onto the quiet, deserted street. Quiet that is apart from the shouts from the back of the building which would soon attract the neighbour's attention. Ali walked briskly down Park Lane and across Grosvenor Square, taking one last look at the American Embassy and hoping that some of the mixture would find its way into their water supply.

"Right, Neil, bring me up to speed on what's happening." George shouted, trying to make himself heard over the noise of the surrounding traffic as he closed the driver's window and continued weaving in and out of the busy morning rush hour.

"The contaminated area has been sealed off and they have erected a containment tent over it while they decide how best to treat it."

"Try and get hold of that guy Hassan, Hussein or whatever his name is in Edwards Chemicals, see what he can suggest. I should be there in about ten minutes but we need to act quickly on this. Has the water supply been turned off?"

"Yes, that was the first thing the chemical guys did. They were going to use steam jets to sanitise the area but they need to know what they are dealing with in case they only end up spreading the risk."

"Okay, well, you try Edwards Chemicals direct and I'll have another try at getting hold of Peter Edwards."

George ended the call to Neil and scrolled through the last dialled numbers until he found Peter Edwards and pressed call. The incident at the pumping station had distracted him from his belief that Edwards may be in danger from his own son and he needed to make sure he was safe while they tracked down Aziri.

"Peter Edwards." The response after only two short rings.

"Mr Edwards, it's George Daniels, where are you now?"

"I'm just coming off the roundabout at Chessington, about five minutes from the office, why, do you need to speak to me again?" Peter Edwards could feel himself starting to get annoyed. The fact that someone could tarnish his cherished reputation by considering him to be a potential terrorist, especially when his son could become the most powerful man on earth, did not rest easy with him.

"I have reason to believe that Ali Aziri may want to cause you harm and I would prefer it if you were in our protective custody until we have contained the situation."

"Are you putting me under arrest Mr Daniels?" Peter Edwards was now in attack mode, resenting any and all restrictions on his personal life. "I think I had better speak with my solicitor before I answer any more of your questions."

"No you are not under arrest, Mr Edwards; I just want to get you and your wife to a place of safety while we sort this out."

Peter paused while he gathered his thoughts. Catherine is the innocent party in all this and he did not want her coming to any harm. "I don't think he would want to harm me, but for my wife's sake I will do as you ask. I need to get some documents from the office and then I will meet you at my residence, have you got the address?"

"Yes, Mr Edwards, I will arrange for a team to pick you up in about forty five minutes."

"Make it an hour, please. I'm sure Catherine will want time to take some personal belongings with her."

"Okay, an hour, but please keep your phone on at all times." George ended the call just as he pulled in to Park Lane where a young police constable tried to wave him on down another route.

"Who's in charge here?" George barked, flashing his I.D. card.

"Inspector Lewis, Sir." Mumbled the PC pointing to an incident van parked up on the other side of the road.

George pulled onto the pavement and got out of the car just as Neil Bishop came out of the incident van.

"What's the latest then, Neil? Is it the same bugs found in the States?"

"Well, the initial samples show a strain of Hepatitis so I think we need to assume it is. We managed to get hold of Hussein at Edwards Chemicals and he reckons that CO2 would work better at killing any bugs. He is speaking to the containment team now, it has something to do with fitting a spray nozzle onto the cylinder so that the CO2 comes out as a freezing spray but it only kills on contact so the poor buggers have to dig up any that has seeped into the ground and take it away."

"Has any got into the water system?"

"It has all been contained and they are continually running tests but nothing has shown up yet."

"Our friend Dr Aziri, would you say he was a creature of habit?"

"In which way?"

"He has not visited the UK that often so I wondered if he used the same hotels. What was the one he stayed in before, Fairmile wasn't it?"

"Yes, I'll get some checks run on all the local hotels starting with that one." Neil replied, keying in the memory dial for central desk.

Peter Edwards drove through the industrial estate and into the C.E.O parking space in front of the Edwards Chemicals building. He let the

Bentley purr for a couple of seconds before turning off the ignition and easing himself out of the car. The locking mechanism clicked into place as the beep from the key fob secured the silver, Bentley Mullinger as it basked, serenely, in the early morning sun. He walked briskly towards reception and was about to enter the building when he felt something being pushed into the middle of his back.

"Do not turn around or say anything, I have a gun and will use it if necessary. Just take us into your office and do not do anything foolish. I do not want to kill anybody if I can help it."

"Ali?"

"Yes, it is I… Father."

"Good morning, how was your trip to Wales?" The receptionist asked.

"Fine thanks, Marge."

"Shall I sign your guests in…" She asked as they walked past the reception desk towards his office.

"I'll do it later, it's okay." Peter Edwards replied.

"Would you like some tea or coffee?" She persisted.

"No, we will be fine thanks." Came the response, as the trio disappeared down the corridor and into his well-appointed office.

George Daniels surveyed the Park Lane area and the hustle and bustle of the emergency vehicles as they cordoned off both ends of the street. The local police were busy evacuating the last of the residents just as small, inquisitive groups of people paused to look over the 'Police' tapes spread across the road then moved on, as if it whatever had happened was an everyday occurrence.

"We may have something, George," Neil shouted as he walked over to speak with his boss. "A Dr Alhami was booked into the Fairmile last night and a man answering to the description of Ali Aziri picked her up just over an hour ago."

"That's good enough for me. Get a surveillance team to Edwards' office in Chessington and make sure Peter Edwards and his wife are secured. In fact, there's nothing more we can do here, leave your car and come in mine, you can phone on the way. Just a minute…" George strode over to the incident van and stuck his head through the open door. "Inspector Lewis?" He asked, flashing his badge to the most senior looking policeman at the desk.

"Yes, what can I do for you?"

"I need a police escort to blue light me to Chessington quickly. Can I have one of your guys?"

"Well, yes, I suppose, I take it that it has something to do with this incident?"

"You take it right, but it could get a hell of a lot worse. Who can I have?"

"PC Harris," The inspector turned to the constable at his side. "Take this gentleman to one of the squad cars and tell them to escort him to wherever he wants to go."

"Thank you, inspector." George nodded his thanks and set off back to his car with Neil and PC Harris in tow.

Peter Edwards sat on the edge of his large, neatly laid out desk and offered the two seats opposite to Ali and his lady companion.

"So have you come to shoot me then?" Peter Edwards spoke in a calm, calculated tone, trying to assess the determined young man sat in front of him

Ali smiled as he saw the look of surprise on Safia's face. "I would not do much damage with this," He took the folded jacket off his left hand to reveal an extended index finger. "I did not think you would speak with me if I just turned up."

"And this young lady is…" Peter Edwards asked as he studied Safia's features.

"This is my sister, Safia."

"I should have guessed, she has your mother's smile, how are you my dear?" Peter asked as he lent forward and offered his hand.

Safia shook his hand and smiled warmly. "I am fine Mr Edwards and you?"

"Well, I suppose I'm a bit confused at the moment. Here I am, face to face with a son I have never got to know. But Ali, are you really involved in all this mess? They believe you are the instigator of all this trouble."

"What trouble, Ali?" Safia asked, her caring voice full of concern.

"Nothing for you to worry about, Safia, it will all be sorted out soon."

George Daniels weaved in and out of the bustling lanes of traffic as he struggled to keep up with the brightly marked police Range Rover Vogue.

The blue flashing lights and wailing sirens carving a path through the queues of cars, nearing the end of the busy, morning rush hour.

"Edwards isn't at home George, I have tried his mobile and it rang once then went dead."

"Try his office, though he should have left by now." George had an uneasy feeling, he should have persisted trying to contact Edwards the previous night. He would have been safely tucked away by now. "Neil, better get some uniforms around to the Chessington office and tell them to be quick about it."

The traffic eased and they were soon hurtling down the dual carriageway, moments away from their destination.

"So what are you going to do now?" Peter asked, a genuine concern in his voice. "I will help you whichever way I can but you know you will have to account for what you have done." Peter's phone rang once as he cancelled the call and turned it off.

"I am ready to account for my actions, but I wanted us to be together as a family."

"I regret not being there for you. I loved your mother very much but I had to make a decision, probably the hardest decision I have ever made and I do not know how I can put it right, not after all you have done."

"Ali what is it?" Safia placed her hand on Ali's arm, "What is it you have done?"

The sound of sirens echoed in the distance, getting louder and louder. "I assume those are for me," Ali stated, looking out of the window into the clear, blue sky. "I just wanted one moment as a family." He continued, rising from his chair and outstretching his arms. Peter stood up and walking towards Ali, wrapped his arms around him in a fatherly hug.

"Come, Safia." Ali beckoned her to join them as she rose from the chair to be absorbed by the newly acquainted father and son. The trio stood in the middle of the floor held in a group hug. Ali slipped his hand into his pocket and feeling around the small, oblong object, flicked the steel switch and pressed the protruding, red button.

George was relieved to see the Edwards building as he followed the police car through the open gates of the car park. The distant, thunder like sound was quickly followed by shards of glass that peppered the car, causing both occupants to duck as they screeched to an enforced halt.

"Shit, what was that?" Neil shouted staring at the dark plume of smoke escaping from a large hole in the side of the building.

George was already out of the car and running to the reception area, closely followed by the two officers from the police escort. Two more police cars were speeding through the estate as Neil clambered out of the car and ran after his boss.

The shocked receptionist was staggering around the front of the desk in a complete daze, her long auburn hair stuck to her head as the sprinklers sprayed down from the blast damaged, suspended ceiling above. George looked towards the corridor and Peter Edwards office. It was now one tangled mass of doors, walls and rubble. He carefully picked his way over the pile of debris and peered into the dust filled hole that was once an office. He took out his handkerchief and tried to cover his mouth and nose as the dust started to irritate his throat and lungs causing him to cough uncontrollably.

"George, we need to get out of here, until it's made safe." Neil suggested, grabbing George's arm and trying to pull him back. George resisted, straining to see through the dusty haze until he could make out several mutilated, body parts, confirming his innermost fears. He relaxed, allowing himself to be dragged back and guided out through the doors into the car park.

The receptionist was sat on a low, red bricked wall being comforted by a police officer, his jacket draped over her shoulders. George made his way over to her and bent down as he quietly asked, "Mr Edwards? Was he in his office?"

Marge looked up, tears started to well in her eyes and her lip quivered as she slowly nodded, unable to speak. George gently patted her shoulder then turned to walk back to his car.

"What would you like to do now, Sir?" Neil asked, changing his usual personal approach for a more official line. Somehow it just seemed more appropriate.

"What would I like to do now?" George repeated. "Well, for a start I'd like to turn the clock back twenty four hours, but as that can't happen, we had better get back to the office. You can drive; the keys are still in the ignition." George turned to have one more look at the bomb damaged building before moving around to the passenger side and getting into the dust and glass covered car.

"So what's the latest then?" Brian asked as Kane finished his call with Bill Johnson.

"Dale Edwards' father was killed by a suicide bomber believed to be Ali Aziri. They are still running tests to confirm that and both of us are off to Afghanistan. But first, we have to meet up with agent Morrison who will brief us on some joint mission or other. Bill and Tom are going to join us on a conference call so it must be pretty big."

"Someone's going to have to take the flak for that one. I wonder if that will affect Dale Edwards' presidential campaign."

"I'm more concerned with this next mission. Bill didn't sound too keen on parting with any information so I think we are not going to like what we are letting ourselves in for."

"Well, just remember, it's your turn to get shot this time."

Lightning Source UK Ltd.
Milton Keynes UK
UKOW03f2039040913

216547UK00012B/144/P

9 781908 586292